D0993486

Patrick Farrelly was born and raised in rural Ireland. In his early twenties, he followed in the footsteps of thousands before him and immigrated to New York. In the years that have followed he has travelled extensively all over the world, appeared on stage from time to time and worked in many fields meeting many colourful characters. He currently lives and works in Brisbane Australia.

My Bohemian Muse

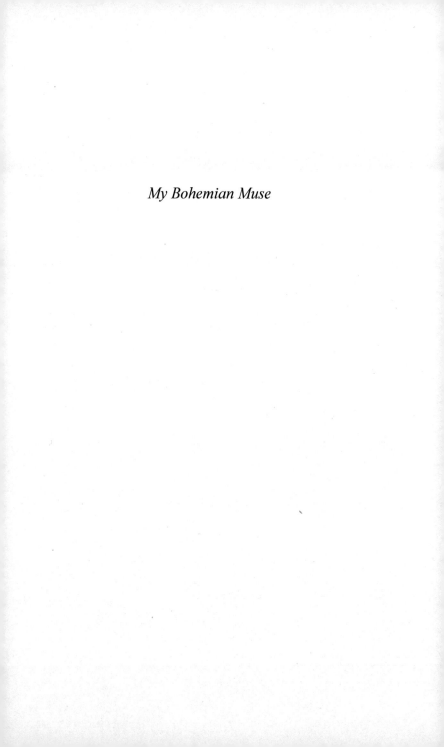

Patrick Farrelly

THE EXILE

AUSTIN MACAULEY
PUBLISHERS LTD.

A CIP catalogue record for this title is available from the British Library.

ISBN 9781785547515 (Paperback)
ISBN 9781785547522 (Hardback)
ISBN 9781785547539 (eBook)

www.austinmacauley.com

First Published (2016)
Austin Macauley Publishers Ltd.
25 Canada Square
Canary Wharf
London
E14 5LQ

Acknowledgements

My Bohemian Muse, who kept the faith alive in me that I could indeed complete this.

My family, whom I love dearly

My brother. You know why as do I.

My uncle David, recently passed, who always listened and never judged, missed everyday

Patricia Shaw, very accomplished author, who graciously took of her time to read a manuscript and in doing so, justified mine in writing it.

Mo & Lynne who suffered a would be writer to sit in their beautiful *Three Bowls café*, for hours on end absorbing the peace and tranquility of their most wonderful space, thank you friends, I am gaining enlightenment – I think. We can talk about that too!

All the wonderful friends I have made in Brisbane, you bring vibrancy and joy to my life

Savior For Me

Savior me,
savior see me, savior me
for I have lost the way.

Through verdant pastures green-hoofed
I flew, blonde and browned by a sun
never set. All around me love burst
forth from every bough.

Inconsequence never came forth to
make me bow. Intransigence lived
within me like an unborn litter in
the belly of a sow.

Here now I come to realize how,
control, the illusion we all hold to,
can in chains of thrall
make others see us bow.

Not I, no more shall fear to be free,
within the vaults of self.
Once free within then free without,
savior for me, I am now free, fear is
gone, the shadows past.

Patrick Farrelly. April 2002. New York

Chapter 1

Lost

He was alive and frankly, he was surprised. He never truly had the guts for suicide but had engineered his recent past life so that he could dance with death at least once a day, a lot of the time it was more. There are many forms of death, physical death is the one irreversible form, true to a point; but he had died in his head, heart and soul many times over in the last nine months. In a way, he still died a little every day. He was clean now and always would be until the day physical death called time on his tango, but the taint, indeed the very taste of those many flings with crack lived on. Maybe it would perish when he did.

Cocaine does not lever your mind out of a box, as some would suggest, it destroys the boundaries that help you to define the personality, the self that you believe you are. When you are in the free-fall that precedes a crack binge, you tend to find out just how lonely life can be. You just cannot believe that the mass of humanity around you does not understand, does not see things with the clarity of a mind getting penetrated by the glass dick in which you burn your rocks, cannot understand the lustful compulsion, the sexy disregard for everything normal, the simplicity and complexity of life spent in the pursuit of *Quills*. The almost demonic tinge that the world has when you have *broken night* again for a grand total of eleven days straight. He would assure you, that when you have been awake and high or in the pursuit of a high, or many other situations we will get to later, for over two hundred and sixty four hours, you are but a passenger on a psychotic train, the smallest kink in the rails will spill you off and career you down the embankment into all of the hells ever conceived in the span of mankind.

He read avidly, on the fourth day of the aforementioned eleven; he picked up Dante's divine comedy, the *Inferno*. Divine comedy indeed, for somebody watching him perhaps, but with the bonds on his psyche loosened via pharmacology, it became a terrible strobe light in his brains' reality. The pages before him seemed to shimmer and buckle out of the present into the icy heart of hell; he pushed his arms out away from him while leaning the rest of his body back, away from that beckoning abyss. No matter how he tried to restrain it, his mind gained a velocity and intensity likely to burst every vessel in his brain, then he seemed to get sucked out of his avatar through the eyes locked on the shimmering surface of those well-thumbed pages. He felt himself elongate, compress and expand all at the same time. He wished to die to avoid the pain; his spinal column became locked as though he were having a fit. Movement was no longer an option.

Do you have any idea how terrifying and agonizing it feels? When you are convinced that after your mind has extruded itself through the venturi your pupils have become, your spinal cord will begin the same journey. Every nerve from your heels to your scalp flows with an ever-increasing momentum like grease-laden dishwater heading down the sinkhole. Welcome to eternity. He felt he would have probably met the devil himself, or at least a demon of the seventh circle, if only his companion had not re-entered the room to borrow his *Stem*. That being the street-speak for the aforementioned glass dick, the quarter inch diameter glass pipe about three to four inches long with a pair of tightly packed and compressed metal smoking screens in one end or the other.

She could not find it, so she nudged him to ask its whereabouts. The lights flickered, the room shifted and it all came to a crashing halt. For one brief tottering instant, he feared that all recently vomited mind and matter stuff would reverse course and re-enter by the same route, popping his eyeballs like bubble-wrap. Blindness the true fear, he screwed his eyes shut, willing her to go away 'Hey what-cha reading?' He swam in the void; he knew that if he perceived light he would know pain. 'Hey you!' Pop, up came the eyelids, reality, light, air, all return to his body. He became more aware as the seconds passed, punctuated by a shuddering diaphragm that tortured his lungs with the fluctuating pressure differential. He looked up at her pretty but empty face. 'What did you say?' arose from a throat you would swear just emerged from the Sahara after days without water. 'Listen Poppi, I needs to borrow your stem, mines is broke too much flame, you look like you need a hit as well Poppi, wanna shotgun?'

A year earlier a statement like that would never have entered his three-bedroom, nice neighborhood Queens location. Now it was like a lifeline. He looked at the pages again, normal now; obviously the Devil does not like an audience as he draws individuals out through their eyeballs. 'How long have I been reading?' He croaked. 'Poppi you only opened the book as I came in

3

the room'. He was stunned 'that's not possible!' he breathed, 'Whatever Poppi, can I have the stem now?'

He put the book down while being both appalled and drawn at the same time by the power of the mind to compress and in this instance, to expand time. He produced the stem and fished a fresh dime bag from the bundle on the table. She was lithe, as most crack whores are before they begin the final descent from the last landing of addiction, she leaped into his lap and as she pulled off her shirt to expose her breasts said, 'While I take a hit Poppi, will you lick my nipples on the very tip as you do, it makes me orgasm every time!'

Of course he obliged, she would reciprocate in a different way while he took his hit, and there-in lies the real problem with Crack, it makes you horny in so many ways, sexually, belligerently and the most costly of ways, it brings empathy for whatever is the subject at hand, be it a pair of tits or an imagined demonic fit. The hit was good as always.

That was only ten minutes more or less out of day four. Imagine what he was like on day eleven? But now don't waste time, just reflect on nine months of it. One person he met in this period of his life was smoking crack and sniffing *smack* with the same enthusiasm as when they had first started, twenty-two years ago. Let me tell you for that you need the constitution of a bull and the greatest amount of illusory control of your mind. He did nine months, he knew ten would kill him, a year he never would have reached. I shudder to think what has passed before those eyes, both real and imagined in twenty-two years of using.

How many lies had they told both themselves and the people they came in contact with? How many conspiracies? How many crimes? How many violations

4

of self and others? How many compatriots dead in vicarious ways? Was there a soul left at all?

Maybe soul only was left. Ah! You might think a soul at least is something. Well, to a point you are right, but a soul in which the last vestiges of self are merely spots on the surface. Beneath it is one great infinite space into which, at first, you are infinitely satisfied by filling it with a few intense experiences. Maybe as a foil to some ones you wished you never had. Life experience you see, the visceral sort, is as good as any rush you can get - sometimes anyway.

He had been wounded much earlier in life and had tried to get a handle on it, so much so that it became a game of truth within him that eventually disguised the truth as fantasy, and fantasy as lies so that there were no boundaries, only rough ever widening borders of grey shading. So as long as the lies remain unrecognized and your own council you keep, it seems enough for self-growth and inner scalable expansion to a point of infinite size to such comprehensible extent to seem to be at one with the ultimate, eternity.

But as he had found, that's normally a ways off, far enough yet near enough that he knew he would not reach that promised land of peace until the dull ache of lifelong wounds were cauterized by – well, by something! Drink, his compatriot's normal panacea in distress didn't do it for him so then he tried weed, nice cool mellow high. That was enough for a while and then it developed one night in a rush of time and circumstance that he was not even aware of until it was too late.

He was away with some so-called friends, upstate New York, on a blue-collar ski weekend. He was flushed with the day outdoors, the feeling of speed over the snow, the past seemed a long way away, almost

5

forgotten entirely, he was relaxed and she was risqué and attractive, immediate and there. The lodge was heaving with people, adrenaline and hormones. So the après ski horny kind of toasted on chocolate weed or maybe primo hydro-weed, he'd forgotten which, penis like a baby's arm holding a tennis ball as she brought him upstairs, away from home, an inner desire to point his arse against the wind and fart at the world, while outrunning the stink in the opposite direction kind of way, took over, simple as.

He was Captain under God of this particular ship, the girl whose name he remembered long enough to enjoy the full extent of the après ski sexy stranger, never will *ever* see again, sensually outrunning her own flatulent aroma in his direction, right now, sort of why not, I'll take a blast off her pipe just once, kind of no big deal… 'Oh my God, the rush!' he remembered later. Suddenly, instantly- it was good 'rock' and he couldn't even put a time frame on the body rush, to the top of all the extremities of his avatar, a sensory overcharged orgasm, "I say avatar because Yep! I was not there no more, you is gone boy, and you could give a fiddlers fuck if you never came back 'cause Whoooaaa!! You never even fantasized in your best wake up shooting western dream teenage youth that you could possibly experience such bliss of both mind and body,' and then it hit his soul, 'Shit, I'm bloody hooked.'

He needed to go and see if that was even real as an excuse to push it beyond register. They screwed and smoked, smoked and screwed all night. Much later, years in fact, he explained it to a friend thus; 'For a gossamer moment I was a God, kind of a singularly-focused- on- one- thing- at- the- moment kind of God, but still a God. One that never will give a shit about the faithful because in the instant you feel its power hit you and then melt away giving you your first taste of the *Fiending,* that incomparable and indescribable urge to use, which comes later, you know it will only ever be about you and the high. If you have the money to get high, you have power, because most crack heads will do anything for a hit, therein lay the source of my divinity to all the inferiors I was about to spend a lot of time with,' a pointed description indeed.

The rush will let you see outside of yourself and how you handle the view will determine how your time as a crack head will ultimately come to fruition. Note I say 'fruition' instead of end because it never ends no matter how long you are clean- it comes to how you use the experience as a guide to the future. If you wallow in self pity or recrimination, you will go back to the pipe in a moment of weakness and everything can be a moment of weakness when you are trying to stand up like a wobbly newborn foal slick with the afterbirth of a nightmare, oh yeah! This shit will leave you shaky for a long time. You either survive or you die. The best outcome is resolution and that is something that when you feel you have achieved it you can never tell anybody, because the demon that is in stasis in your soul is just waiting for that admission of security that always brings a loosening of the bonds you have restrained him with, and pop goes the weasel.

You see, when you go through the process of telling people that you have a problem that's tough, then you fight the problem and everybody has a different pain threshold hence the fight has many outcomes for each individual, then you get some clean time under your belt, you look and feel better, people who matter look at you with new respect and as you claw your life back their respect for you grows. They might not say it but you can see it, feel it. If nothing else, crack attunes your senses to people if you look at it that way, it's a natural way that the mind deals with the paranoia which comes with using.

It's like a hungry feral dog ravening on carrion after days without food, at the first sound he freezes and seem to reach out with all the senses, but he will not leave his meal, the hardwired mammalian response mechanism of 'fight or flight' becomes 'fight and fight'. The 'fight' part becomes the part that overcomes all previous life conditioning and reasons that if you are going to be challenged for your food, your basic urge to feel it fill your belly will make you fight things that would normally make you run. You will fight to feel that belly expand even though previously, just like the dog, you would have run away to fight another day.

Dying with that feeling of expansion is better than existence searching for it and being unfulfilled. But the senses are so much more enhanced, the feelings, the emotions, everything. If you ever let that demon out and start using again then the shame you feel, the perception you think you know is right, that people, even when you were still clean, thought in the silence of their souls that it was only a matter of time before you fell off the wagon.

Once you smoke crack you give people an automatic sense of superiority over you even if they don't realize it themselves, but you can see it, smell it off them just like a dog smells fear and you have to learn to deal with it. But when you fail, God when you see all that in their souls, you reason to yourself that 'Well they never believed anyway, they will never trust me again so to Hell with them!' and you justify your use, kind of a punishment of others for their daring to judge you. This lasts just long enough to ensure you are fully hooked, that is the true power of the demon to make you rationalize everything, make you believe everything is possible, and then drive you to seek it out more and more while keeping all these false self promises up as a carrot to yourself to keep you justifying your use and as a barrier to the truth your loved ones are trying to get through to you from the outside.

If you go through this a couple of times you are dead and you know it's leading you there but you just cannot help it, you keep putting your hand into the fire, until all the flesh is gone and the skeletal remains are all that's left. Finally, even you cannot justify your use but there is nothing left to save and the demon stops driving you then because his work is done. He will leave you with just enough of yourself to really know hopelessness and enough time so you can feel true loneliness and despair before dying cold, hungry and forgotten in a gutter. The best you can hope for is to die mad; consciousness at that stage is true damnation.

It was terrible for him one day when he wished he had been born just a little less gifted. Then he would be able to lessen the guilt which overwhelms him at those moments of crashing down from the precarious high that he no longer had the money to sustain. He had many experiences while he smoked crack cocaine, but he can say something that most cannot. He never stole anything in his life before crack and he never stole anything for crack and God there were times when the pain was so bad he really had to reflect upon himself. In the end this is what saved him ultimately. If he had crossed that line inside himself, he knew he would have been lost forever. The second thing is that he never exchanged sex for a hit, again, something he was proud of. He fought this addiction for nine months and while he basically ruined his life at the time in doing so, he did not lose his dignity and he remained functional for most of that time.

He told someone much later that 'I am blessed to have people in my life that love me not for what I can do for them or for what I can give them but people who love me because they see who I truly am and what I am capable of even if I do not always see it myself.' When you smoke crack it's very hard to hide and he concealed it beautifully for all that time. That was part of the reason for him he supposed, the challenge to him to maintain the mundane everyday life he had come to hate himself for leading and live in the shadows of society by night, and then in the morning go to work with people who had lots of money and conservative opinions by virtue of position not experience, an unshakable belief in their own superiority, even though they would not call it that.

They loved having him work for them, he was gifted and intelligent but also socially adept and he did have great physical presence, six foot three, blonde and blue eyed. It used to amuse him no end when he would be summoned to solve a problem. He made himself totally and had a gift for adapting, but they just assumed that that was who he always was. He had lived on different continents, seen some of the most horrible things man can inflict upon his fellow man, he had done many different jobs in many diverse places and he learned from them all something different. But the most important thing he ever learned was 'That the sun will come up in the morning Man and if it does not, we are all screwed anyway.'

One day when he was with his boss standing on the street outside the office in the Bronx not far from Hunters Point, a noted area for drugs, prostitution, violence and hopelessness; a busted-out, bedraggled woman shambled by, emaciated, filthy and vapidly staring at the world. As she approached he looked at his

10

boss who was watching her with a look of disgust and revulsion, already his body language was telling Thomas that if she stopped in front of them he would be uncomfortable. She did and asked in unintelligible tones for something so she could get something to eat.

The man became agitated in a restrained way like a prince who had been confronted with the true reality of the peasantry in medieval Europe. He ignored her in such a way so as to make it clear, that to him, at that point she did not even exist. Thomas turned and looked her straight in the eye, she was not used to having a white man look at her as an equal, he quickly produced ten dollars and gave it to her and said 'God bless you love.' She wavered for a moment looking at the crisp bill in her time ravaged and shriveled hand. Gently he closed her fingers over it. For another moment their eyes met, she had tears beginning to form, they both knew what that ten dollars meant to her, a chance to get high in the middle of the day without having to risk anything, or turning a cheap trick for it.

She was gone beyond any hope of recovery, her body ravaged by disease and life. She knew he knew and tried to say something but he cut her short and said 'It's ok love go on now and be safe for a while.' She nodded and shambled on her way. He lit a cigarette as he turned back to where his boss was standing; he was looking at Thomas with an expression of disbelief and total incomprehension of what had just taken place before him. He said, 'Why did you give her ten dollars?' His reply was simple 'I had it to give and maybe some day I'll need someone to give me a few dollars without judging me for it'.

Thomas could see that this just would never make sense to him. He was a good man in his own way, was honest in his dealings and respectable but he just had no

11

idea of what it is to live life with no security net, always one step from imminent disaster. Charity was something you gave to the church in a brown envelope a couple of times a year and let them deal with its distribution. 'But, but, ten dollars!' Thomas looked at him, he was a millionaire and would buy coffee in a deli or the nearby bodega instead of Starbucks, because he didn't believe that a cup of regular coffee was worth a buck eighty-nine at the time. 'What price a moment's dignity?' was Thomas's reply. 'Just when I think I have you figured out you always throw me a curve ball' the boss came back with, he let it go at that point. Thomas could have explained it to him but it would have taken hours to make him see all the connections that he had had to learn, whether he wanted to or not at the time, and then his conditioning would not have allowed him to see Thomas as the same person, he would have become an indefinable, unknown quantity to whom money was nothing more than something to put a roof over your head, food in the belly and the odd luxury to be savored, not squandered.

For most people if it's unknown, it's dangerous. It was he supposed, a basic animal instinct in all of us. If you are confronted by an unknown in a situation outside of your normal envelope of security, then you tend to lash out at it, how strongly or meekly does not matter it's all relevant, in the hope of provoking a reaction and based on that reaction you then hope you can classify the previously unknown as follows, threat or not, friend or foe, superior or inferior, controllable or not. 'Just like the pinging of an active human sonar.' Thomas liked reading Tom Clancy novels too.

Rarely does 'Can I learn something here or not?' come up. When Thomas started to work for him, he knew he was intelligent and could do what he was hired to do. When he learned that he could do all the physical work as well as sell the jobs, could weld like a pro and had spent time as a steel fabricator, could do engineering calculation and presentation quality engineering and architectural drawings to a higher standard than most who had been doing it for years, he automatically assumed Thomas had gotten a college degree at some stage and probably had done some graduate work as well.

When he revealed he was self-taught, he was impressed but in a way threatened. Thomas did not bother to tell him that the skills he was so impressed by were only the ones that applied to the scaffolding and construction industry.

Thomas was only thirty-one years old and did not have the boss-man's money and therefore his access to knowledge and power as he saw it. That was fine by him, but if he had pointed it out to him he would most definitely been seen as a threat from that point forward. The boss never likes to be shown up whether it was intentional or not.

Their interaction with the woman on the sidewalk was just another instance of this, for him life has always been there to be lived and experienced because that's the way it just had to be for him. Most people pay lip service to this ideal but never really risk anything to live it. When you have no choice you learn how to think outside the box very fast, and when you reach full maturity, if you are lucky to survive that long, then you know the real truth, there is no box, just life. Live it or be carried along by it, love it or die bitching about how you never got what you deserved.

Thomas thought he was lucky, he was strong, and he had experienced many things prior to his arrival in America that hardened him in a way so that he could survive what he was currently calling life. This life that was fast becoming a blueprint for flirting with crack and other drugs and living to tell the tale. As he once reminded himself in a moment of clarity 'you do not flirt with crack like a teenage sweetheart behind the schoolhouse on a summer day. No, with crack you either fuck or get fucked and that's in the biblical sense.'

It was beginning to get that way.

Chapter 2

Beginnings

It was a day he knew was coming but chose to avoid within his mind. She was moving out, leaving him, 'leaving us' as he thought of it. It had been coming for quite a while but that was irrelevant now as he smoked a joint on the balcony. The moving guys had come to take away her treadmill. God how he had hated that treadmill, ever since she had bought it in Sears a couple of years before. It was a noisy bastard, especially at 7.30 on a Sunday morning after he had worked a ninety hour week to keep the bills ticking over and save some too.

Directly across 58th Street from the apartment in Woodside, lay the New Calvary cemetery, the largest in the five boroughs. He did not care that it was a place full of dead people, it was green and as it lay to the west of their, now his balcony, the sun would set most days beautifully streaming through the leaves of a reasonably majestic Sycamore tree. A reasonable tree because this is Queens we are talking about. Thomas had nothing against Queens but let's face it, his view was not westward from the fifteenth floor of a building on Fifth Avenue overlooking Central Park! But then as he would truly come to realize later, his view, no matter how limited compared to some on the Upper East or West Sides of Manhattan, was a hell of a lot better than the view out of one of the many ghetto buildings so many unseen New Yorkers have to call home.

Anyway she was leaving because, well to this day he cannot pinpoint the exact reason, but I have my suspicions along the lines of he just did not fit the family bill for future security and success, and perhaps not coming from a quantifiable and known respectable gene pool, one that would suit Marin County Persian mafia standards. He had of course fit these particulars perfectly when he moved from San Francisco in the summer of 1996 where he had dated her for a few months. They had been in love in that let's screw all night and talk shite all day kind of way that you normally are at twenty-four.

They were full of dreams and hope for the future as most young couples tend to be, they did not see the hurdles as insurmountable and they really did love each other, they had really tried for five years. Anyway, he had helped her to move the majority of her stuff to her new apartment in Greenwich Village on Thompson Street, just off Bleecker. It was hot and humid as he recalled and she was so upbeat and all he could think of was 'what the bloody hell am I doing here, doing this?'

As he sweated he began to think back to his arrival in New York. He landed at JFK from San Francisco on a one-way ticket with three hundred dollars in his pocket; it made sense in a way because that was pretty much how he landed in the USA back on June 4th 1994 in San Francisco. Then he was on a one-way ticket as well, the only difference was he had six hundred dollars then. So there he was at JFK, knowing his Grandfather, one of the most pivotal figures in his life was terminally ill back home in Dublin. He called home feeling pretty despondent, he had never been to New York before and all he had was a phone number for a guy who might have a job for him.

He made the call to Dublin and discovered that Grandfather was indeed dead and he was already buried, the family was in the midst of the wake. The previous night Alia had left him at San Francisco International Airport with the promise to follow soon, they would make a life together. He did not have the money to fly home to say goodbye to his Granddad, to Bee Bop, so he had sat and cried his heart out silently, letting the tears roll down his cheeks, while the taxis jostled for business outside the arrivals hall and some rude bastard had complained he was on the pay phone too long. He tried manfully to overcome his trepidation at where he was in his present with the reality of the death. It was truly one of the most difficult days of his life, up until then.

He survived the day and made it to Sunnyside Queens where he got a bed for a few days and a job. He sweated long and hard learning a business he had never experienced before, scaffolding and he did it well as far as he could see. He quickly moved from being a *mule* as the men termed, humping planks and beams and the like, to fabricating because he could weld. He was an outsider in every sense, he did not have any direct family in this new city and all the guys he worked with were from a different part of Ireland to him. To this day he can't trust people from certain counties, he knows it makes no sense, but hard lessons, hard learned, have a habit of sticking with you.

He worked night and day at fifteen dollars an hour and slept on a couch in an acquaintances' apartment. He paid half his rent for the privilege of that couch. Every night Alia would call from California and they both would cry a bit, her in separation, he in loneliness and the fear of adjustment that was well, less than gentle, let's put it that way.

He worked harder and harder and after two months he had enough for a deposit and first month's rent on an apartment of their own in the same building. He was so proud. Alia would not wait, she wanted to be a writer and New York was the place for her. He went out to La Guardia to collect her on the night she arrived and it was strange, they had not seen each other for almost three months and she was scared of this big change in her life too. But she never noticed just how scared he was. He had worked so hard to get that apartment and wanted her to wait a little bit longer so he could furnish it, make a home of it, but she would not be dissuaded.

All the way back to Sunnyside in the cab there was this apprehensive silence, a pregnant silence. They were lovers but they were also strangers in a strange city. She had been to New York before she met him, but that had just been for vacation purposes with her sister and her sister's friend. That apprehensive silence would prove prophetic, which would not become apparent until much later. He could smell the change in the air but he readily chose to ignore it. You see, he always had this fear of ultimate loneliness. He could handle it beautifully most times but when he lets himself open up to let someone into the zone where he feels love, then all bets are off in a way. She was so there, and he did not have the intestinal fortitude to say 'Alia, why are you here, really?' But no, he wanted it all and thought that he could provide it all as well.

They really did have good times but sitting on that balcony right then, they all seemed so ethereal and far removed from his present, like the ghost of a former self at the funeral of his corporeal reality. He had been brought up to be honorable and he had no intention of ever changing that, it was and is part of who he is and as such is one of the pieces that he will not easily discard, if ever. He had a responsibility to her that was more than he could bear at the time, but he had said it was ok for her to come out and live with him, so in a way he had to 'fish or cut bait'. He had been so proud of the one bedroom apartment that he had secured with his blood and sweat, it was a pristine sepulcher of white walls and freshly polished wooden floors that in its own stark way was beautiful, it was his, theirs. It really is not fair to judge her reaction on first seeing it, she was no longer living in Marin County, that bastion of northern Californian wealth and privilege of which he always did say in her defense, she was no fan of and did not subscribe to in any way. But still her family lived in a great house in San Rafael and it was very far removed from the reality into which she now walked.

But by New York standards it was a good apartment and a good area too, it just took some adjustment. He had an air mattress on the floor as the bed he had ordered and paid for had not arrived as promised, and he had scrubbed the place from top to bottom the night before, an extravaganza of *Lysol*. He had bought flowers and made the bedroom as nice as any twenty-four year old, a long way from home trying to make a new home, could.

They made love, but it was more like she gave in to him when he was not really asking. He felt so bad, so unsatisfied, so unfulfilled and so betrayed in a way. But he put it down to her nervousness at the new situation and place. He had always enjoyed the company of Women, but they have to feel comfortable and secure if it is to do anything for him, no doubt a legacy of his own insecurities. He respects women and if they don't feel comfortable and sexy then he just has no interest at all. With Alia, he had been so looking forward to the night of her arrival as he had shared something beautiful with her when he lived in San Francisco and had worked so hard for what he thought 'was us.'

It was never to be the same again, she would be thrilled by his advancement and he really did leap forward in what he was doing, she tried hard and began to work in publishing and he finally began to believe that it would all work out. They hit a kind of stasis that to this day he still cannot explain, she blamed him for not trying enough and he blamed her for being a weight around his neck. Sometimes duty and honor have absolutely nothing to do with expediency. She thought about him a lot and was always there for him in some ways as he was for her, but on a basic level it was just bound not to work.

Now five years later as he sat on the balcony smoking that joint, all he could think of was 'Why the heck hadn't this happened some years ago?' But even that was irrelevant now; at this stage of the game it was merely window dressing. After all the effort of putting up with and dealing with both her shit and his own, here he was on the verge of abandonment. 'Well why should the pattern change now?' he thought as he delved into the mysteries of good hydro weed. She was so upbeat it made him feel so used. How many ex-boyfriends would spend six sweating days transporting her shit from Queens to the Village and then hauling the shit all the way up to the fourth floor in the middle of a New York heat wave?

Not many is the true answer, he did not look for accolades or a ribbon like a prize pet, that was just how he was reared, built. That sense of duty, guilt and responsibility would later both save and haunt him and still does a bit. For almost four years he had had the most boring and unsatisfying sex of his entire life. But being

Irish Catholic that was to be expected wasn't it? For Alia, physical relations after the initial rush of a new love were something to be both avoided and endured. It was not her fault they were just different. She was a secular Muslim, and later he would laugh and irreverently say 'That's ultimately just an Irish Catholic from a better climate with more sun, less rain, but the same amount of guilt about having any sort of fun'.

He had had to learn to be comfortable with his own sexuality, because of a gift bestowed upon him in his childhood, but few indeed he has ever found to share this deep reality of him, but then have any of us? As a result of this he has always had this secret desire to experience things, the somehow forbidden things and feelings, outside of the normal envelope of time. In other words, that's when he gets bored or frustrated to the extent that he becomes self-destructively activated in a strange and sometimes alien way.

He would just get this urge for sexual fulfillment no matter how hollow it might be. To satisfy this he would use an escort service, because it was painless, guaranteed in a way, and most importantly of all for him, he could be who he wanted to be for that hour without being an asshole and all the while treating the woman with respect. Sometimes the girls would be surprised that he wanted them to feel relaxed before they did anything and if he did not feel like she was ok then he would do nothing but talk, smoke a few joints and maybe jerk off after she was gone.

Due to his experience many years ago, he learned that sexuality and gender are related but distinct, that what you experience in life with one person should not necessarily influence how you interact with others later. He could have picked up women at a bar, but that seemed callous to him. To have a one-night stand with someone means there is a certain lie associated with getting laid in that fashion. When he called an escort it was not a lie, everybody involved knew exactly what was going to happen and he made it clear he would have respect for them and in turn they would respect him. Also he could preselect in a way, what was going to arrive.

He would smoke a joint and have a shower, feel sexy and have a good positive interaction, at least to his mind, with the woman. Everyone is different and a different approach was required for each one. He would rarely see a girl more than two or three times, he found they would become attached to him, expectant somehow and would drop hints about seeing them outside of their agency and so on and so forth. He was flattered but how could he tell them that he just needed physical intimacy, without all the emotional baggage that had brought him to this point as it was?

If he told them that stark truth, he would be guilty of using them too, which in a way he was anyway, but no more than he was used in return; it was an acceptable form of mutual use and abuse. It was a lie that was bigger than a little white lie but was, as said earlier, a lesser evil than pretending to really like someone just long enough to get into their knickers. So on this, the night that Alia was finally 'moved out', he went and bought a six-pack of beer and sat on the balcony, called his friend from upstairs, and the pair proceeded to get drunk and mellow in the evening warmth.

That was four days before 9/11. There would be much to reflect upon soon but at that point he did not realize just how foolishly unconcerned he really was, how much he did not relate to reality at the time. Truly he had no idea just how bad it was about to become. After Thomas and his mate got stoned and he staggered his way up the stairs to his own place, Thomas called an escort. She was beautiful in the playboy 'I was born to be used as a sexual object!' kind of way, she also smoked crack and he had tried it with her once before, but his wariness of it after 'the upstate mission' as he referred to it precluded him from taking a really effective hit.

This night was different, he was feeling really abandoned, lonely, high, horny and trapped so he needed, and at least he thought he did, to escape. She arrived and he was in his robe after a shower, he had the candles lit and the music on, she stepped in and straight away stepped out of her dress, he gave her the joint he had in his hand. She turned and rubbed her thong-encased butt against his penis as it emerged from the folds of his robe. She fetched the *stem* from her purse and gave it to him.

He was already in that mental space where he would justify anything to himself. She purred like a happy cat and took his cock in her mouth while he hit a full dime bag. For the first and last time he ejaculated while exhaling the first hit of a session, he had never come so strong in his life before, it plastered her hair all over her face and she was both shocked and really aroused by it. He showed her to the shower and apologized for coming all over her in that way, something he would not do without being asked to do so or seeking permission to.

As she showered he sat and then lay down on the couch as he took another huge hit. He floated in a void that was beautiful and creepy and powerful. He could see everything now, the clarity, the reality of who he was, the reality of who he was becoming. He bought all the crack the girl had, about a hundred and eighty dollars worth and then he let her shag him as she wanted to, he had really turned her on earlier with his explosion and she already was well high upon arrival. She wanted him to almost dominate her, he did not like it but he took a hit and did it, as she wanted him to, for a few brief minutes, he could not come again, he pulled out appalled at the reality of where he really was and what he was doing. The urge to ejaculate began to ache in the top of his cock like a demonic heartbeat, that was the first time that he got a hint of just how bad having sex with crack would be in the future. But the two are inextricably linked; at least they were for him.

'The more you smoke the more mentally aroused you became and the more you wanted to come and come and come again, but you just cannot maintain an erection on crack, you nearly have the pull your stomach off yourself as you masturbate so hard,' was a later reflection. Once you come though, if you are clever you will have kept a couple of hits for afterwards. Then you can mellow out and let yourself fall asleep reasonably contented. If you do not then you begin to *fiend* for it and once you feel the *fiending* you know without any shadow of a doubt that you are now a crack addict, and the first time you give in to that *fiending* and you go in search of somewhere to cop a couple of dimes then you have reached the inverse pinnacle of addiction, you are now officially a crack head.

For Thomas, life was just about to get really interesting and scary beyond belief, 'Will I live or die?' echoed across the firmament of his mind, then he realized he did not care, he had begun, he was becoming something he would either comprehend or die from trying to, he was the epitome of a man in search of truth, then it started to get interesting, but then again the really big lies you tell yourself sometimes, lend themselves to that.

Chapter 3

A Ghetto Education

To Thomas the word 'ghetto' evoked remembered images from childhood of grainy black and white documentaries of the Second World War, millions of Jews being forced onto trains to death camps. He had seen and experienced many of Europe's finest slums in his travels as a younger man; Marseilles had a few beauties, Munich, London and let's not forget some of his native Dublin's finer residential slums. They were all different yet similar places where the unwanted, the forgotten of society found themselves. Mostly though they were full of people trying to get on in life, up to where the commercials on television were not just a window into the impossible dream of fiscal solvency, but real attainable goals, the place where the donkey finally gets to eat the carrot without having his ass reddened by the stick.

Yes, he knew in theory what a ghetto was, he travelled through them going to or from various construction sites, but he had never really experienced the reality of an American ghetto or thought he would be getting better acquainted with one. The first thing that struck him was that this place existed only a few minutes' drive from where he lived, from where all of his neighbors could recline on their couch and feel secure while watching the news at night and commenting how 'Those people are no good and only a drain on our hardearned taxes, and what do we get back for supporting them with our shining welfare state? Violence, hatred, murder and rape, all sorts of crimes and yet again at the end of the year a bigger tax bill. Tsk! Tsk!'

Sure, the ghettos produce all of these things, and more, but they are a direct result of humanity's evolution into a city dweller. Not everybody gets dealt the same cards, no-one gets to pick their gender, race, the intelligence they are born with and probably most importantly of all, their parents. You need a license to drive a car, own a gun or a dog, but you do not need one to have children. Thomas once at a party, set collective hackles rising with righteous indignation by saying that 'some people, irrespective of color, race, religion, education, prospects or financial status, should never be given the chance to have children.' Thomas was confronted with this old argument of his, as he parked the pickup just about fifty yards from the corner of Troutman and Starr Avenues. He would walk from here, better to see which way the cops were cruising about tonight, he didn't need to get pulled over with a big bag of rock shoved down his crotch and spend the night in Central Booking.

Yes, Troutman and Starr, that was the intersection where it all happened for him. This was the place at night where the action mostly began and not just for him, he was a bit player, a cog, a mere planetary gear orbiting its axle as it ground away lives and hopes and dreams. The night was warm and New York Summer sultry, the woman was strutting, as only a Brooklyn hooker on the local track could. He knew her and she knew him, he knew she was good at her trade, experienced and as trustworthy as any could be, who smoked crack and sucked dick to pay for it. She was no fool though, was clean of all the major medical issues that one did not want anywhere near one's crotch and only went with a certain clientele, johns just like him, her own personal party crew. She could read people too, had to, to survive. She knew that some day it would all end in disaster, that was the choice she made the first time she smoked crack and took it over the life she was about to leave behind. But for now it was controllable to her, manageable, once there were a few like him about to fund the mission. Friendships like these could last not longer than six months as most ran out of money quickly or developed other problems, issues that lead quickly, normally, to death in one of its many guises. Some very few had the wherewithal to keep it going, to sustain 'Life on the Rails'.

'He could be one of them' she always thought, when he paged her or cruised up beside her in the truck, its sapphire metallic-like liquid in the sporadic sodium vapor glow of a street lamp. Sammy saw him as she strutted and came over to him and kissed him on the cheek, a sign to the other wildlife on the corner he was cool. They went to the bodega and bought five glass stems and screens, they wouldn't serve a white guy like him unless someone like her was with him, no matter how often he was there, he looked too much like an undercover cop. They walked the few paces back to the truck. Once she was aboard, they would drive straight up Starr to the south side of Troutman on the next block and smoothly she would get out and go into the four-story walkup that was 237, with the cash. He would drive a lap of two to four blocks, always turning east to check for cruisers, it was a hot neighborhood after all as far as the cops were concerned, and pick her up again when she emerged, all with no fuss, all done smoothly. She had two *Eight balls* of crack and the *Play* for being both large and regular, at least compared to the other locals. As he pulled away from the curb the choices were the shithole Hotel where no questions were asked on Bushwick, her crib or his place? Tonight it had to be as cool a place as could be and yet unrestrained. Her 'crib' was her mothers' place, who also smoked crack along with her friend, the sexy forty-something widow from across the street, called Dena.

They all knew one another by now, smoked together, sometimes watched others fornicate or try to fornicate together, while one or other of the ladies would provide a running critique of the participants and their technique. To say it was surreal was an understatement, but it was reasonably safe and never dull. As he had plenty of money for material on this particular night, he didn't mind going there. Also it was the best education in street Spanish you could hope for. The patois that was spoken there was both clipped, hurried, pointed and crude, hopeful and warm with moments of joy interspersed with the reality of what all its denizens were actually about.

Sammy was a heroin addict, and she was never really into crack, only as a sideline if she couldn't get smack. He knew she had gotten a wrap or two for herself when in getting his material in 237, that was just how it worked and he didn't care, now upon arrival at her home she greeted her mother and Dena and then said she was taking a shower before getting ready to go out again, but not to work. She would be shooting up in one of the bedrooms first.

He was greeted warmly and made himself comfortable on one of the three couches in the living area, the kitchen was off to one side separated by a unit suspended from the ceiling over a counter, so you could look out and talk back into the main area. In the middle of the room was a glass topped coffee table of respectable size, organized but laden with all kinds of paraphernalia. Mama G was sitting legs tucked up on one couch beside Lowell, her son of about twentyeight, Dena was laying on her side with her head propped on one hand, smiling at him on the other. He sat alone on the third.

Mostly the place was ok, depending on who was actually there on any given night. There would be a new face every now and then but Thomas was a regular, liked, wanted and even if the new faces were known to others present, they knew not to upset the status quo. Also he was security for Mama G when Lowell was out doing his thing. Not five minutes after he sat down, a slag from the Bronx arrived and asked 'who the big motherfuckin Cracker was.' Lowell had her hustled out the door before the last syllable was out of her mouth. Thomas just watched the scene unfold, knowing full well it was a fine line between being welcome and getting the door for causing trouble, so he said nothing. He was not worried too much as he could well handle himself and had to often enough, since this odyssey of his had begun, but a gun could handle anyone. After much wailing and pleading from out in the hallway, Mamma G asked him if he minded if she came back in, he didn't, anything to make the racket stop. The Housing Police could be on their rounds, not likely but still all the same, a concern. The slag came back in; her name was Tray as it turned out and she had to be known to Mama G or else she would never have been there in the first place, she had a pipe and only one dime bag of material. She was all over the place with apologies, like a puppy that had just had its snout nipped by the alpha female of the pack. 'Whatever' he thought and smoking swiftly began. He put almost a full dime into his pipe, lit up and inhaled it in one long slow luxurious burn, being careful all the time to not over burn the material or crack the end of the glass stem, twisting it back and forward as he drew on it.

He was good at this now. He held it in for a long time and then sat back and slowly exhaled, the rush was excellent, bliss. The new arrival he noticed, was in her twenties, looked in her thirties but had a slim body and a pretty face. The talk resumed as he floated in the happy place but he was perfectly aware of everything being said both verbally and otherwise. Body language was universal, especially in a crack house. He sat up a bit and loaded a pipe for Mama G and Dena to share, that's how they liked to do it sometimes, half and half. Lowell got up and made his excuses, as he got ready to leave. He was a low / mid level dealer who looked after three different corners in the hood for the main local guy and he had work to do. He was also a handy contact when it suited. Thomas got up and they clasped hands and back slapped street style with the salute 'Good looking out man' He kissed his mother and handed her a small packet saying 'that's for the big man' meaning Thomas, however, because Tray was there he gave it to her instead as she wouldn't know who it was for so then couldn't be nagging to get some of it. As he went to the door he turned 'Man I'll be back with that bundle before you go, say an hour or so, ok?' That would be the other $100 worth of good material he had ordered via coded text message while on the way, that he would be taking back to Queens to end the night well.

'Yeah no worries Lowell, be safe' was the relaxed reply. He still had nine from the bundle Sammy had bought for him plus the four dimes Mama G was holding for him. He would let her keep those. After the door was locked again the three women loaded up and he did the same. The Bronx woman looked around the room, hoping without saying it for a piece from someone. Thomas was no fool; he had four dimes on the table and the rest safely tucked away. He turned to Mama G as her daughter and her neighbor lit up their lighters, warming the ends of their stems before smoking. 'Mama G, how much play we get?'

'Four Poppi, same material as before' that was good and the material was good as well, strong and not cut with too much speed or other shit. 'Those are for you Mama G, thanks for the hospitality as always'. She smiled knowing full well he would slip her a few more before he left. Sammy came back in the room, got a quick hit from her mother and went back towards the bathroom to finish getting ready. When she did eventually go out she would score some heroin two blocks over. That was they way she did it usually, once she knew Lowell was on the corner she would pass by, get it there and go shoot up with a few other girls who worked the same track together. They would not be turning tricks tonight. Even hookers need a night off he reckoned. She came back out and gave him the false hug as usual, 'Page me Poppi, when you coming again ok?'

'Yeah, of course babe", she also kissed her Mom and the neighbor and then said to the Bronx girl 'You coming Tray?'

'No I got to go work tonight' that drew a look and then a shrug and she was out the door. Mama G knew where this was going already and said 'Tray, don't you sit there begging off my Irish son with those eyes,' while

31

waving an authoritative finger for emphasis. She could play a room with the best of them. Tray shrank a little at that. She had already scraped out some of the crack residue from her pipe onto the glass tabletop and repacked her screens into the opposite end. She loaded up the pipe with what she had and warmed it slowly with the lighter. The rest of them loaded up and smoked, all leaning back in their own way as the rush washed over them. Tray smoked her bit and did the same sitting on the floor with her back to the wall. He discretely watched Mama G out of the corner of his eye, he knew she liked girls and obviously Tray was here to get smoke, in exchange she would be staying to please Mama G.

'Why don't you get comfortable Poppi, me and Dena kind of like it when you do' the two old friends laughed, they had an hour to kill with plenty of smoke before Lowell came back, he would be coming and going all night in intervals of an hour or two, either to stash cash or collect more material from his stock stash. The women looked at each other knowingly; they had their desires while getting high too. He agreed and took off his jeans feeling much freer now in boxers and a tee shirt, Tray just played with her stem trying to get more residue out of it. He took another hit and stretched back feeling the rush and sexy.

Dena was forty-something but a good-looking woman, she got off the other couch and sat beside Thomas and stroked his crotch while Mama G watched and smoked. They were both getting turned on and they chatted randomly as his hard-on grew tingling inside the cotton. He fished a dime off the table for himself and Mama G loaded a pipe for herself and Dena. The stroking continued, softly, gently as Dena became more aroused herself. He put half the dime in his pipe and then said to the Bronx refugee 'Wanna hit?' She smiled a hungry smile and was over to the couch like a shot. He gave her the other half still in the bag and took his hit while she got ready to smoke, as he lay back for the exhale and rush Dena and Mama G took their hits then Mama G took his pipe and started to reload it for him from her own stash. He exhaled slowly feeling the tingle amplify as Dena continued to stroke him and at the same time started to play with her nipples through her top.

Mama G handed over his pipe really full and as he lit up to smoke it, Dena pulled out his dick and looked at the Bronx girl, she was on it like a dog on a sausage exhaling her hit out around the top of his dick before closing her mouth over it and beginning to suck wetly. He exhaled his hit and loved it. Dena got up and moved to Mama G's couch, they were more than just friends and as Mama G watched Thomas getting his dick sucked she opened her legs and Dena started to lick her pussy. She came quickly and never once took her eyes off the show on the other couch. He lit a cigarette as Tray continued with gusto, more to delay the orgasm than from any real desire for a fag.

Dena and Mama G loaded up all the pipes again and Dena brought his back with her to the couch, she had managed to leave her mini skirt and panties behind. She knelt beside him facing him and took his left hand and put it on her pussy, he knew what to do and how she liked it. He obliged her as she lit his pipe for him, Mama G was stroking herself violently now about to come again but not yet, she was enjoying the show. Dena put the hot stem down in the ashtray hot side up as always and he held the crack smoke deep in his lungs as he played with her clit, she had her tits out now and as she let her hit trickle slowly out of her nose, she was pulling her nipples and thrusting her hips against his fingers rapidly. He exhaled and as the rush washed over him he tapped Tray on the head to signal he was about to shoot his load and give her the chance to get off his dick in time, she dropped her mouth down and licked his balls which he loved and directed his cock away from her head with her hand, he came strongly and as he did so both Mama G and Dena climaxed as well almost simultaneously.

'Fuck yeah that was good' he said while the other two women moaned and purred and muttered in their own way. Tray sat back up, looking well pleased with herself, took his cigarette and smoked it. He swam in the beautiful post-orgasmic void, enjoying the view. He took another dime and handed it to Tray who straight away got ready to smoke it, he told her to use it all as he would give her another. She smiled, delighted as each dime bag would give about three or four good hits depending on how you smoked and your tolerance for the material. He sat forward and reached down between her legs as she smoked, she was surprised but happy too, he pleasured her as he had Dena, getting turned on by seeing his hand disappearing up beneath a strangers hemline, Dena and Mama G again watched and called encouragement to Tray as she came too. Now they were all satisfied he got up to go to the bathroom, he didn't bring his jeans with him but whilst trust had its limits in a crack den, Mama G and Dena would have his back when it came to watching his stuff because he looked out for them, he wasn't selfish; swings and roundabouts applied, even here.

He washed himself off and came back to the room to put on his jeans and boots. He looked at his watch and realized that Lowell would be back inside of fifteen minutes; time always did fly when one was having fun. The three women were now all on the same couch stoking and smoking and oblivious to the fact he was there. Suited him fine, he had one more hit then wrapped up his stem in clean tissue paper and stashed it along with his material. He went to what passed as a kitchen area and made an instant coffee. He smoked a cigarette while drinking it and watched the ladies play.

As soon as they were done, Dena got quickly dressed from a medium sized overnight bag she always had with her here, and Tray went to the washroom, Mama G fixed herself up, her real son would be back soon and this was not a show for him to see, some values still held true in the fog of drugs, but not many. He had left a bag on the table for Tray. 'Dena was a sexy bitch, no doubt' he thought as she sat down opposite his kitchen viewpoint showing off her fresh white panties to good effect. He brought his coffee over and lit another cigarette as he sat on the very end of the sofa. 'The dime on the table is for Tray' he said, 'Here's a nice one for you'

'Thank you Poppi' Dena chimed as she put her hand on his crotch again 'Steady now babe, let's not start something we can't finish' She feigned a pout of disappointment but he knew she'd get over it. He looked at his watch and as he did so they heard Lowell's special knock, right on time. Dena got up and went to the door, checking first through the special peephole which was large enough to see more than just a narrow view of the hallway beyond, it was also tinted so that whoever was outside could not tell if it was being used or not. A pricey little piece of optics but necessary in Lowell and his mothers' line of business. She unlocked the door and he slipped quickly in to the short hallway beside the kitchen. All seemed well by the body language.

Greetings were once again exchanged and he handed Thomas the 'bundle' of crack in exchange for the cash, he also slipped him another five-dime bags of 'play'.

This night was shaping up nicely and it was only just gone midnight. Lowell turned to his mother and they spoke in rapid fire, Thomas caught most of it. Lowell was saying he was going out again and would not be back until at least dawn, big deal going on later at his gangs' main bagging crib, that being the place where they cooked the crack and then sorted it by quality and bagged it in either bundles, dimes or nickels. A 'nickel' was five dollars on the corner and normally was the poorest quality with the most 'cut' but then again that's where a lot of the business at the street level was. Brought a whole new meaning to the term 'Nickel and Dime' Thomas reckoned. Lowell turned and asked Thomas if he was staying, he was worried if he was gone about people calling to the apartment and no man he trusted being there to look after Mama G.

Before he could answer, Mama G said 'He's going Poppi, but I'll be ok I'm locking the door for good until you get back, Tray is in the shower and she will be staying for a while, I don't want no-one else coming tonight'. Lowell seemed happy with that answer and grunted in assent. Turning he gave Thomas the back slap street hug and as he again turned to his mother to say goodnight, Thomas could see the .22 caliber pistol wedged in the waistband of his baggy jeans almost obscured by his Knicks vest but not quite, yeah the boys were definitely up to something tonight and he was glad he was not hanging around. The spy hole was again checked and Lowell slipped out the door as smoothly as he had entered. Mama G asked 'Poppi, why don't you take Dena with you? She's been hanging around all day and might want to get away' this was said with a smile, a knowing smile. 'Sure, why not?' he replied even though he had had every intention of doing just that anyway, but still better it happened this way. Dena was delighted, she loved going to party with him, she was not a hooker per se and did not turn tricks, but she had come to like Thomas and especially going to his place in Woodside. The three bedroom balconied place he had was to her like a Manhattan duplex would have been to him, clean, large and most importantly, uninhabited.

Tray re-emerged from the shower in a large reasonably white towel, Mama G looked at her speculatively and he took this as his cue to move. He went over to her and gave her a kiss on the cheek, she embraced him with a strong hug she did have genuine affection for him, as much as anyone who smoked crack regularly could. 'You take care Mama G and thank you' he said as their hug parted. 'Don't worry Poppi, I'm going to see you in a few days' she was already moving to the door with him, as Tray sat on the couch and started to take one of the screens out of a pipe to begin the process of cleaning it, getting ready for what was to come. Again the spy hole was consulted and Thomas slipped out into the hallway, Dena close behind. Once over the threshold there were no more goodbyes or chat, the door had been swiftly closed quietly, locked and bolted, they were on their own until they knocked again or the sun rose, whichever came first.

Moving surely while aware of all the sounds he had come to expect in a building like this at this time of night, the busy trade time, they moved to the elevator and Dena pressed the call button. They only spoke in hushed tones, both listening intently for the slightest sound out of place amongst the ambient of domestic bliss and terror combined. The elevator arrived, both were already standing either side of the doorway when it opened, it was empty. He reached in and pressed the button for the ground floor and as the door closed again they both hurried in a measured way to the stairwell. The controlled dash from the fifth floor took less than a minute and as the elevator arrived they were already walking swiftly across the lobby and out to where the truck was parked. It stood out in the neighborhood, but less than the blinged out cars of the players or the wannabe players but that was ok, out here everybody who could be a problem knew who drove it and that he was tight with Lowell & co and that was that.

He had learned early on that the problem areas and times were inside the buildings, the hallways and lobbies, the unfamiliar apartments, plus as he was a tall well built white guy he was assumed to be an undercover pig first and to someone looking at a third strike in the federal pen for the load of drugs and illegal gun he just might have on him, like Lowell earlier, that meant shoot first and run second. He opened the door of the truck for Dena to get in, both from the same side and had it started and moving in a matter of seconds, all very controlled with a measured haste and normal speed. Once they turned the corner and headed west on Bushwick they could relax a bit, check for cruisers or tails and light a cigarette. Dena reached over and rubbed his crotch and smiled as she then turned on the radio all with the same hand, 105.9FM the 'loco' Spanish station that did his head in, suited where they were though. Soon he was passing down Woodward to Metropolitan and then on to Grand Avenue direction. He was driving down 58th Street past the NYPD garage where they fixed all the police vehicles which always made him sweat and chuckle simultaneously, no-one ever wants to see over a hundred blue and whites while carrying enough crack to do ten years if the judge was having a bad day. Within ten minutes of starting the truck, it would be parked outside the apartment on a side street off 58th just south of Queens Boulevard, no more than fifteen minutes since he said goodbye to Mama G in her Den. Ten minutes to travel from one Galaxy to another.

The difference in atmosphere was huge in the small space of time it had taken to make the transit. Here the night was warm and safe, the smell of freshly cut grass wafted over the retaining wall of the cemetery and gave an olfactory counterpoint to the reduced hum of the night-time traffic heading its way east and west on the boulevard, the neighbors' window-mounted air conditioners added their own background baseline as he opened the main door and stood to one side as Dena entered with a smile ahead of him and went up the stairs to the door at the second landing. Inside she turned and gave him a long lingering kiss before heading for the shower. He kept the place very clean and tidy mostly, unlike his mind, 'Perhaps that's why' he mused as he put on the stereo and selected Massive Attack's *Mezzanine* from the menu before walking across the polished oak floor to open the patio door leading to the balcony. In the background he could hear the shower running and the happy humming of Dena as she enjoyed herself. He was as happy as he could be at this point in his life. He hated it right now, all of it, himself, what he was doing, the people he was cavorting with, the drugs, all of it but at the same time it was exhilarating, fun and in a very frightening way, fulfilling.

Out on the balcony he looked up and he could see Mars and Venus, he liked that but his favorite was Orion and that was a delight of the winter months only. He went back inside and lit candles in the living room, kitchen and the master bedroom, a lot of candles, some for light and some for aroma and light. He lit some joss sticks in each room as well and then got a beer from the fridge as he sat down at the kitchen table to roll a quick joint from the five-ounce bag he kept in the freezer. The shower continued its rain dance as he rolled and *Dissolved Girl* filled the space with its melody, the lyrics a strange echo of his current reality. He quickly rolled a second and then brought the first and the beer out to the balcony. He settled in the old chair he'd gotten in some yard sale a while back, it was weatherproof but big and comfortable to him as he gazed at what little of the heavens he could see through the light pollution all around him. He contemplated the stars and constellations, thinking back to when he would listen to Carl Sagan describe the Cosmos in a documentary that he and his father would watch together. The Cosmos and Antarctic Exploration were two legs of the stool of education that his father had been denied by circumstance in his time but had made up for by his own efforts, the other being poetry which he could recite at will or request to suit any situation. Thomas had a deep desire to understand who he was and where in all of the vastness of the universe he would find a place, meaning. This chair on the balcony was his observatory and drugs were the mirrors upon which the images would form so he could try to grasp the meaning of what he saw, night after night. He felt safe in that chair looking at the sky, as he had sitting in another chair beside his father all that time ago. Back then he had absorbed the language of science as he had his mother tongue, easily, naturally with the innocent zeal of a child. To him the Stars were suspended in vast transparent aspic, clearly visible but somehow beyond the impenetrable barrier of the atmosphere, the sky. There was poetry too, in the imagined and visualized movement of suns and solar systems, galaxies as they twined about each other dancing and colliding on a timescale that made his span a meaningless speck on a quantum scale.

The cosmic filaments that contained galaxy clusters and super clusters separated by dark matter that when imaged by mathematical simulations designed by impressive minds on supercomputers and released on scientific websites, looked to him like a 3D image of the neurons in a human brain. The inter-connectedness of it all was a wonder to him as he felt so disconnected from everything he had believed was correct, what he had been 'educated' to believe. The limits of his learning could only allow his passion for an answer to overcome his understanding so much, then like elastic would inexorably pull him back to his own reality and bathe him in recrimination and regret once again. He sipped at the beer and pondered the sky as a brief pause of music from the CD's changing their relative positions within their own unthinking mechanical dance, allowed him to hear the shower was no longer running. The moment was passing yet again, but it left him feeling as though he could recapture it later, like an aroma in a deserted kitchen that said while the table was bare there was a freshly made pie beckoning, hiding, somewhere.

The music started again, the jangling intro of *Sour Times* by *Portishead* that always made him think of Cold War spies and their various missions as described by *Le Carre* et al. He could feel rather than hear Dena coming across the polished floor barefoot, he turned in his observatory chair and watched her silhouette approach outlined in the nimbus of candle light, the flickering shadows dancing as the flames bent with the air still moving, but much more gently after the rain storms passing.

Chapter 4. Risky Sources

A simple ashtray can often tell you more about a place and what's been cooked, smoked and toked in a room inside the last hour, than anything else. Cardboard rectangles of *Rizla* packet covers, raw tobacco from ripping cigarettes open to roll joints and their discarded filters, the smaller plastic packets scattered around the ashtrays periphery, evidence of the more serious stuff. This particular apartment had a coffee table, rather a good one, matched to the rest of the room. It was a typical Upper West Side condo; doorman, plants in the lobby and the elevators, hallways quiet, unadorned and evocative of a sterile national motel chain. As he had entered the building earlier and exited the elevator to walk quietly but briskly to his destination, he had noticed the subtle scent of incense, very faint but present nonetheless, as he passed several doorways, there was more than one *Party* resident it seemed. But back to the ashtray, crack and weed, both of good quality is what the debris told him.

The resident of this particular place was called Steve, or as Thomas liked to think of him, *Shelob* the spider, sitting in the center of a web of illusory power. There were several other denizens present, but they were of no concern and certainly no threat to Thomas, well no

42

physical threat but they could get troublesome by being stupid, which was always an issue in situations like this. Thomas had seen a few of the others when here before and basic nods of acknowledgement were exchanged when he had entered the room, beyond that nothing, just as he wanted it to be. Steve, of course had been effusive in his welcome, but he had been expecting that, the false joy of seeing someone who at this time of night, would be a vehicle to get more rock. Steve was typical of the breed even though he thought he was special, very special indeed. He was an addict but a slightly more upper-crust one, who as a result, had no place on the streets either buying or using. He would have been chewed up in an instant and spat out like so many others before him. Because he had a place he actually owned and some sort of income no matter how small, left from his trust fund or disability or whatever, he had made a web connecting users just like him, who needed to get their hands on stuff, but outside of using him as a conduit, didn't know how or were too scared to find out themselves. He played them all like a mad puppet-master, the coke sweat beading on his brow as his beady little eyes gleamed with a fervent desire to get high, to feel the power, out from behind the glasses encased in what had once, no doubt, been hip designer frames.

Thomas had come across him by chance via a hooker he had met a few months previously while out on the town one night. She had mentioned him as a source for really good stuff in Upper Manhattan, when they had run out of material while partying hard. He had his own contacts down in the Lower East Side but you had to be careful and not high, to go shopping or collecting there, after nine pm. He had agreed, as trying to find rock in a neighborhood where you were not known or did not know the ropes, was a dodgy proposition to say the least.

43

Since then Thomas had come here several times, more for the sake of variety than anything else as there was a great difference in the taste of material between the various boroughs of New York City sometimes. But the main reason he came here was to develop some *cred* as a regular and to get in with the dealer, which could be a tricky process at the best of times. Steve knew Thomas would look after him with a few dime bags which was way above the odds for a transaction like this, but Thomas always tried to be cautious and would rather drop a few dimes and be safe, than stay and smoke his head off with a group of head wreckers, who would ruin the high anyway. Steve also knew not to mess with Thomas He had tried that the first night by doing a swap on the coffee table - one bag of stuff for a bag of shit. He had not expected to get caught and certainly had not expected to be told in a calm chilling voice to return it before he got hurt. There had been a moment of tension when eyes locked. Steve thought about protesting, but he saw in Thomas's eyes that he was not to be trifled with, so he had relented and been even more surprised when Thomas had not made any more of it, and gave him half the bag saying 'That's the first and last time you try something with me, now have some of that and when I call again we will pretend this never happened, agreed?' Steve made eye contact again and quietly said, 'agreed'.

There had been no issues between them since, but for sure, there was a very uneasy and subtle tension. Thomas didn't mind, as he knew it kept Steve in his little box and himself on his toes. Steve could play his little God games with his other clients, getting dime bags or blowjobs, or both, off the other scared former rich kids who came here to get their stuff, but he knew Thomas was not to be messed with. What Steve did not know was that this would be the last time Thomas would be coming here. There were several reasons, but foremost was that if the expected dealer showed up tonight, Thomas would be getting his number as it would be the third time they had done business, and he always bought bigger than the other creatures present who bought dimes and fifties at the most. Steve never let anyone call the dealer or page him, that was his imagined power, but Thomas had already let the dealer know the last time that he wanted to deal direct, with a note slipped to him with the money. He had received a text from a throwaway phone, saying in ghetto speak, that the third time was the charm, and hence he was here. The other big reason was, he had been here several times over the last few months and that was pushing his luck on several levels, the doormen would recognize him now, even if he was well dressed and together when he came here. They knew which apartment he was going to and they knew what went on in there for sure, they only turned a blind eye because they either bought some stuff or sold Steve some weed themselves every now and then, it was after all, a city of entrepreneurs. The other reason was you never knew when a place like this was getting staked out or one of the neighbors had decided to call the cops about people moving quietly late a night on a constant basis, or the smell. Even now Thomas was not happy at the amount of smoke in the place and it was only 11pm, and he had no idea of what kind of nutcase Steve might have had up here recently trying to get a hit. Even the most disciplined of users, had a tipping point, where the *fiending* for a hit outperformed their well developed and subtle eccentricities, each one existing to cover their using as best they could. By the evidence surrounding the ashtray and the amount of smoke in the place that point may well have passed for Steve a few days ago. Thomas had decided when he arrived and took in the situation, that if the dealer was not here in ten minutes, he was outta here. It was, after all, only a matter of time before shit just simply caught up with you, the perfect storm of a bad night, bad choices in both material and cohorts and the next thing you knew the cops were battering down the door. For Steve, that would be the end. As soon as New York's finest were putting the chrome bracelets on and he began his journey towards Rikers Island, he would be finished. Life, or what he had left of one; job, family, friends, trust fund, no matter how it might pretend in the movies, rarely survived the first trip through the criminal justice system. This knowledge was also another reason why Thomas no longer wanted to be here; who was to say Steve hadn't already had a visit from the boys in blue and turned turtle, which he would have done, at the first sight of a badge? He would sing like a canary to avoid even one night in Central Booking. 'Yeah,' Thomas mused to himself 'Time to blow this particular Clam-bake'

One of his fellow 'Travellers of a reasonable Caliber' as he liked to think of them, had been collected in a raid on a place just like this, the guy who ran the place never saw the inside of the squad car. The cops put him straight back in business as in a few months' time, when all the fuss had died down, another raid would offer up a few mid level dealers and a group of high caliber users and the precincts stats would get a nice boost. His fellow traveller had the unfortunate pleasure of having enough good quality rock, paraphernalia and tainted cash on him to keep the Devil himself entertained for a week in Vegas. 12 years in upstate New York was not what Thomas would call a humorous outcome. Shelob Steve caught Thomas's eye for the briefest of moments and he smiled in that twitchy way, Thomas was instantly on high alert, that look, in that instant, told him that this place was on a long slow heat and it could flame up any night now, perhaps even this one. He reflected on what he had observed on the way here. He had taken the subway to Central Park West and walked briskly, purposefully, for four blocks in either direction before approaching and entering the lobby of the building. The cops normally preferred the hours of 2am to 5am for their door bashing; those were the hours where 'life on the rails' in all its forms, was normally in full swing, the occupants of their objectives were normally well high and less vigilant. Still, even though he had not seen anything obvious on his route here, that did not mean the place was not being watched or worse, on the list of places to be mined that night for information and a few easy arrests. The tug of love that was the war on drugs, playing itself out at the local level.

Thomas had stayed clear of most kinds of trouble so far in that regard, he had had a few close ones along the way but he was pretty sure he had never fully come to the attention of the law. Be polite and people were less inclined to drop a dime on you when the law came calling, plenty of candidates in a city like this, no point in volunteering to one of them. If there had been a girl close to the building who looked like she would hang out and party with you if you were willing to share, that would have been bad news and a dead giveaway. This was for sure not a place to linger and enjoy the fruits of the night's labors, no matter what the smell of incense told you in the hallway. The 'Gut' was never to be ignored and Thomas was getting that tingle, as he surveyed the room, that said while the telegraph key was not tat-tat-tatting out news of his impending doom, the line was live and open.

He swept his eyes about the room again to be greeted by the usual nods and shuffles, some names exchanged and of course no handshakes, any SOB who extended his or her hand in that manner, to a stranger in a place like this, a Judas for sure. Thomas wasn't feeling this place tonight at all, but a few minutes was worth the wait to get this contact sorted. He lit a cigarette and smoked carefully, he would not smoke anything else here no matter what anyone else would do. No one had pulled out a stem since he arrived, so the place may well be tenser than he thought initially. He contemplated abandoning his carefully planned night's entertainment, if he had to. While that would indeed make for an uncomfortable night and a sleepless one at that, this vibe was not sitting with him. He drew purposefully on his cigarette and pondered, hyper alert on the inside and muscles almost fully coiled to strike, if need be. Smoking in a nonchalant manner was an art form at his level of vigilance. He checked his watch again, two minutes was all he was going to give this enterprise, and then he was gone. Right then it came, like a Klaxon blaring, full of adrenaline flooding into the middle of his thoughts. Steve picked up his trembling and wailing cell phone and muttered a quick 'yes, ok' that meant the dealer was walking into the lobby right now; allowing for the elevator and the walk, he would be at the door in about 130 seconds, you counted and remembered stuff like that if you wanted to stay out of jail while smoking crack. A quick glance and study of Shelob's face in Thomas's peripheral vision as he flipped the phone closed told him all he needed to know. This time it would be all right, no surprises were in the elevator – as far as he knew anyway. Right on time there was a knock on the door.

If nothing else, the logistics department of 'Life on the Rails Inc.' tended to be punctual. The dealer was typical, dressed on the nightclub side of street fashion, which would have made him passable for going and coming to buildings just like this one, all over the Upper West Side. The dealer gave him a nod, barely perceptible, but there nonetheless. In the note Thomas had slipped him the last time had been a street name for a dealer down 14th Street direction, from another crew. That nod told Thomas his name had checked out and the word was good. This guy was a lieutenant and would only be there if the word had been good and he thought it was going to be worth his while. Thomas was so damn happy that his parents had reared him to be polite; this kind of acknowledgment was a close as this lifestyle came to a karmic compliment. He was simultaneously sure his parents would rather he used their good rearing of him, for better purposes. He would be getting great quality stuff and only buying two *bundles* off of the dealer here. That would be four big, tasty, fifty rocks and maybe two or more, dime bags of play. The play, two of them and no more, would be for Steve and then he was out of here for good, he only needed the dealer's number after all and then he could call him in fifteen minutes or so after getting out of Steve's place and buy the rest of the stuff he wanted for the night's enjoyment. The dealer would still have his number from the last occasion and a simple call would be all that it would take to close the deal, no one here would have a clue and that was very, very important. If Steve got wind he was never coming back it would get ugly quick, desperation would make him demand more than Thomas would be willing to give and that would end badly for all involved, a fracas in a place like this would have no winners, only losers.

The dealer exchanged a few words with Steve and moved to the connected kitchen area, where deals could be conducted out of sight but an eye could be kept on the congregation. As soon as Steve was done, it only took a few seconds, as he was buying damn all, Thomas moved smoothly over and was doing his deal before Steve had reached his La-Z-Boy recliner and sat down again. Quick as that the deal was done. As Thomas moved out of the kitchen area the next customer was moving in, the rest forming a line, like homeless folk at a soup kitchen. He took the two strides or so, over towards Steve and in his outstretched hand he already had the two dimes secreted, the dealer had given him six which was another good sign, as he shook hands with Steve he palmed them off to him. His eyes lit up with a feral hunger as he received them, Thomas said 'Catch you in a few days' time Steve.' He did not even have time to think of a reply before Thomas was moving across behind the line of supplicants queuing for the kitchen. The door was smoothly unbolted and closed firmly and quietly behind him after he stepped through into the quiet hallway. He reminded himself to move at a normal pace and keep calm as he approached the elevator, which he did despite the pounding in his chest as his unconscious tried to get him excited enough to smoke some of the really good material he had just purchased, right now! He ruthlessly pushed that feeling deep down inside, while at the same time marveling at how his own body and mind would happily have him betray himself by smoking his crack pipe, right here right now, just because it knew it was good stuff. 'My God!' he thought as the elevator doors swished open in front of him, 'Part of me really wants to smoke right now, and to hell with the consequences, Damn!' he could hear the Demon, deep inside, cackle a mad laugh in his direction. The elevator seemed to not move after the doors closed with him inside for what seemed like an age, the Demon was messing with his perception of time now, just for fun, just because it wanted to feel him taste the object of his addiction, right now. The stainless steel box, complete with plastic foliage, began to move downwards and as it did so he heard a door close, not quite a slam, but louder than it should have been. He only had four floors to descend and that took less than thirty seconds. The fire escape was alarmed so no one was going to get down that way. He waited until just before the elevator doors opened into the lobby, and pushed the buttons for the first three floors. This would ensure he got a five-minute head start; as the elevator stopped at each floor on the way up and went through its cycle of stopping, opening, closing and subsequently moving again, before anyone else was getting out in the lobby, he would only need two minutes.

Those two minutes saw him down the street and into the opening of the Subway stairs like a mole dodging a fox. He would just make the last train, he could hear its rattling approach as he swiped his Metro card and went trackside. The F train would have him back into Queens quicker than any cab would, even at this time of night. The train was anonymous as always as it picked up speed, heading from 69th across beneath the East River towards 21st Street in Long Island City. There were a few people on the train but not of his concern. He got off the train and hurried up the steps like any other New Yorker getting home later than normal. He was around the corner of the Boulevard and into the familiar, safe, side streets of Woodside, where cops and firefighters lived, alongside people just like Thomas.

The evening was warm but comfortable. He opened the patio door onto the balcony enough so the curtain swirled slightly with the breeze every now and then. Rain began to fall steadily, it was that time of year after all. He lit the candles about the large room and the adjacent kitchen, ran the bath – hot, and went to put some music on. He twirled the dial and found NPR's Classical Live from the Metropolitan Opera house in New York, a playback of the earlier recorded performance. He undressed and as the full tub cooled just a bit, he took out the new stuff and took a hit. It was every bit as good as it looked and burned in the pipe. It tasted the way he always hoped crack would, in the moment just before putting the lighter to the end of the stem for every hit he'd ever taken. It also made him gag and nearly puke, all at the same time, which was a sign of really high quality stuff. He relaxed into it and lay naked on the bed, the mild nausea would pass and he had a follow up hit from the pipe as it started to do just that. It felt like he was swimming even though he was perfectly still as the music washed over him. The bath would be ready now. He rose and gathered his stuff on a tray he had for nights like this. He could soak and smoke, stretch and contort himself yoga-like, luxuriating in the sheer physical and spiritual side, as he thought of it, akin to some sort of pagan ritual, enhanced by the Druids' knowledge of the local Fungi. He pondered this and thought of where it would take him tonight. Would it be to new awakenings of the conscious mind and the fabric of reality? Or would he think of Demons again which he could never seem to vanquish, no matter how hard he tried. 'That was the deal though' he reconfirmed to himself, 'Surely if you have the sheer arrogance to question God, while indulging all the base lustful aspects of life, would you not expect a reminder from the other side of the fence?' The Devil would have his due; that was the hope that kept him believing, he would snap out of it soon and leave the life behind and get clean.

He sank into the hot scented water and felt a thrill as his balls began to float, that was a hello from the lust side but not now, maybe in a bit. A fresh stem and a pre-loaded follow-up were to hand and he took the full half of the pipe in one hit. He swam in the void momentarily as he exhaled, he lit the pipe again, when it was loaded like this, the double shot approach was best he thought. The second burn would slowly fill his lungs to capacity after fully exhaling the strike off the first burn. After inhaling the second strike, he held his breath, put the pipe down on the tray in its spot and laid back in the hot water. After about a minute, he exhaled the lot in a steady stream split between his mouth and nasal passages. As the rush overtook him, the void opened and he floated through a rift, as he saw it, in his mind's eye. He felt as though he could float free of his corporeal self. The light of the candles danced with the shadows as the rainstorm intensified outside. He was so much more aware of everything at this point. The small vibrations as the metal tub cooled and contracted in some places and expanded in others, the subtle intensity of the rain driving on the roof above and from across the street as the sound came in through the tilting ceiling window. The coughs from the audience as there was a brief pause between movements of the Opera emanating from the radio. The faint beep of the Nextel phone charging in the bedroom, as it reminded him of the passage of another hour, just like a metronome for a piano teacher, the hours could click away that fast sometimes too, time was a thing you could not take for granted when smoking and travelling at this level. He had had to train himself to keep track of that beep, to avoid falling asleep, as was always a temptation with the really good stuff.

He rested his ankles up the wall above the taps and pulled his legs towards his head with his hands behind the knees, the stretch of tension slowly advancing up his spine, focused as he visualized the joints, the tendons, the ligaments and muscle groups. The effect took hold as his back popped in several sequential locations, one by one, until he felt incredibly limber again. The physical arousal from these stretches or *Crack yoga* as he thought of it, 'My own version of Tantric' not that he had any real clue about Yoga of any form, but the concept made sense to him, the idea of joining body and mind in some sort of a dynamic symbiosis. The images in his head slowly passed by, not forced, but random. When he was this relaxed the mind could bring up the most amazing memories and encourage the most astounding questions, almost God-like in their brilliance; but that particular blasphemy was well under control now. Why? Because he had learned that something was there, that you deep down did not want to believe existed.

One night, not too long ago, he had met a hooker and to make a long story short, he had not gotten the best of vibes off of her. She had just happened to be at one of the local street level buy dens on Starr Street. She was hot-looking but with an edge he could not define, she had bought her own material and had her own money from agency work the night before apparently. She offered to go down on Thomas because she was as horny as all damnation and wanted it, 'Great,' he thought, 'A real dyed in the wool enthusiast for dick' However; when he slipped Julio the $20 bill for the use of what passed as his bedroom in the crack den, for an hour to have fun with the enthusiast, he caught her boring her gaze into him with the most terrifying, malevolent, predatory and casual concentration. Her eyes gleamed with amber and crimson fire just for an instant and every hair on his body stood on end, their follicles quivering with primordial fear, it was enough for Thomas. He demurred her offer and quickly left with what he had come to get in the first place and nothing else. He had not yet smoked that night but he was sure of what he had seen and felt. He never forgot that face, and for all that he could not explain exactly how he knew, there were Demons in the world he lived in now. What better place to find the revelers in human misfortune? A place where a soul could be stripped, whipped, humiliated, broken and consumed by a willing weak-minded fool with a drug habit that would allow them to do anything. For all of his sins and the reasons behind them, he still knew that basically while he was dancing a fine line, he had not crossed it just yet. He knew that his Guardian Angel gave him a nudge every now and then, no matter how he might view the situation he was undertaking the intervention for as deplorable and distressing. No indeed, Thomas had learned a lot he would never be able to explain to anyone, except maybe a person just like himself. It was not the kind of question you posed to people over coffee 'Seen any Demons lately then?'

He just knew that that particular night he had been given a glimpse, a not so subtle and real reminder, that there were more than just human and chemical fueled interests at play on this level of life.

The water was at its apogee of his personal temperature curve. He turned on the hot tap to prolong the soak while he took another hit. After a few seconds the heat washed down through him again. He turned off the faucet and after drying his hands, twirled the second stem in his fingertips, careful to not let the load fall out of its tip. He contemplated the liquid light reflecting unevenly along its glass blown length, as he deliberately fully exhaled and emptied his lungs. He placed it to his lips and slowly used the very tip of his lighter's flame to warm the outside of the stem where the screen held the rock, as he slowly rotated it back and forth about its long axis. As the rock inside began to crackle and sweat smoke, he continued to twirl the pipe and began to inhale as he moved the tip of the flame to the opening at the end. The flame bent at right angles to itself as it was drawn in to liquefy and burn through the rock, the remains of its shape melted and folded into the screen as on the other side it vented thick, luscious smoke, that billowed down the now fully clouded pipe, into his lungs. He timed it perfectly when he released the lighter button and stopped inhaling. He rotated the stem briskly between the palms of both hands to dissipate its heat, before quickly and expertly wrapping it in clean tissue paper to protect it while the *Res* or residue, formed inside the pipe. He placed it standing, vertically, on the tray in a receptacle designed just for that very reason. This only took 20 to 30 seconds and all the while he was holding his breath and the full rich hit, deep inside. He lay back and after a moment let the hit out and the rush take him, as it did he felt his penis grow hard and throb with the sheer wave of pleasure waxing through him. He enjoyed and ignored the erection all at the same time.

The reason he *farmed* the residue so carefully and placed the stems just 'so' after taking a hit was twofold. If you had a few pipes on the go, and he always did for really good stuff like this, then as you alternated your way through them as you smoked, after a while you would get lots of residue building up inside the pipes and if you were careful with how you used your lighter as you smoked, it would be a lovely greyish color with no black resin in it. Every now and then you would scrape this out with an appropriate instrument. Pretty soon you would have a nice pile of residue, almost the size of a fifty rock, or bigger depending on how much you were smoking. The second reason to *Farm* the residue, was simply because it was some of the best material you could possibly smoke and as such was to be jealously guarded. More than one smoker had gotten the crap beaten out of them for touching a pipe with residue in it that was not theirs to begin with. Thomas had seen this happen more than once and one night in particular, Mama G had beaten the living daylights out of a guy one of the girls had brought home to do heroin with. It was not a pretty sight by any means. No one had batted an eye though.

He got up out of the draining tub and toweled off, his skin red like he had been too long in a sauna. He put on his bathrobe and went out to the couch. He lit a cigarette and watched out of the window, as the clouds seemed to get darker. The Opera was almost over now. He thought long and hard, as it seemed to him, about what he was going to do next. He was lying to himself by pondering that question, playing the game; the decision had been made earlier as the water had lifted his balls in the tub. This shit was really good and that meant it would be awesome with the right woman for sharing company. But there was no rush on that decision just yet. He decided to roll a joint, that would place a nice mellow undercurrent of arousal while taking a hit every half an hour or so, 'Ok maybe fifteen minutes' he mused. The high was good, prolonged and what he termed an *Up* high, not a *fiending* more, mad scramble to smoke a ton of crap, trying to get exactly where he was right now. Bad shit could drive you crazy, add into the mix the

57

speed it was most likely cut with and you were in for a bad, psychotic, expensive and very unfulfilling night, but not tonight.

On this material you could do anything, theorize, act out, stand and to the awestruck audience of one that you were, make fiery rhetorical speeches like some great historical figure. He had done that a few times and each time wished he had recorded the results, so impressed was he with his rhetoric. He would often, at moments like this, get lost in reading out loud from Shakespeare or Homer or even one of the poets whose work he loved. His musings were interrupted by the dulcet tone of Leonard Lopate's voice emanating from the speakers, an advert for his talk show *New York & Company* on NPR. Time for Thomas to change the music as the Opera was done; somehow he had missed hearing the extended bout of applause that normally marked the end of such broadcasts. Now he needed something to fit the mood. He looked through the stack of CD's as he lit the joint he had just finished rolling automatically. 'Oh Yeah' he exulted to himself as his shuffling revealed Massive Attacks' *Mezzanine* from the stack. He put it on and savored the beat and samples, as music filled the apartment once more. He went in to the bedroom to get ready. The black opaque hose went on first and he loved the texture of them on his skin. They felt good and made him feel sexy and desirable in a bold way, the role-play in his head was making him horny. He was not bisexual or a transvestite, he just loved pantyhose and women wearing them with him. A minor fetish in the great scheme of things and his only one, surprising really considering how much partying he got up to. The way the nylon kissed the instep of his foot and the top of his thighs, they way they looked on a nice rounded, not too big female ass with no panties underneath and how that view felt beneath his hand as he caressed it slowly, carefully.

'Wait a minute!' he was losing the run of himself here, anymore down this line of thought and he would be jerking off. 'Not going to waste a perfectly good orgasm all by myself tonight' he thought knowing that the prospect of good company was not too far off. He pulled on a black tee shirt and put his robe back on. Thomas walked into the kitchen and opened a bottle of red and poured a glass just as the track *Angel* filled the room. He relit the joint as he contemplated who he would call to join him on his quest for tonight, would he need more stuff? No, quality outweighed quantity on a night like tonight. He would relax after he made the call and by the time his date would arrive, in about thirty minutes from now, he would be really aroused, ready for some professional, no nonsense female attention.

As he picked up the phone to make the call, a dim, distant, very faint part of him began to cry yet again and he could not shake that quantum sized sorrow, no matter how he tried. Thomas somehow knew it was his soul, and he could not seem to help hurting it, he knew he could not help hurting himself right now. Thomas hated himself really.

Chapter 5

The Theft of Innocence

At five or six years of age, innocence is your stock in trade. There are certain things you take for granted: love, food and shelter, if you are lucky enough to come from a good home like Thomas did. There was nothing else in his young life except love and security. His parents loved he and his other siblings equally and without question. His father and mother worked hard to run the family business and they were very good at it. Thomas grew up simply understanding that his parents seemed to be known by a lot of people and he accepted it as normal that he would meet new people every other day. Of course he was a blonde, cute child and whether it was merely people being polite to impress his parents, or because they themselves were parents, Thomas was often being complimented and having his hair ruffled during business hours, when he was on the premises and not in school. This was just one of those things that seemed quite natural to Thomas and in a way he enjoyed the attention, every kid would have. The customers of his parents' business came from all walks of life, farmers big and small, professionals, laborers and people of the cloth. As far as Thomas could tell, everyone in the whole world knew his Mammy and Daddy, and that was fine by him.

Each day had a rhythm and an informal sort of routine that adapted itself to the seasons and what was going on in each one of them. For Thomas, school was a recently discovered joy that seemed to take up most of his life, as he thought of it, but he loved the summer holidays as they seemed to last forever and the sun shone for him most days. However, included in everyday things like a core thread connecting all aspects of life was religion, in Ireland the Catholic Church held sway, like no other institution before or since. It pervaded throughout the very fabric of daily living. Each day was started with prayers, each period in school with one too, at twelve noon the Angelus bell would ring out over the fields from the village a mile or so away and everyone would stop and cross themselves and say the angelus. The bell would ring out again at six pm. Before and after each meal grace would be said and every night, no matter what, the family would kneel down and say the rosary together. Each and every Sunday was begun with the stressful rush, as it always seemed to him, to get everyone spit and polished and out the door on time, to get the usual pew in the Church before the parish Priest emerged from behind the Altar, as punctual as an atomic clock, to begin the Sunday Mass. Thomas was never a big fan of the Sunday rush but he did love the Sunday roast and he enjoyed helping his mother from start to finish with the cooking, a love of which he carries to this day.

He asked sometimes 'Why it was so important that everyone pray so much each day' and depending on which parent he asked and what time or place he chose to ask the question, would of course heavily influence both the tone and content of the answer. He had learned very young that questions of any sort were not to be asked in the Church itself, especially when it was full of all the other parishioners looking and projecting their Sunday best. He especially was concerned why, regardless of what was happening, that the Rosary must be said and everyone on their knees to say it. He pointed out one evening that 'God most get tired of all these people praying on to him all the time each and every day' his mother had given him a look that was only short of flaying the skin clean off of him. It was better than the look his Father had directed at him, but he had managed to ignore that and maintain eye contact with his mother, even if it was uncomfortable. After the rosary was over that night he was packed off to bed with no supper. As he had pondered his fate, he had decided that questions relating to religion were not to be posed, full stop. His mother had had a fresh tray of scones cooling in the kitchen for supper that evening and even as he lay in bed, he could smell the butter melting and the fresh tea being poured. 'I won't be missing that again for a question' was the resolution he fell asleep with rolling about in his head. He did of course not feel his mother and father tucking him in later and kissing him on the cheek and forehead. He was already far away in dreamland having a great adventure in which every meal was hot scones with butter and tea. He would know the following morning at breakfast that everything was all right, and in his family it normally was.

At school it was even more frowned upon to utter anything that would be remotely construed as being questioning of God, his Church or its activities. At school you could get a wallop of the teacher's ruler for those kinds of questions, or worse, you could be sent to the headmaster's room and he had a much bigger and thicker ruler and more size to swing it with too. He also did not seem to be fussy about how times you got a lick, Thomas was convinced the man could not count as 'six of the best' could be four or eight depending on the victim or the mood of the Master. He of course did his best to avoid such unpleasantness and would say nothing when a classmate got their marching orders of doom, to head down the hallway, to stand in front of the fifth and sixth class kids as they laughed at the master's jokes about the offender. The shame would often be worse than any belt of the stick. Thomas had been sent there, once, for a minor transgression. Between having to stand in front of a room full of what seemed to him, howling and braying animals, and the fear of the stick the Master was casually pointing in his direction as he conducted the chorus of derision, Thomas began to cry softly with fear, he was only five after all; this only served to increase the howling and braying and the thumping of the stick on the wooden desktop. Thomas was terrified as the sounds washed over him and he wet his pants. The noise and derision reached a new crescendo and Thomas thought it would never end, however the master called order and sent Thomas on his way back down the hallway of doom to his own classroom. He had a female teacher and she would sort out his 'accident'. As he closed the door to the headmasters room and turned to walk away, there was a renewed burst of jollity and he had no doubt it was for him. The shame he felt was like nothing else he had ever experienced. He was wracked by silent wrenching sobs and just stood there, pants and legs wet, in no man's land, lost and afraid. He had been fixed up by the teacher from his classroom, but he was quiet for the rest of the day, he knew all the other kids knew, he knew in a child's instant understanding that they all knew it could be them next, so no one laughed at him from his class. By the time the last bell rang and he packed his leather school bag to leave, he was simply exhausted by the stress and he just wanted to go home, curl up with his dog and go to sleep. His mother had known something was wrong but he said nothing of what had happened. While it had never happened to him, he knew that some kids after getting a slap of a ruler in school got a thick ear if they said it to their parents when they got home, just because they no doubt deserved it for being bold at school in the first place. He was not going to chance that even though his parents never hit any of their children, it was a day to be forgotten and fast, but its lessons regarding authority in Irish society, would linger, especially as he was just turned five years of age when it happened.

One of the many people who came to his father's business was a Priest by the name of Father Brendan Smyth. He was not unique in that, a lot of clergy came to do business with Thomas's father, as he was honest and respectful of the church and its teachings. In another regard Father Smyth was very unique; he was a pedophile. The true extent of his depredations would only become apparent many years later but by then the real damage had been done, to literally hundreds of children. His exposure in those later years would precipitate the fall of the Government of the Irish Republic, but a Government feels no pain and there will always be another one elected and installed. A child only gets one childhood and for a terrifying, lingering portion of his, Thomas got Smyth.

Thomas knew that Fr. Smyth would be about the place every other week. His was a roving ministry that took him from the Abbey in Cavan where he was based, to hospitals and orphanages all over the country, both north and south of the border. He always had the big sweet shop sized jars of sweets in the boot of his car and boxes and boxes of lollipops. These were of course his currency of abuse. In later years, Thomas often wondered just how many times the monster had casually walked into places and institutions, where children were supposed to be safe and protected, with armfuls of this currency, to be given a private room so he could hear confessions and the like. No one would have dared interrupt a Priest, let alone a Priest hearing confessions. He would have been able to do whatever he wished for as long as he wished in those rooms, and he did. The sweets used to groom the new victims into his web and soften the reality for the ones already there.

Sex was another of those things that was taboo in the Ireland of Thomas's youth. Even the hit TV show Dallas was not considered suitable to be watched in a God-fearing home, too many infidelities and divorces, affairs and harlots, lots of unabashed greed and lust. Countless women who got pregnant out of wedlock, whether by choice, rape or sexual abuse at home, were sent to places later called the Magdalene Laundries where they were no better than slaves, to be worked day in and day out and no doubt further abused in many ways. Sex was a subject that never was to be discussed, even more so than tricky questions as to 'Why do we have to go to Mass every Sunday?' Anything to do with the body beyond its basic health, fitness for work or ability to play Gaelic football for the local team was off limits. So much so, that when Thomas was first 'touched' by Fr. Smyth he just knew, he had been conditioned, to keep it to himself. This was of course, the greatest source of pain to Thomas later in life and one of the big reasons Smyth and others like him, got away with it for so long.

It was a lovely sunny day, warm and comfortable. Insects were buzzing from place to plant and back again as Thomas knelt in the long grass behind the cottage he called home. He was very busy trying to figure out how the tie the knot on the fishing hook exactly as his Grandfather had shown him. He almost had it twice but the trick to it eluded him. Still, he knew it could be done and he had all day to do it. He was not aware of the approach of someone, so intent was he on the task at hand, until his name was spoken with confidence and familiarity. 'Thomas, how are you today?' asked the shadow above him, Thomas looked up and recognizing the shape silhouetted against the sunshine replied 'Hello Father Smyth, how are you today Father?' he said waiting on his eyes to adjust, 'I'm good Thomas, I'm good. What are you doing?' he asked as he gestured to the hook and line in Thomas's lap. 'I'm trying to tie the hook on the line how Grand dad taught me, so I can set a fish trap in the river later.'

'I see,' said Smyth as he settled himself down to sit close to Thomas in the long grass. 'Our Lord was a fisherman you know Thomas?' posed Smyth in those unctuous tones that Thomas would later come to hate, instantly, no matter who used them. 'I know that Father, it was on the Sea of Galilee with the twelve apostles Father.' Smyth smiled a slow smile that never reached his eyes 'Yes indeed it was Thomas, the Sea of Galilee, very good Thomas, now I have to talk to you about God and what you have to do to be a good Christian Thomas, your parents asked me to talk to you about this and as a Priest it's my job to teach you these things'. He seemed somehow, to grow a bit in all dimensions as he said this and Thomas had a flutter of something deep inside that he had no idea about, he did not recognize the instinctive alarm nature had provided him with because he had never had need of it before, his life was safe. 'What things Father?' was his innocent reply. 'I have to teach you how to be a good boy that does what he's supposed to do for God and his Church, his priest. You have to learn and as all boys do, keep it secret between you and the priest just like in confession. You've learned about confession haven't you Thomas?' Thomas was getting a sense of foreboding, but he had no reference for it, no understanding of it. He was becoming aware of the man smell, of Smyth, growing stronger and feeling more uncomfortable as a result. 'Yes Father, we are learning about it for my first holy communion next year Father.' He answered quickly, less sure now. 'Very good Thomas, now in confession you tell your sins and you have a lot of sins Thomas, that's why we will have to speak with each other and do things together, to get rid of your sins Thomas because you have been bold Thomas, very bold.' this last was delivered with a rising pitch and glaring eye contact that made Thomas shrink where he sat. 'I'm a good boy Father, everyone says so' he replied with a noticeable tremble in his voice. He was not getting sweets from the priest today it seemed and why had his parents asked Smyth to talk to him? What had he done? Were his Mammy and Daddy mad with him? Question after question, tumbled and rattled through his mind, and he was afraid.

Smyth reached out and pinched Thomas hard, expertly, on the bicep 'Don't you dare answer me back boy when I'm trying to help you, now stand up boy!' Thomas stood, shaking and feeling like crying. 'Now open your pants boy and show me your bottom' this demand was delivered with another pinch for emphasis. Thomas did not know what to do, so he did as he was told, he was a good boy after all and a priest was always to be obeyed. 'Now boy, you will learn how to get rid of your sins and you will keep it to yourself or you will be taken away, to a school for sinners, do you hear me boy?' said Smyth as he kneeled behind Thomas and spoke dangerously quietly into his left ear. His hands started to slowly touch Thomas's bare buttocks and up between his legs. Thomas had no idea what was going on, except he was scared. Smyth pinched him again, painfully and expertly enough, so as not to leave a mark. 'Do you hear me boy?' he rumbled. 'Yes Father, I hear you.' was the quivering reply. 'Every boy must learn how to serve God Thomas and I am here to teach you, you will not talk about this with anyone, anyone at all, or you will be sinning so bad you will burn in Hell, you know about Hell don't you Thomas?' The hands were now sweaty on Thomas's skin, clammy like a fish freshly caught, sticky almost as they gripped and stroked and pinched and prodded, this was a sort of Hell as far as Thomas was concerned; a Hell made up of not knowing what was going on, not having a clue what to do, a Hell of not knowing why? 'The Devil lives there Father' he managed to get out while screwing his eyes shut against the tears and the growing pain as Smyth's hands got bolder, more urgent, in their raping of Thomas's innocence. 'That's right boy, now close your eyes and don't you dare look at me, don't look at me do you hear boy?' This last delivered with a particularly severe pinch to a place Thomas had never been pinched before. 'Y-y-y-yes Fr. Smyth' was the quivering reply and Thomas screwed his eyes shut as he felt Smyth push him down on his hands and knees. He could hear and feel the man as he moved on his knees around Thomas until his crotch was at Thomas's head, all the while his hands rubbing and stroking Thomas's back and buttocks, pinching lightly at his small penis and where one day his scrotum would be. Thomas kept his eyes screwed shut even as the tears seemed to be at a pressure to burst past his eyelids like a broaching dam in a flood. He felt Smyth grab his head lightly but firmly enough and press his head into his crotch 'Keep your head there boy, and don't you look at me' said the beast in a more hurried and breathless tone. Thomas felt his head being released and then a shaking and tussling up and down, up and down, beside his right cheek. He had no idea what was going on, he was too young to know that Smyth was masturbating, all he was aware of was the musty stink of man smell and the ever more urgent and sweaty grabbing of his bottom by Smyth's other hand. The shaking and rubbing seemed to get faster and faster and the man stink got stronger and stronger and the rubbing and grabbing and grunting increased as well until suddenly Thomas felt one of Smyth's fat man fingers, plunge straight up his bottom and it hurt. He let out a mewling sobbing cry and got an angry 'don't you dare move or look at me boy!' as the finger was pushed in again, hard and violent and probing. Smyth's panting rose and the shaking and rasping of his furiously masturbating hand kept battering the side of Thomas's head, then suddenly it stopped and the monster groaned and grunted and jerked in a few spasms and the man stink almost made Thomas puke, but the finger was hurting his anus so much he decided to keep crying silently instead. Then as suddenly as it had entered, the finger was withdrawn and Thomas felt him move away from him and heard the sounds of clothes being fixed and a few grunts and coughs of satisfaction. Thomas stayed where he was, eyes screwed shut but leaking salty tears, on his hands and knees, terrified. After what seemed a long time but really wasn't, Smyth said 'Well done Thomas, you are such a good boy after all, you have done really well for your first day's training, God is happy with you'. He also mumbled something unintelligible to Thomas and years later when the memories were allowed to come back fully, Thomas would realize it was Latin he had heard, but never distinctly enough to understand or translate later in life. 'You can get up now Thomas, you have done very well, here have a lollipop' he said it so smoothly, so perfectly safely and angelic that even at six years of age, Thomas knew it was too good to be true, but he got up and quickly fixed his underpants and shorts back to where they should have been. His anus hurt so much he still wanted to cry, but somehow he knew not to allow this man see him cry, not to feed that gleam in his eye. He took the lollipop even though he hated sherbet and lollipops in general; he knew he had to do it to appease this man he dare not refuse. Finally that instinct that he had never had need of before was in full flow, that instinct that tells children there is danger in some adults, that instinct once tasted in the throat in the form of gut wrenching stomach churning fear, revulsion and terror, that changes everything. That taste once known can never be forgotten, that moment that innocence was ripped away in tatters, never to return. Thomas stopped crying.

Chapter 6

Learning How to Be Different

Once Thomas started to try to cope with what had happened to him, he felt different. He had no term of reference for why he felt this way but it was obvious to him that he was. He saw and understood even though he could not explain why, that he knew something the other kids did not.

He knew what adults were capable of, well some of them at least, the majority of people that he knew, grown-ups, seemed to still be ok, not different, not threatening, but somehow now he could sense the ones to steer clear of, to be wary of and even here in his formerly safe world there were others who had that look, that *stink of Smyth* about them. It had not taken long at all to develop this new awareness; having a grown man's finger forcefully pushed up your bum while he jerks off against the side of your head, will have that effect on you. The thing for Thomas was how did he deal with this? What did he do? After all he did not have the benefit of a frontal cortex at this stage of his life and development, but when he did, it would form with all of these new unexpected pieces of knowledge to help it along. He would always be attuned to any kind of predatory behaviour, be it in life or business, sports or romance. But right now he had to learn how, without fully understanding why, to seem normal and not the pariah. Kids after all, tend to be crueler to their peers than Adults ever could be to each other, Thomas was not going to be the wounded fish in a schoolyard full of sharks, and he would not be bait.

The Primary school he attended was of course Catholic; you would have to look hard in the Ireland of the seventies and eighties to find one that was not. This meant that at least once a week the local Parish Priest would arrive at the school and make his rounds of all the classes to see both the teaching staff and the children. His name was Father Coleman and to Thomas he was the complete antithesis of Smyth. Father Coleman was in his later years and he exuded a sense of peace and safety, he was a saintly man in his manner and scholarly in his nature. He would come to Thomas's classroom and regale the children with stories not just of a religious nature, but also from Irish mythology; Finn and the Fianna, the ancient High Kings of Tara and great stories of the various Saints of the Church, there were a lot of those as far as Thomas could make out. In fact there seemed to be a saint for every day of the year, but he didn't mind because Father Coleman had that gift of communication that was a joy to be engaged with. Thomas never ever felt in any way threatened by Father Coleman but his recent experience with Smyth had made him wary of anyone with a white collar. This was sad to Thomas because he greatly enjoyed his Parish Priest's stories and the sonorous rolling of his voice as he wove the tales about their young and eager heads. He did not have to act any differently now; for the most part anyway, he was just more aware, tuned in if you will.

There had been a door wrenched open within his head and it could not be closed now.

He found himself watching the older children much closer now. The ones who were twelve and thirteen years of age, just on the cusp of going to secondary school, just in the early stages of puberty and all the hormonal confusion that brings with it. Thomas observed that the boys and girls behaved differently around each other in fourth and fifth classes, and by sixth class it was a very obvious gulf between the sexes. The boys and girls his age just all mucked in together, sure the girls had their dolls and prams and the boys their tractors and action men, but they still mostly got along. The teacher would sometimes punish a boy by making him sit beside a girl in class, which to Thomas's mind was a bit silly really, but some of the boys almost went spastic when threatened with this most grievous of punishments. He had no time for dolls and prams mostly but if he was stuck for company, he could hang with the girls if he had to. However now that this new reality post-Smyth was upon him, he noticed all the subtleties a child should not have to concern itself with.

He saw one of the sixth class boys kissing a girl from the same class. He saw quite clearly the trembling blushing nature of the encounter, and was fascinated by it all. They both obviously wanted to kiss but they didn't have a clue how to go about it, they nearly leaped out of their skins each time either their hands or lips touched the others, and their eyes were sort of glowing with an inner fire. Thomas shuddered when he saw their eyes, it reminded him of the look Smyth had in his eyes when he came at Thomas, but at the same time he could see it was different between the boy and girl, there was no greed in it, no predatory lilt to it, it was more of a clumsy tenderness.

He listened to how the older boys would talk about girls and women and sex. He got very good at listening and hearing what he was sure he was not supposed to be hearing. He watched the grown ups about his Father's business and he was aware now of the new way he saw men and women interact. He noticed the way some of the men would look at the women who either worked there or came and went in the course of the day. He could tell after a very short amount of time, thinking and seeing the world in this new way, who was liking whom or as he put it in his own head 'Who wanted to kiss who.' This of course mostly still filled Thomas with revulsion, the idea of putting his lips on someone else's lips was yuck, and as for what it would be like to tangle tongues with a girl, like he saw some of the boys do in school behind the hedge, was simply double yuck!

Every two weeks or so, Smyth would arrive and no matter how Thomas tried to disappear or change his movements, Smyth would find him. Even his fiercely loyal German Shepherd, Dino, was taken out of the equation. Thomas made sure he was with him one day when Smyth arrived on the scene. The dog had nearly, nearly savaged the aberrant priest and Thomas who was supposed to be in charge of Dino that particular time, was in no way inclined to stop the dog from doing so, in fact he was almost on the verge of exultation when his Father had called the dog to heel at the last moment. Thomas was disgusted but kept his peace. He still had not figured out the whole 'Your parents asked me to talk to you' bit that Smyth had hit him with the first time he abused Thomas. He knew his parents loved him dearly but there was a gulf between them recently as Thomas did not know how much they knew about his 'cleansing sessions' with the beast. He was still very much trapped by the social norms he had been brought up with and of course the skilled and well practiced manipulations of Smyth were hard to deny or overcome, no matter how much Thomas's little heart screamed at him that all of this was not right. That one occasion that Dino lunged at him was perfect for Smyth, because from now on when he was around the place the dog was automatically put in the pen. There was no way a man of the cloth would be denied even the most trivial of considerations for his comfort. In looking back much later in life Thomas knew the bastard had planned it that way that day, just another obstacle to him getting at Thomas that he maneuvered out of the way, another subtle manipulation of circumstances, to enable his depravity.

Thomas had hardened over the course of the first weeks and months that Smyth was abusing him. The pattern was fairly familiar, the abuse pretty much the same as it had been the first time, but the pain was not as bad now as Thomas had gotten used to it. He never cried now or pleaded for him to stop either. He had figured out that that only added to the disgusting gleam in Smyth's eyes as he was about what he was about. Over the next two years or so Thomas never gave him a single thing more than what he was still afraid he had to, and strangely enough, the number of ' cleansing and training sessions' seemed to diminish. One day Thomas saw Smyth drive on to the forecourt of his father's business and instead of the usual gleam of lust in his eyes as he looked at Thomas there was something else; he looked haunted and was hurried. In the passenger seat of his car was a grown woman and in the back seat of the car a little girl about Thomas's age. Smyth had hurriedly gotten out of the car and gone to speak with someone in the office, Thomas didn't see whom; he was looking at the people in Smyth's car. The woman had this fixed hot glare, which briefly touched Thomas then had turned back to trying to melt a hole in the windscreen directly ahead of her. Thomas had not felt anything when her gaze had passed over him, he knew she was not seeing him, didn't want to see him. Thomas had walked up to the back door of the car, out of the woman's line of sight and he looked into the back seat. The little girl and he made eye contact and without a word they both knew the story of the other. They both could tell and they both smiled at each other smiles that if an adult had seen, would have both amazed and chilled them. Those smiles did not belong on children's faces; there was no innocence for them to share. Just then the moment was broken by the sound of Smyth approaching the car. Thomas looked up at him across the low boot lid of the car as Smyth made for the driver's door; they made eye contact briefly and then just as quick as he could Smyth was into the car and starting it up, without saying a word to Thomas. The little girl looked back up at Thomas as the car reversed out of its parking spot, he would remember always the deep azure blue of her eyes as she seemed to ask the question of him 'You know what it's like, will it ever be ok again?' He had no answer for himself let alone her but he smiled anyway as best he could, in solidarity. The front passenger window passed by his face, the moment shattered by the cars movement. The woman in front still stared rigidly ahead, and Smyth did not even glance at him. Thomas just stood there as the car stopped and the beast wrenched the gear lever in a seemingly futile search for movement away from here. Thomas did not know how he knew, but something had changed, was radically different, and he knew he would not be having any more cleansings in the near future.

Smyth found the gear he was looking for and as the car swept forward across the forecourt and onto the main road in the direction of Dublin, Thomas looked at the little girl who looked back at him, to this day those azure eyes haunt Thomas's dreams still.

Later on that evening as his mother and father discussed the day's events at the dinner table and Thomas was studiously *not* listening, his Dad mentioned 'Father Smyth has been posted to Washington State in America by the Bishop, apparently he's taking over a ministry there, all happened very quickly apparently and he flies out tomorrow.' Thomas was in love with his mother's cooking, but at that moment all he wanted to do was run to the bedroom and look at the big globe of the world on his dresser and figure out just how far away Washington State was, but he stayed put. One thing he had learned from the bastard Smyth was patience. His parents had continued chatting amiably over the balance of the meal and Thomas and his older brother joined in as usual when expected to. His mother noticed Thomas was more upbeat than he had been for a while and when she asked him why he replied 'I scored a goal in school today, it was a good one.' His parents had smiled at that and there was no more mention of his happiness as the table was cleared and the dishes washed, dried and put away. Thomas had a spring in his step as he fled to the bedroom and the globe that lit up. It was a great globe as he saw it, the countries were all in different colors so you could make out their borders and it had a raised relief to represent the mountains and the like. Thomas loved to have it lit and the room dark, he would spin it as fast as he could and then plunge his finger down onto its surface, wherever it landed he would look at the name of the place and resolve that he would travel there someday. He searched out Washington State and he was happy, really happy, it was far away. Australia would have been better or Antarctica even; but Smyth would not be bothering Thomas without spending at least a day on an airplane, and that was fine with him. He was truly happy for the first time in two years.

Over the next few months Thomas began to feel more secure, but he still had dreams about the 'cleansing sessions' he no longer had to be a part of. There had been no more word of Smyth and his parents never mentioned him. He was more and more sure as each day passed that his parents would never *ever* have sanctioned what had happened, but he still kept it to himself, he did not know why but he just knew, or thought he did, that it was the right thing to do. He maintained his habit of observing the older children and in fact any child he came in contact with, why? He did not know, but he did it anyway, it was a part of him now this observation of people, beyond what his peers did. Each time Father Coleman would come to the school and spin a web of wonder with his stories and rich laughter Thomas was more and more sure that he was not like Smyth, no that was incorrect, he knew Smyth was unlike anyone else. He would often get the urge to approach his parents or Father Coleman, and tell them of what had happened but he was still surrounded by a society that did not discuss such things, so he kept it to himself. He did not want to be *dirty*. When he felt the urge to tell he would ruthlessly push it deep down inside and the more he did this the more he realized that he was pushing the memory of Smyth and his clammy sweaty hands deep down as well, a little bit more each time until one day there was no real concrete memory of those fear soaked hours left in Thomas's conscious mind. Eventually he never thought of Smyth at all, but the door that Smyth had forced open in his rape of Thomas's mind and body, remained so.

Thomas was now almost nine years of age and while he was not getting the first stirrings of puberty just yet, he had been sexualized too early and he was fascinated by it now. He was already looking at the older girls and even at his female teachers and their shapes. He felt a deep thrill run through himself one day when the wind took up a skirt and he saw a woman's panties on her smooth bum for the first time. He had not been the only boy to see it as it happened at the collection area at the end of the school day but he was the only boy of his age to be thrilled by it. Thomas never, at least until much later in life, realized that this was due to what had happened to him. As he went through puberty he masturbated and thought of older women, not the girls he was sure all the other boys were jerking off to. He had this unconscious assurance about what he knew to be true about sex, even though he had forgotten why. This brought a lot of frustration to Thomas when, as all boys did; he spoke with his peers about sex. For some reason, as the other boys talked and speculated about the mysteries of sex, Thomas would find himself becoming detached, bored; almost as though he knew something before he could have possibly known why. As they would laugh and giggle and smirk at their 'Dirty little imagined secrets' as he thought of them, he would go to a far off place and just drift with no coherent thoughts, just images of freedom. He would see a naked ephemeral woman beckoning to him, enticing him, exciting him, as she would draw near to him her breath in his ear as she said something he could never quite capture, would almost trigger a spasm of sheer ecstasy before the dream would disappear like smoke in the wind and he would be back listening to the imaginary knowledgeable conquests of pubescent boys. He would invariably leave the conversation at that point and head off to be alone, to be free of their ignorance, their stupidity. They would notice of course, but Thomas didn't give a 'Fiddlers Fuck' a saying of his favorite uncle, he was never afraid of what a group might think, he was harder than that even though he did not want to be hard.

Literature was a beautiful place for Thomas and he escaped there as often as he could. His favorite book was the *Odyssey* by Homer. His peers were reading Enid Blyton and the like, but Thomas was with Homer and Virgil. He could feel the spray of the 'Wine dark sea' as it washed over him, as he was engrossed; he could feel 'The Immortal fingertips of rose' as the sun would warm his face by the river as he read and re-read the story of Odysseus on his journey back to Ithaca and his fair lady as she weaved and rent, weaved and rent repeatedly the tapestry that was the only barrier between her and her suitors while she had faith her husband would one day return. He dashed across the sand, could feel it in his sandals as he fought for balance battling beside Achilles' against wave after wave of Trojans. In his mind he was free, powerful and safe. When he played football he likened it to combat and was always disappointed when he would discover no chivalry upon the field. Good manners became very important to him, much more so than just what his parents expected of him. He would address adults correctly and in an adult fashion and when they addressed him as the child he still effectively was, he would find himself bridling inside, frustrated as all hell. Thomas, as far as he was concerned, just could not grow up fast enough. He was bigger than most of his friends by a long shot but he was also gentler too. He had empathy.

Bullies of any stripe got him inordinately agitated and at school or on the football field he would be swift and hard with any one abused the weaker kids. This was noticed one day by a teacher and he was asked why he had defended the child who was being bullied by this particular teacher's pet, who could and would do no wrong in front of adults, but with no grown ups about was a terror to a timid child. Thomas simply said 'Because he is a pig!' This resulted in a trip to the headmaster, but Thomas was long past wetting his pants or thinking of the considerably shorter hallway now that he was bigger, as the path of doom. He had knocked and entered and recited why he had been sent to the higher authority. There was no ruler or stick, no six of the best; the Headmaster had seen the altercation in question earlier and as far as he was concerned Thomas was developing into a fine 'Lump of a lad' for knocking the opposition about on the football field like skittles. As usual of course, the headmaster was wrong when it came to the reasons behind Thomas's reaction to the bully, but Thomas didn't feel like expanding on those reasons either. After a brief unspoken moment of complete miscommunication on the headmasters' part, Thomas was sent on his way and that was fine by him. If playing football kept him happy then he'd play football. This was how it was now for him, he observed, he ruminated on what he observed, he acted when he thought he should and stayed quiet when he thought that was appropriate too, but he never forgot a thing.

Eventually as he approached the last year of his primary education he learned that he could entertain and gloss over so many things with wit and charm and he honed these skills with a ruthless precision. Being around adults in a place of business helped immensely in this regard as he had an unending audience for whatever character he was playing that day. He learned how to make people laugh because he wanted and needed them to. Laughing was good, it was happy and safe. Pretty soon he became so good at it that he forgot completely why he had started all of this, what the driver was. Thomas, ever more frequently now even forgot who Thomas was, who he was supposed to be, he was by the time he went to secondary school, the perfect emotional chameleon who patterned himself to fit the situation and the people in it. Thomas could blend in anywhere with anyone.

Chapter 7

The First Addiction & the Gateways Created

Smoking cigarettes was still cool when Thomas hit secondary school, it was *hard* and if you wanted to be *cool* and *hard* you smoked, simple as that. Being hard was a straightforward concept, no one messed with you and your peers respected you, a good combination when you made the transition from a small country village school with a total of one hundred students, to an institution that had several hundred. Kells was a market town and three miles down the road, give or take, for Thomas and his cohort of other locals boys cycling their bikes daily, in all weathers, into town for their day's education. Mostly it was fun to ride your bike to school but when it rained in the wintertime, it was a mournful experience. Gloves were a luxury that any of the boys could never seem to make last. Their hands would be bright red from the stinging cold sleety rain that was propelled by a wind that always seemed to be in your face as you went up hill, coupled with whatever velocity they were able to maintain against it. Such days meant the first hour in class being a slow process of gradual thawing as hands stung with returning circulation and the other equally exposed bits of skin did the same. Thomas was always disgusted by the complete inadequacy of the school uniform to provide any warmth at all. Grey trousers, grey shirt, navy sweater, a god-awful maroon tie, black socks and black leather shoes. The Christian Brothers were maniacal in their insistence the full uniform be worn each day. Each day though, no matter the season, the bike shed beside the school was a perfect place for a surreptitious cigarette, normally shared between at least four boys. As they would be there a quarter of an hour before class began, the smell would be disguised by the teachers who would be walking and driving in to the adjacent yard, the majority of them having a few last puffs of a Major, Carroll's or a Rothman before their day of opening young minds to knowledge, or in some cases closing, began.

Thomas had parents who neither drank alcohol nor smoked cigarettes, but he had a Grandfather who did both, but respectfully. Most of his uncles smoked at the time and a good portion of his aunts and older cousins as well, Thomas had a lot of cousins. So getting his hands on a few coffin nails was never really that hard of a proposition. However hiding such contraband at home always presented a problem and cigarettes, while not that expensive at the time, would still put a hole in your pocket money. To the rescue in this regard was the sweet shop right next door to the school. It was small and pokey and a goldmine for the owner Mrs. Smith. Down the back of the place she had a basic extension into which was wedged a pool table, jukebox and several arcade video games. There were a few old church pews scattered against the walls to allow seating and when Thomas would get down to the bottom of the place, he would nearly have to duck to avoid hitting his head on the ceiling. Mrs. Smith also sold single cigarettes at eleven to thirteen pence a go, and she did a brisk trade indeed. In fact she was effectively his first drug dealer. But of course cigarettes were not put in the same category as drugs in the 1980's although they should have been. Across the town about a quarter mile away was another sweet shop, a mysterious place where all the girls from the convent school would hang out. They had no pokey arcade down the back of the place like the boys did, but the proprietor Mr. Sean Mclafferty was equally happy to sell single cigarettes to his clientele. It was a brave lad in a Christian Brothers uniform who would enter Mclafferty's shop on a school day, when it was full of the girls in their blue uniforms. It just wasn't done.

The routine was quickly established between the boys in their first year of secondary school. They would arrive at the bike shed, secure their vehicles in their usual spots, post a lookout to check for teaching staff and to also provide visual intimidation for any squealers who might be about, there was a lot of those types in the junior ranks, as Thomas had discovered. If they had a cigarette between them then it was sparked up and passed round. If not, money was pooled and an emissary dispatched into Smith's to procure one. By the time two or three lads had a go at the cigarette, the red glowing tip ash would be huge and the cigarette ruined from the practically constant drawing upon it. Pretty soon each and every one of them was smoking at least two, maybe three cigarettes a day. This went on for the first two years of secondary school, but by the time they were fifteen years of age, they were regular hooked smokers. Once in a blue moon the head Christian Brother would launch a sneak attack into the den at the back of Smith's. He would swoop in with the black cassock trailing behind him in the wind of his passing and the shrieking of Mrs. Smith at him to get out would raise the alarm. As he would enter, the assemblage would just as quickly be exiting by various routes, like cockroaches fleeing a switched on light. He would retreat after catching one or two of the slower, thicker students a quick cuff on the ear, and a hurried exchange of rhetorical assertions between himself and the proprietor about respectability, sale of single cigarettes and blah, blah, blah. The lads quickly figured out that these sneak attacks only occurred after some parent complained about the smell of tobacco smoke on their child's uniform or they had seen their child actually smoking outside the shop, which of course was a beginner's mistake as far as they were all concerned. There would be huffing and puffing and various noises from the parent teacher council about smoking and the sale of single fags to minors, and within a day or so, just like everything else in Ireland, it was back to the status quo and business as usual.

Thomas remembered all of this after one particularly bad night of drugs where the material was shit and he felt like shit and even the weed he had at the apartment was shit. He was fidgeting with his rolling papers as he tried not to let the negative thoughts overwhelm him as the desire inside him to get a decent high was rising to a crescendo. He was literally fighting for his life inside his head as he knew if he went searching for stuff in this particular state of mind he would make mistakes, it would be dangerous so he had to just suck it up. A part of this mindset was the inevitable asking of the questions inside his head he normally tried to avoid or ignore, the ones that either started with or ended in 'Why'? What had ever possessed him to start down this path? Why had he begun to smoke drugs of any kind? Why did he feel the need to smoke over twenty cigarettes a day? Why?

Why? FUCKING WHY? 'The merry go round of self-recrimination and self-loathing was gaining a good pace tonight' he thought out loud. He knew why but he just couldn't remember why. There was something just out of reach, like an itch that was always a few millimeters from your fingertips no matter how you contorted yourself. He could sense it deep within himself, feel its presence and even get a glimpse of its nature by the repulsiveness of the void surrounding it. He began to try to excavate it out of himself, just to keep his mind off where he was at right then. He peeled a layer of the onion back and the stink inside his head almost made him retch, he withdrew quickly from the endeavor. Grasping the packet of cigarettes in front of him he hurriedly lit one, swiftly inhaling deeply. The nicotine only served to make him want something harder, something to make him high. He had a bottle of whiskey in the house, so he drank that instead and eventually became aware again of being curled in a fetal position, on the floor in front of the couch, crying silently to himself in the horrors of drunkenness and of withdrawal. Oh the lamentation that was echoing about inside his skull, the self-pity, even pissed as he was he recognized it for the crap that it was. 'Or was it?' He straightened himself up so he was sitting legs outstretched with his back against the base of the couch. He stared into the silence for a while and just let the images coalesce in front of his mind's eye.

Quickly, even drunk, he concluded that it was all about gateways, pure and simple. Smoking cigarettes had provided him with the first one, the one that got him used to smoke in his lungs, to inhaling at different velocities and depths within his chest, to the satisfaction of a chemical rush. Then when he had first travelled to America, he had been exposed to weed in San Francisco at the youth hostel he stayed in. Because he smoked cigarettes, he could withstand the sharpness of the weed hitting his throat and lungs much better than those who did not. When the first tingling of the chemical and physical high came on, it was just like the rush from a cigarette if you had not smoked for several hours. Of course then being high meant your boundaries were redefined when it came to what was acceptable or what you would try. That in turn had led him to the fateful weekend in upstate New York where exactly because he was both drunk and high on weed, the offered crack pipe had not seemed like such a bad idea, after all they were in a ski lodge with respectable people, they were not in a crack den in the arse end of Brooklyn or Long Island City. When he remembered that particular line of thought, which in turn led him to give himself permission to take the crack pipe for the first time, he shuddered. He could see the faces in the ski lodge, the well-appointed bar and rooms and how safe it had been and instantly then he saw a quick slide show of all the hovels he had been in since to either buy or smoke crack. He limply raised his right hand as he stared into the space between his position and the wall in front of him and snapped his fingers 'Just like that,' was the thick-tongued mumble that accompanied the motion. Indeed, just like that, it had gone from being cheaply purchased cigarettes outside of school, to weed, to crack cocaine. The years in between those steps were irrelevant, it was the process, the path that had been a large part of bringing him to right here, right now. He gave up on trying to stay ahead of the slowly advancing tears down his cheeks. Their warmth and sting seemed in a weird way to expiate some of the guilt he felt, the shame and the loss. Indeed he was becoming aware of just how big a sin he had been committing for the last nine months, he was denuding his soul one day and one pipe at a time.

He reached for the bottle to see if there was anything left in it, only a drop but he drained it anyway. He lit a cigarette and as he did so he became aware of the mess on the floor around where he had been curled up for God knew how long at this point. It was dark outside but that was no indication anymore for Thomas, he lived his life, the one that seemed to matter to him now, in that darkness, every day merely punctuated by the daylight activities that led to a paycheck, so he could pay for this, his empire of lust and shit and hatred and all for 'FUCKING WHAT...!' he suddenly bellowed into the silent space in front of himself, no doubt scaring the living shit out of anyone on the floor above or below him or even outside on the street in front of the building for that matter. But he did not care anymore; in that moment he did not care or even know if he was really alive or dead. He was living in a purgatory of his own construction, how he got there was one thing but how he got out of it was completely another. Now that he had given himself some brief mental and physical release by roaring loudly he clung to that fleeting feeling and resolved to find a way back, out of the shit. He let his head roll slightly to the left, unconsciously, sickeningly, enjoying the impaired ability to control his neck muscles, his mind-set had indeed led him that far. On the shelf between the television and the door that led onto the balcony, he saw something flicker and reflect the light from the street lamp outside. He focused as hard as he could on what this could possibly be, no joy though. He was going to have to move if he wanted to see what it was that had captured his attention. Thomas automatically commenced the mental conversation that all addicts have in one form or another that allows them to justify pretty much anything, whether it was doing a particular drug or in this case, trying to rationalize why he should ignore it and just stay here, parked on his butt surrounded by shite. The echoes of his roaring into the silence were still with him, so he forced himself up to his knees and then his feet. He swayed a bit for balance and felt discomfort as blood forced its way through vessels previously denied to it by the way he had been arranged on the floor. He allowed his eyes to adjust to their new perspective of being six feet above the hardwood floor instead of on it. He shuffled a step then strode purposefully over to the object, which was now fully pissing him off with its dangling, gleaming dance of annoyance. He reached the shelf and whipped the item into his right hand, neatly enough except for the several books he scattered and knocked clattering and thumping to the floor. This annoyed him even more and he raised his hand to hurl the object out of the window without even looking at it, he drew his fist back past the right side of his head and just as he bunched his triceps to fling it across the void between his doorway and the streetlight below, part of it smoothly slipped out of his tightly balled fist and presented itself to the corner of his eye with a calm reflection of dull light. He froze recognizing instantly what he was holding, about to throw. It was the Rosary beads his mother had given him when he first had left home for America; a lifetime ago it seemed now. The shock of recognition made him stagger back a step and his breath caught in his throat, images whirled madly inside his addled head and he stumbled backwards again all the way to the couch, and flopped into it. He held them lightly in his open hand now and as they draped themselves over his fingers the images inside his head slowed down and he could see. He saw his parents and his older brother, kneeling on the carpet saying the rosary together, when all was safe and beautiful and full of endless possibilities and he could smell raisin scones cooling on the rack in the kitchen.

He was dumbfounded and Thomas started to cry like he had never cried in his life before. Thomas was mourning his very soul. Eventually he cried himself out, his stomach sore from the wracking sobs and he drifted off to sleep, seeing his mother's blonde hair and beautiful face shimmering in the firelight, his father's strong hands as he passed a plate of scones across the table towards him, the smell was beautiful like he had once been. As sleep took him completely, he felt it inside, he would change his destiny again no matter what it cost. He slept hard and dreamed of things he could not remember; he just knew they were good.

Chapter 8

Dreams & Nightmares

'Run you stupid bastard, Run..!' his own voice screamed through his head as the blue lights flickered in the corner of his eye accompanied by the wail of fear that seemed to simultaneously emanate from the siren and all of the denizens who were already fleeing the place by the nearest opening they could find. He had his hands full as he tried to secure his stash in the slot he had previously sewn in the cuff of his leather jacket, exactly for that purpose, and at the same time avoid the mayhem erupting around him everywhere. 'Run' his mind said to him again but he knew he had a few seconds yet, to act correctly. The other ten or so crackheads were all over the place, both high and stupid as a result, as they streamed out into the rear alley knocking each other over and falling down. Thomas stepped out calmly just behind the melee and made a small jump vertically to grab the bottom rung of the fire escape ladder just above him. In a flash, quietly, he was up and climbing to the roof three floors above. He was lucky; he had been here a few times before and knew the lay of the land. Once on the roof he resisted the urge to both run and look over the parapet at the scene unfolding on the streets below. By now the cops were well on their way in the front door and had a paddy wagon and a couple of cruisers at the rear. They had been here before. He slowly and silently crept his way across the adjacent rooftops until he was almost at the end of the block. He settled down in the shadows to wait, while the cops rounded up, arrested and began to process, all the mice that had tried to flee. 'At least it isn't raining' he thought to himself as he snuggled smaller into the space he occupied, nestled beneath an air-handling unit that hadn't worked since Nixon was President. The noise from the street began to calm down a bit as the cops secured the area and the *caught* gave up on the whole trying to run away from them bit. The *caught* would have all been through the system before, some would have outstanding warrants, others not. Most would get a day or two in Central Booking and those unfortunate enough to have warrants would get a month or two in Rikers, depending on the charges or the judge, that could be much longer too. Neither of those two options to be found on Thomas's to-do list.

The cops would be happy enough now, some good arrests, no injuries, some material confiscated and most importantly, a positive impact on the precinct's Crime Stats for the month. He was really glad no fool had pulled a gun or knife on the cops. That tended to upset New York's finest no end. It also would have meant the building and most of the flea-bitten block being sealed off for almost a whole day, more if someone had wound up getting shot, but worst of all for Thomas in his current perch; it would have meant a helicopter and that would have been that. 'Can't hide from a whirlybird,' he mused as he listened to the sounds of the cops going into the final phase of the night's operation down below. In less than an hour the show would be over, the curious onlookers would leave and the cops would be back for another raid in about a month or so. Thomas wanted a cigarette but he wouldn't give in to that urge until he was out of the danger zone. He waited. There was a sick symmetry to the system which all depended on how much drug trade was re-established in this place, how quickly and by whom. It worked for all involved; the cops knew where to bust for a quick surge in crime control figures and also when not to come near the place, the problem location was known and contained in one particular spot and the dealers knew that if they kept things quiet amongst themselves, they were mostly going to be left alone in return. Thomas also knew that every building on this block had at least one informer in it, maybe more. He waited and waited and waited…

As he became conscious of waking up, his eyes rolled as though through sand paper, each tenth of a millimeter of movement a torture of rotation. The way his tongue cleaved to his palette behind his dry lips right on the very point of rupture. This feeling was reinforced by the distant alarm from his medulla that he was dangerously dehydrated. The hunger pains the neurons in his stomach were busily communicating to their brethren in his head, did not rate notice just yet, he could survive a long time without food but no more days without fluid. 'How long had it been this time? Thirty-six or forty-eight hours?' he wasn't sure; which worried him more, the riot of information his body was communicating to his consciousness from a variety of sources, about his need for water in ever increasing waves, now that he was tuned back into the here and now. 'Friday, it's Friday,' was the wispy thought that fluttered across that window, slightly wider now that the sandpaper curtains had parted a bit more. 'Why does it matter what day it is?' he asked himself angrily as he shifted a bit from the prone position he was now aware he was lying in. The tendons and other related ligaments in his back and shoulders thrummed like badly played guitar strings. He would be 'Dealing with that side of it too' he mused. Slowly the room regained some semblance of focus as he tried to turn a heavy head on a loudly protesting neck. 'Screw this for a game of soldiers' he croaked to himself, finally upright in what he imagined would have been the style of Dr. Leakey's Lucy from the Rift Valley. He fought his way upright and shambled, zombie-like, to the open and lit archway of the kitchen area. The closer he got to the faucet, the more impetus his primal urge for water gave speed to his shamble. Reaching the counter top he grabbed at the large plastic tumbler with the motor skills you would expect from a zombie. It held about twenty fluid ounces of liquid. He had learned to put the glass items away while on a binge, a long time ago. He filled and drained it twice in a row before he took a breath. His tongue was still swollen, but decreasingly so. He envisaged the crimson canyons across its surface as rivers of fire, coursing where fire did not belong, as the water welded his tissue back towards something resembling normal – which would take an hour or two.

'Time, it was all about time' he told himself 'What you felt at whatever speed you chose to live life at', another piercing insight from the obvious as far as Thomas was concerned. The soles of his feet were clammy with the forty-eight hours, or less he hoped, of partying since he last got out of the bath. Floor tiles strangely tingled through the hyper-sensitive soles of his feet via the invisible membrane of cocaine-tinted grime.

The rumble of his stomach as the water expanded it nourishing him, but now his body wanted, needed, food energy. Time. He did a slow steady stretch by arching his back from the hips upwards and rotating his shoulders back as far as he could, tensioning the muscle groups down each side of his spine, until he felt and heard the multitude of pops, the tension releasing. He shambled, a little faster now, towards the bathroom. He washed his face deliberately, vigorously, in the cold virtuous water. The mirror was not consulted. He had a French shower of Degree antiperspirant, sourced clean socks and lounge pants with a tee shirt to match before heading back to the living room. Light was streaming in at the edges of the floor to ceiling and wall-to-wall curtains, like the corona of the sun during an eclipse, the curtains themselves glowed like the surface of the Sun as presented on a Nova documentary, before the eclipse would end by his parting them, the room needed tending.

The balcony beckoned in his mind for his recovery to a sentient state, but he knew he needed to come back into someplace tidy, ordered, ready to allow him to get out the door at some stage and interact with the rest of humanity. If he didn't tidy up he'd be laying his own honey trap for himself by leaving temptation openly about. He knew there was still plenty of material about the place. He got a clean trash bag and over by the coffee table began, with precise well practiced motions that removed the evidence to the casual observer, like magic. He automatically separated what could go in the trashcan outside the building, and what had to be disposed of discretely. Shattered crack pipes, burnt smoking screens and fistfuls of the little Baggies or glass vials the material came in, did not go down well with the other residents or the cops either for that matter, and anyone in the building would call the cops if they found any of that crap in the trash cans. Well, some of the other residents at least, plenty of times he had smelt the wafting presence of a fellow herb aficionado from some of the other balconies.

The incense was lit; surfaces wiped down and shit organized in short order. Time, time to open the lungs and feel the outside world wash over him to complete his sobering, waking up to reality. The balcony beckoned again, new tumbler of water and cigarettes in hand, he pulled back the room's eyelid and whatever illusions he may have had about not been fully awake, were seared away by the pulse of light that seared his retinas. He relished it for its intensity, the heat it brought to his mind to help kick start it, from the numbing cold storage he assigned his consciousness too, while in the midst of indulging his baser impulses and desires. The balcony door slid easily open the rest of the way as he stepped through, out onto the warm smooth concrete. He sat by the small table and put on his sunglasses; the sunshine felt so good, so pure, the air fresh. The traffic noise was just part of the background ambient of this place. The tree up the street sighed in the warm breeze. As his eyes adjusted he could see the sun was well above the horizon and the sky azure. That never ceased to amaze him, coming from where he did, that you could have weeks on end when the sun shone every single day, all day with not a cloud to be found.

It was at least 7am he knew, he also knew that he didn't have to work today, in fact he was off until Tuesday morning. He luxuriated in that because it kept the fear away, the fear of failure, for now. He drew deeply of the fresh air and reached for a cigarette. Time, the day was his; he had no entanglements to worry about until Tuesday, until then. He thought about the bath again and how long ago it was, yet he had known as he was stepping into it, that he would be sitting here right now remembering it as if it was only five minutes ago. It was *the time bubble* again. He had closed the circle on it, yet again. He slipped back and forward through the reality of the last forty-eight hours and it seemed to him that this insight should be accompanied by a suitable fanfare from a symphony orchestra conducted by Carl Sagan himself. No, he had accepted that moment of precognition as readily as he had immersed himself in the hot water, knowing he was going to have fun on his party night. Accepting the waste of that time and all the dangers of its devouring and the guilt about doing so, he could never shake off – about anything. The never-ceasing analysis continued.

He put the question away by thinking of the time, at light speed that it took to travel to the Sun, eleven minutes or close to it and then the vastness beyond that. Even as there were no stars visible, except the Sun itself, in the azure expanse above him – he knew they were there and that he could still, at any time, fall off the edge of the world.

The old Asian lady across the street came out the front door of her building to deposit her daily bag of trash; you could set your watch by her. The sound of the trashcan lid pierced the meniscus separating him from the rest of the ambient sounds of the neighborhood, time for a shower. On the way through the apartment he detoured to switch on the coffee maker. Soon the water steamed away the grime of excess as the shower worked its gift upon him. He could smell the coffee as he toweled dry and finally consulted the mirror, a respectable shadow on his chin could be shaved later or tomorrow if he felt like it, the shocking state of his bloodshot eyes he could do nothing about. The coffee was gurgling and puffing its best 'come hither' aroma at him. He was refreshed yet tired, but in a mellow way, the first mug of coffee was as good as it promised to be. He put on some toast and boiled an egg. Sitting at the table he enjoyed watching the second pot brew its way to perfection as he buttered toast and dipped it in the gold. The food was wonderful, simple and he would not have changed it for anything. He thought about anything and nothing all at the same time, like a passive voyeur through a window. The beauty of the food coursed through his body and he was thankful to God for it too.

The thoughts of God brought back memories of the last time he had gone to Mass. It had been in St. Patrick's Cathedral and he had been with Joan, whom he loved deeply, completely passionately, but had not loved her or him enough to stop using the drugs that were driving them daily apart. He had of course made a complete bollix of that relationship with his addiction and the behavior that went with it. She had her demons too though and the big one was an ongoing divorce. The long and the short of it was they were toxic for each other even though they tried very hard not to be. It had ended with them breaking each other's hearts, the pain and regret lingers in Thomas's memory to this day He still loved her in this moment he realized. The tears had the inevitable taste of salt as they flowed freely down through the stubble on his cheeks to flavor his eating of the egg.

Strangely and quickly, he resolved to do something about stopping once and for all. He was done, over it, like the bad smell of a fart hanging around in a phone box. But he honestly reflected that it was not the first time he had had such an epiphany either, 'What a head-fuck all this really is' he admitted to himself.

He thought again about that last time he had darkened the doorway of the Cathedral. He had sat in the area to the right of the nave as he faced the Altar. The glorious Gothic difference of the interior as it suggestively vaulted its way towards heaven, compared to the architecture of the rest of midtown outside, moved him. The Ecclesiastical aromas of frankincense, oils and melting hot candle wax that he remembered so well from his childhood days serving Mass, had transported him to a place of inner peace. The coolness of the space and the reverent hushed movements of the people as they moved within it, even the bloody tourists, all had had a calming transformative affect on his inner self. Prayer of the unconscious opening of the spirit kind, had seemed to wash slowly about him, gradually rising, pulling its tidemark along where he imagined it touched his skin, eventually over his head. He had swum and floated there for a while that seemed interminable at the time and he had cherished it. It allowed him to feel whole and normal but more importantly, honest, as sitting there in the house of God there could be no secrets and he was safe from the Demons guarding those self same secrets, in this place at least.

He stayed there safe in that void of scents, sounds and ever-increasing peace until he had been gently shaken from it by a touch on his shoulder announcing the arrival of his beloved. He opened his eyes and stood immediately to greet her and allow her to access the pew. He was old fashioned in those ways; after all it had been the way he had been raised, another rock he often clung to in the storm of chemical dependency. She was beautiful and the smile she wore was simply stunning.

He felt his heart almost break with both the joy of seeing her and the glory of her symmetrical facial features, her smile and twinkling brown eyes. Her hand found his gently and she lightly kissed him on the cheek as she sat, they had the well-polished pew to themselves. 'Hello Thomas' she almost breathed the greeting he thought as the scent of her breath mingled with the others that had being transporting him before her arrival, and again he felt a rush of love and desire for her and the fear of her which he always suppressed, further and further, deeper and deeper each time he saw her, kissed her, spoke to her on the phone or made love to her. Theirs was a complex relationship and that was being kind.

'Hi baby' was about all he could manage as a reply, still reeling as he was from the assault on his senses she always unleashed. She was everything a man would aspire to desire, smart, intelligent, she was a doctor after all, beautiful, sexy and incredible in bed. However she was not his to fully have and she was not free enough within herself to be with him either. She had told him she was getting a divorce when they had first met but that had been a stretch of the truth on her part, she was only separated and as he had found out way too late to stop himself falling madly in love with her, still attending relationship counseling with her husband who was a lawyer in the city. There were other lies and sins of omission along the brief but passionate road they had traveled together so far, but they faded away as they always did when he was this close to her. He was screwed and he knew it but just like crack, he was making a conscious choice to ignore the consequences.

'Sorry I'm late, mad day at the practice, it was butt to belly with patients all day' he saw in her eyes that she was not being entirely honest, but he hadn't seen her face-to-face in two weeks and he didn't give a damn where she had been, she was here now that was all that mattered to him. 'That's ok J, I am so glad to see you, I missed you… so much' God, there was a piece of him that just hated when he sounded like a love struck, puppy-faced teenager being led about the place by his prick. She had smiled again and caressed the side of his face and once again the spell of her overtook his sense of self, he wanted to believe, so badly. He knew though that this was just another variation on his recurrent theme of escape.

They had made some small talk but they both knew they were avoiding the elephant in the kitchen, he would want her to come back to his apartment and stay the night, making love and feeling secure in that sliver of time they shared, before she should would disappear once again, only reachable sometimes by text, even more rarely by phone. She was there because she wanted to go with him, but was torn by the fact he represented such a real danger to her respectable life. She desired him, wanted him inside her the way she had wanted no one else, but he was damaged and dangerous to her place in society. Thomas had come to know this of course but weakened fragile fool that he had become, he hung in there in the vainglorious hope of a fairytale.

Extra-marital sex and the excitement of thinking she was getting away with it, was her drug. She had gotten away with it until she had banged a college friend when she was at a conference somewhere, somehow or other she had decided within herself to not cover her own tracks so perfectly anymore and slowly a wedge had begun to separate her from her husband. She had been banging her personal trainer when Thomas met her, but somewhere in the swings and roundabouts of getting to know her he'd assumed she was separated at the time, of course like all his assumptions over the last nine months, it was wrong.

He was in fact, a tainted modern facsimile of Lady Chatterley's lover who got high on drugs and powerful engrossing, well-practiced on both side of the equation, sex with this woman rather than the imagined breathless excitement, longing and whatever else passed for forbidden love in the nineteenth century, just like him he would ultimately wind up being discarded and destroyed by it.

He shook off the memory for a moment, as he felt himself losing his grip on the recently rediscovered reality provided by egg yolks and coffee. He needed more of that. Rising he placed the crockery in the sink and poured another mug with one hand while reaching for a cigarette with the other. Feeling better for having moved, he readjusted his chair and sat down again, lighting the smoke and inhaling deeply as his eyes wandered distantly out through the window and across the street again. He sipped the coffee and smoked and soon he was back in where he had just been, the smell of her hair as vital and real as that of the coffee he held in his hand. He had always thought and had told her so, that to him, her hair smelled of summer meadows.

As he had often found, once a line of thought was broken, it was next to impossible to re-capture its thread, its intensity, if you tried to, especially if you forced it, yet when it came to his memories of Joan, perhaps because of love or lust or whatever the emotions really were, this was not the case. Once again he could see almost with his waking eyes, her eyes, as she looked at him, her voice chimed softly in his memory just beyond the edge of hearing and the images flashed by blending into one kaleidoscope, of her. Mass went quickly as it had been midweek and therefore no long sonorous sermon before the Eucharist.

They had left the city on a train and hugged and kissed like a lovestruck couple all the way to Queens. They had gotten off the 7 at Woodside and sat in Shane's Irish Bakery just round the corner from the station stairs to share a big pot of tea and scones freshly made. They had bought whiskey in the liquor store and walked arms linked to his place where they had made love again and again, high on life, high on each other. They could not stop laughing almost manically after who knows how many times they had sex. The whiskey flowed and he recalled how she liked a cigar, they both did sometimes as they drank a dram or two. They had watched the sunset and the moonrise from his observatory chair, the perfection of it all as it came back to him, made his eyes moist once again. She had stayed and he could feel his arms around her, her scent filling his lungs with every breath the enjoyable pain in his groin from too many ejaculations and the warm slow drifting to happy exhausted sleep, the high point and culmination of it all.

In the morning she showered as he made coffee, she was sweet and kind but trying just a little too hard to be so, because she was leaving and he would be left there hoping, dreaming he would see her again. He was such a fool for her he even had what she called *His Shrine*. Ages ago it seemed, she had left a toothbrush, some contact lenses in a case and saline solution behind one morning. He had left them on the side of the sink beside the tap, there for when she would return, fervently hoping that she would, a little thing to make her feel welcome when she did, a tilt at pretending they were a real couple, not two people acting out and screwing each other for their own reasons, ignoring the thinly disguised lie that it represented, making light of adultery. He pondered the fact that he rendezvoused with a person in a church he had just been recently asking God for help in, then promptly took that person from the same church and happily indulged in some of the seven deadly sins while breaking one of the Ten Commandments all at the same time. Did he have to wonder perhaps why he might not be getting answers to some of his prayers?

The reality of his choices and more, the convenient way he could ignore what he needed to, like it had never happened, hit him hard and he came back to the reality of his now, coffee somewhat colder in his hand than when last he was aware of it. He swallowed a last gulp anyway and splashed the remainder into the sink. His cigarette had lain abandoned at the ashtray and rebelled at his inattention by falling onto the Formica tabletop, burning a black lane with nicotine coloured borders for what had been its full length. He contemplated that and compared it to its fellows, 'Just one more milestone on the road to Perdition' he mused knowing full well what he was trying to ignore, an old prompt from his gut; it was massaging the edge of his consciousness incessantly now, refusing to dissipate, no longer willing to allow him to ignore it.

'Damn it all to hell anyway' he breathed almost silently and turned to walk the few steps to the bathroom. Yes there they were, still enshrined, where he could ignore them or implore them, depending on how lonely and sorry for himself he might have been feeling at the time. He pondered the way the bristles on her toothbrush had gained that curvature all of its species seem to develop after being used for a bit then left high and dry, unwanted and forgotten, pretty much like he was.

Finally, the mirror was consulted again and he leaned close in to it, grasping the side of the sink with his strong hands, gripping until his knuckles were white with the effort of it. He looked deep into the irises of his light blue eyes and the sparkling fire he saw there gave him strength, power, hope. He could see himself in the deep, mysterious liquid black of his pupils as he flicked his focus minutely from one to the other. He was whole there, a complete silhouette possessing shifting indistinct contours, as colours scattered from the ever-shifting reflected light between his body and the mirror itself.

An image of possible action flashed in his mind's eye, his hand backhandedly scattering the contents of the shrine like so many skittles, across the space towards the tub, his face contorted with rage as he roared his disapproval at his abandonment, his anger at his fate. But no, he slowly and gently collected the toothbrush and the contact lens case, the bottle of saline solution and walked back to the kitchen where he consigned them to the garbage. It was a tiny victory for him, for in that moment he was not avenging himself upon the memory of her discarding him, he was placing her and all the sins they had committed firmly in the past. A little catharsis was a good thing he realized.

The rest of the detritus scattered about the apartment that needed to be discretely disposed of was placed on top of the former constituents of his shrine to true love. 'What a fool, what a bloody fool' he said aloud to the apartment, calling upon it to witness his awakening from the dream. After all there was no one else to hear him say it. He tied the garbage bags closed with a somewhat restrained viciousness and felt better for it.

He showered and shaved then quickly dressed in casual day of don't-give-a-shit-what-you-think-of-my-couture, pair of shorts sneakers and a black tee shirt. He grabbed his phone, keys and cigarettes from the table, putting them in the ample cargo pockets the shorts were equipped with, he found his wallet close by and grasped the garbage bags by the scruff, restraining the urge to joyfully kick them down the stairs to the front door like a vandal kicking severed heads after a battle. 'Seriously Man, where do you get these images and thoughts from?' he thought with the hint of a smile as he locked the door behind himself, then nimbly rushed down the stairs and outside to his pickup truck, determined to avoid any of his neighbours.

Once he had deposited the trash in the bed of the truck and put the cargo net quickly over it, he bounced into the driver's seat and had the key in the ignition, the seatbelt on and the sunglasses out of the overhead pouch, all in one series of automatic fluid motions. Putting them on his face he felt better as he sat back in the seat and turned the key. The V8 fired up immediately and he sat for a minute or two enjoying the rumbling smoothness of its power, as he allowed the engine to warm a bit and the oil to circulate properly before moving off. He lit a Marlboro red and opened the driver's window, tapped the button to deactivate the CD player and engaged gear, checked the mirror and pulled away from the curb and coasted the ten yards at engine idle to the corner of 58th Avenue, where it made a ninety degree right and led up the hill.

Once he was past the apex of the corner and he had the beast straightened up, he smoothly floored the throttle, luxuriating in the feel of acceleration, the sound of the engine note rising as the transmission held a lower ratio a fraction too long, before changing up. The wind poured in through the open window buffeting his hair, this was freedom and he always felt secure and purposeful when driving, especially with intent. He backed off, just a bit as he approached the crest of the hill to allow for any oncoming traffic, then when he could see the next apex of the corner leading around onto 58th Street, confidently pointed the truck at it, let it take its *set,* then sank the throttle once again. He was rewarded with a beautiful, fast and yet discrete power slide that required just a hint of opposite lock to collect, before he slowed to the legal limit and began the cruise to his destination.

A big grin was struggling to spread as he admired the sun dappling and rippling across the metallic electric blue paint of the bonnet after being filtered through the trees high above to his right, the long eastern retaining wall of the Calvary Cemetery supporting them skyward, its limestone blocks blackened by decades of fumes, stretching away in the distance all the way to the railway bridge a good half mile away, where he would be turning again for Rust Street. He felt a growing happiness and flicked the CD player back on to enjoy some music, he didn't care what and he couldn't remember what he had left in the thing, the speakers revealed that it was the Stereo MC's. The song *Connected* seemed to suit the mood so he cruised on, happier still.

Soon he arrived at his destination, the heavily industrialized area surrounding the Gowanus Canal where the scaffolding company he worked for when he had first arrived in New York, was based. The area was a dirty 1940's era warren of single-storied warehouses, yards and the like. Barges had once traversed the canals to and from the East River, bringing materials to the

Brooklyn Navy yard which he could see a mile or two away, framed underneath the high span of the Brooklyn Queens Expressway as it became the Gowanus Bridge, the Manhattan skyline beyond. What a view of such a different world for the wretches who shambled and eked out an existence nearby. 'May as well be a different Galaxy' he mused as he turned off the engine and got out of the truck. There was not much activity about the place and he parked just down the street where the big forty cubic yard skips were. They were full of all kinds of crap, even waste that should have been disposed of carefully, like asbestos, everyone knew it, even the hobos who called some of the abandoned lots home, and so no one ever went through the rubbish inside.

When they were full, the private and no doubt mob-connected garbage company came, pulled them onto the trucks designed for the purpose, and the contents were never seen again. He got back in the truck and after a quick U-turn was heading back the way he had come, glancing in the rear-view mirror at the rapidly receding vista of neglect behind, he made a vow not to drive down this way after sunset again, this was one of the routes that led to crossing Flushing Avenue and then shortly on to Troutman Street, where he so often went to get all the supplies of debauchery including the women.

'Fuck me but I'm over all this' he reminded himself as he lit another cigarette comforted by the deep rumble of the engine and the thrum of the tires as they passed over the concrete road surface beneath them. He concentrated his eyes forward on where he was going, not where he had been. He had some calls to make, and one of them he hoped would change his life. He was going to get help and rehab was the only place he knew for sure he'd find it. The nightmare had to end and now.

Chapter 9

Taking Action

The rehab at St. Luke's Roosevelt Hospital on the West Side of Manhattan was not quite what he had being expecting. It was of course a typical American hospital enterprise, there to make money as much as to provide care to its patients, or in Thomas's case, customers. He could not help thinking of it this way, as he paid $65 for the first session at the reception desk of the addiction unit on the sixth floor. 'No pay, no play, just like the street corners,' he mused to himself. The seventh floor was the inpatient floor, where basically you got locked up for weeks of therapy and cold turkey; the length of time involved would be dependent on the individuals' access to funding and severity of the addiction involved. Thomas had found his way here because Joan had recommended it to him. In desperation, he had reached out to her, to ask her opinion and advice. In spite of their history, he knew she would tell him the truth on this and her directions led here. When he had called he had held a small hope the conversation would extend itself with a life of its own, just like it would have done effortlessly when they first met, but he was to be disappointed as the line clicked dead once the information had been imparted, maybe it was for the best but he did not feel it was so. At least she had not hung up when she first heard his voice or recognized his number.

The first day he arrived on the scene, he was as he always was when he went anywhere, well dressed, albeit casual. The director of the place had interviewed him and almost straight away, as he took on board Thomas's dress and manner of speaking, asked if he wanted to see him privately. 'No sentiment there, straight for the money,' thought Thomas as he politely demurred on the offer. This initial intake interview was over shortly after that. He was directed back out to the reception area and after answering all the questions, there were a lot of those, and filling out questionnaires on wooden clip boards, there were a lot of those too, was issued with a rectangular green plastic card with rounded corners. Embossed into this card in the most rudimentary manner were his name, date of birth and his social security number; that was it. Thomas was sure the color of the card had some hidden meaning to do with what he had said he was addicted to, or something equally paranoid. He had had to exert a lot of control over himself to actually make the trip to this place, and he exercised that control again to suppress the paranoia of that thought. He was directed over to the waiting area just opposite the reception desk, which had high backed leather chairs and a television bolted to the wall. The nurse had told him he would be called to join his new group at six pm, so he had a quarter hour to kill. He considered taking the elevator back down to the ground floor and going out to the little garden area the hospital had out front for a cigarette but he decided against it. As he settled in to one of the chairs, he swept the room discreetly with his eyes to get a sense of the other people in the place.

Over in one corner was an old man with drool slowly dripping down the left side of his jaw; his eyes were the vacant windows of a catatonic. Quickly, a nurse arrived, cleaned his face and cooed a reassurance of some sort, then swiftly wheeled her charge down the long corridor to the elevators. There were a few other people of varying race and age scattered about the waiting room in a seemingly random fashion, but Thomas could tell they had selected their seats carefully just like he had, not too close to any of the others but not too obviously far away either. This told Thomas both everything about them and nothing at all, so he decided to wait and see, observe and try to select who would be in the next session with him. He could tell the gulf in socioeconomic backgrounds between the people; their dress, their posture and their manners. One woman, quite striking really was cleanly dressed but obviously nervous, she used a handkerchief to stifle a sneeze, a large African American man did the same in an almost delicate, genteel manner soon afterwards. A white teenager who was wearing expensive clothing rent the air with a hugely loud fart and looked incredibly proud of his flatulent explosion. Thomas had a sudden urge to go over and give him a smack on the back of the head, but he decided not to. The stink was gross however and the silent shuffling and readjustment of bums in chairs that followed it was almost comical. Thomas wished he had chosen to go for the cigarette after all. Fart boy, still very satisfied with himself, got up and went over to the television to try and change the channel. When he reached it a nurse told him not to touch it from the reception desk, he ignored her and changed it anyway. Thomas decided to ignore him, he had him pegged. A rich waste of space kid who never had to work for anything and probably got his first line of cocaine at one of his parents' parties, never would have been a street purchaser either, strictly high-end order and delivery, right to the door.

Over on his left side was a small guy intently trying to look like he was reading the well-worn National Geographic he was holding, but Thomas could see he was watching everyone in the room, Thomas caught his eye and he gave a little twitch of surprise and buried his pointy nose further into the periodical. 'Ferret' was the thought that popped into Thomas head, 'He looks like a ferret.' He was not being mean by thinking this, just honest. He was proved correct a few minutes later when Ferret suddenly burst up out of his seat and with an obviously twitching nose, did a seamless about face and walked rapidly down the corridor towards the elevators. He stopped equally suddenly, rotated to his left then disappeared from view, all without a sound and all very bizarre as far as Thomas was concerned. He was sure Ferret would be in his group as would Fart Boy, but then again he didn't really care who was in the group, he was only people-watching to pass the time.

Eventually he was called softly back to the reception desk and advised where he had to go. He was well aware that it was going to take a while to overcome the awkwardness of a new sort of territory, finding out where things were. Thomas hated looking out of place in the way that meant you got noticed, it was the little subtleties and hesitations that telegraphed to others you didn't have a clue about where you were or where you were going. After his recent months traversing the various depths of danger he was, well sort of, overly sensitive to that sort of thing but being aware of something meant you could try to understand it, which in turn meant you could try to control it, hence he was here; to understand his addiction, or more importantly, his perceived need to have an addiction in the first place. Walking slowly down the hallway he stopped at the indicated doorway and looked through the opening as though he was about to jump out of an airplane with a parachute. The hesitation only lasted a few moments, then he stepped through into what he dearly hoped would be a new beginning.

The first thing he noticed was that Ferret was already inside, sitting in one of the twenty or so chairs positioned in an arc around the room, which was quite large. This told Thomas that the corridors obviously looped back around the perimeter of the sixth floor as Ferret had disappeared in the complete opposite direction. It also said the man had some sort of OCD, and had a quirky little ritual at a set time to *allow* himself to come into this room in the first place. While this still resonated as strange to Thomas, he reminded himself again that he would not be the only person here with problems that required solutions, he would not be here to care about anything that went on except understanding what was driving him to continue using drugs, and how to stop. The well-dressed woman came in as Thomas was stood to one side of the doorway, still absorbing the fact he was actually here. She gave him a glance and then went to sit on one of the chairs. Thomas decided that anywhere really would do, as the whole point of the chairs being arranged thus was to engender a sense of equality amongst the participants. He sat with his back to the window, so the late afternoon sun would not blind him and he could also watch the remainder of the group enter the room. People began to arrive almost in a kind of rush together and Thomas could smell cigarettes off nearly all of them. A few looked at him, most did not. Pretty soon all the chairs were full, twenty in all. There was some light conversation between a few people and

Thomas was surprised by this, but then realized he shouldn't be, they were here twice a week for these group sessions and surely some would get to know each other well enough after a while. The councillor came in then, a late middle aged man with grey hair and thick rimmed glasses in a slightly rumpled three-piece suit, but the shoes were well polished Thomas noted.

'Good evening everyone and welcome, for those of you who are here for the first time my name is Stanley, or Stan for short' Thomas didn't think he looked like a Stanley. 'Good evening Stan' was chimed by nearly everyone in the room and Thomas contributed a medium pitched 'Good evening' of his own. 'Now everyone, as you have noticed we have several new faces in the session tonight, so a special welcome to them, so starting at my left and moving round to the right we will all say our names, why we are here and how long we have had our problem' Stan continued smoothly with an encouraging smile that did actually reach his eyes, which surprised Thomas in a way. This surprise he felt, struck Thomas as being a sign of a deep-seated cynicism, which he would have to monitor carefully, left unchecked it could derail his ability to concentrate and have a bit of faith in the process. He realized this would not be easy, to convince the Demon deep within him that getting high was no longer a worthwhile pursuit. The first person to Stan's left said 'Hi, my name is Michael and I'm addicted to Heroin for the last four years and I've been coming here for six months' Thomas raised an eyebrow slightly, he was a high functioning addict himself and this guy looked as normal as he did, which if you were injecting Heroin, was a very neat trick indeed. The next addict began 'I'm Rachel and I'm an alcoholic and a cocaine user and I'm in rehab for three months now.' Thomas joined in with the group as they all said

'Hi Rachel.' He noted that alcohol and cocaine was a pretty common combination of fun fuels in the city, it was everywhere. The room seemed to push out of his particular reality a bit, as the round robin of introductions continued, he was not going to remember all the names on the first night anyway and he tuned in to what each person was addicted to. Ferret was on PCP and that made a weird kind of sense, fart boy was on Crystal Meth and the list went on. Heroin, Crack, PCP, Crystal Meth, Ketamine, Ecstasy, Quaaludes, Marijuana and the old reliable Alcohol. They smoked, injected, drank or ingested their particular poison and Thomas was sure each of them had their own ritual of dissipation and excess, just like he did, their own way to convince themselves they were having fun and it was good.

It came to his turn and he said 'Hi everyone, my name is Thomas and it's my first time here. The reason I came is, because I smoke Crack Cocaine.' No one batted an eye as they all said 'Hi Thomas.' This made him feel better, which surprised him and he realized it was the first time outside of the sale and supply end of his addiction, that he had told a room full of strangers that he was addicted to crack and needed help. It resonated and reflected back to deep within, he felt as much as heard the growl of the Demon inside him as it realized it actually had a fight on its hands. Thomas allowed himself to feel better. Stan gave him a nod of encouragement and that was that, the room focused on the next person beside Thomas and so it went on until everyone had spoken. At the end Stan said 'Ok everyone, now that we are all acquainted, let's take a break, coffee at the end of the room and let's all be back in our seats in ten minutes for those of you who will be smoking downstairs.' This was greeted with a pushing of chairs as people rose and either went to the coffee jugs or the door, Thomas decided to follow the herd out for a cigarette. They got into the elevator and there was light banter, more than he was expecting. The doors opened on the ground floor but instead of heading out the front doors, the herd turned right then right again down a corridor to the rear entrance. Once outside, everyone who had cigarettes took them out and lit them; of course a few had none but asked others for them anyway.

Pretty soon the rear vestibule around the door was filled with smoke, the herd was joined by a few people in scrubs with ID tags who also smoked, but very much kept a discreet distance from the sixth floor rejects. There was a sense of a club about the herd, almost 'A Club for the Dammed by their own hand,' Thomas mused quietly. Fart boy was off to one side of the group, talking intently with one of the gay meth addicts. Their body language told him a lot, fart boy had the intently restrained hunch about him any dealer did, when doing a deal and the gay chap had the opposite stance of the receiver who was nervous. Thomas could see there was no drugs or money changing hands, that would have been a bit cheeky considering the location and the company they were in, but fart boy was giving the gay guy a phone number. Thomas knew straight away, didn't know how, just did, that it was not because they were going to be sponsoring one another in the program. He decided fart boy was indeed a complete wanker, a waste of space.

Not feeling so good about being here as he had after introducing himself to the group earlier, he stubbed out the cigarette and went back inside. When he re-entered the room on the sixth floor, he poured himself a coffee and returned to his chair. He thought about what had just happened and knew it was a number for a dealer.

'Bloody Hell' he said loudly within his mind as he heard his Demon giggle, 'Even getting rid of all my contacts will mean nothing, because I can get new ones, right here, in rehab.' He was not happy. Stan came back in, right on time and everyone was in his or her seats in short order. He began to speak about the nature of addiction and after a few minutes, indicated to the well-dressed woman Thomas had noticed in the waiting room. She began to speak and said it had been two days since she had last gotten drunk, to the point of black out, which meant she couldn't remember what had happened to her once she got to a certain point of drunk. 'Dangerous that, for an attractive woman in this city.' Thomas thought, as he listened to her speak; he could see in her eyes that she was hurt and afraid by what might have happened. Thomas knew that she could have been penetrated by several men when blacked out from drink, and she would remember nothing after sobering up, but she would know from how her body felt that someone had had sex with her, perhaps roughly perhaps not, but a woman *would* know.

Not for the first time since his drug odyssey had begun, he was thankful he was a man, the rules were always different for girls especially ones left vulnerable to exploitation by dint of their addictions. He gave an imperceptible shudder at the thought of her being raped by someone who could tell she was blacked out. He was sure it happened to her and also sure she could never tell anyone, she was wearing a wedding ring after all. Suddenly for Thomas, the room was full of the horrors of each individual's addictions. He began to hear all the Demons inside every addict present, join in with his own in a mad cackle of derision, that the fools they all were, thinking they could escape by talking about it. Thomas could almost see the red scaled tormenting fucker with

118

his incandescent yellow eyes, looking up at him from his chest cavity, little tail flicking back and forth as he slowly, deliberately dug his claws a little deeper into Thomas's heart, upon which he was perched. He could smell the sulfuric stench of Hell as the Demon laughed at him 'you do no better Thomas, when you lie with your whores, do you think they like it? Do you think they want you? Do you think they want to be fucked for your drugs?' the mad hellish laughter from the Demon seemed to reach a crescendo ably joined by all the other demons in the room. He could almost see them, indistinct little shapes of pain writhing behind shirts and blouses with equal abandon, all different colors all slightly different in size. For a moment Thomas's mind almost snapped completely when he thought 'They're color coded for each drug and sized for the strength of addiction!' he could feel his mind resisting the cackling madness that seemed about to push it over the edge, breaking his sanity once and for all. He pushed back with a flood of images of his party nights when he was convinced Dena or whoever it was, was having fun, but the images changed on him showing others, not him, raping and taking advantage of those women when they had started taking drugs, when they had become completely vulnerable to their new realities. The claws pinched deeper into his heart and he felt pain, he saw his own rape again at the hands of Smyth, felt the pain, smelled the *Man Stink* as he had called it then. His mind reeled and he knew the sick truth of it, in a way he was no better, he had been perpetrating pain, suffering, betrayal and abuse. He was a Demon himself.

'Now you see, now you know' came the sibilant, scalding recrimination from his heart-locked companion, accompanied by a change in the smell in his nostrils and the taste in his mouth, it was no longer sulfur, now it was crack, pure, fresh, quality crack cocaine, and he wanted to smoke right now 'RIGHT NOW' he screamed inside himself. The demon chuckled on as his tail flicked as though conducting the orchestra of the possessed, the shadows in Thomas's head. 'God and Mother Mary protect me' he begged with a whimper as he sat rigid in his chair seeing, watching the Demons writhe in every other chair in the room, even Stanly's. The urge to get up and get out, to go home to his apartment and smoke his head off was almost overpowering, his mind still creaked and groaned like overstressed steel about to exceed its modus of elasticity. 'Young's Modulus,' he clung to the thought as a lifeline remembered from engineering text books, safer days. The Demon gazed up at him, pinching further, deeper. He still sat locked stock-still, trying to keep a lid on the fear, shame and hatred he felt for all the demons in the room, his own included, then he remembered a prayer his mother had taught him long ago, when he would be afraid of the dark and what it might hold, back when he thought he was not supposed to tell what the Demon Smyth was doing to him, the prayer he had recited over and over and over again inside his head as he had been pawed and raped and played with like a thing, not a person. The pain of the demon's claws seemed to surge but he refused to look; he fought for the first line of the prayer, then the second and he hurriedly began; *Blessed Michael, the Archangel, defend us in the hour of conflict. Be our safeguard against the wickedness and snares of the Devil, may God restrain him we humbly pray and thou O Prince of the heavenly hosts, throw Satan down to Hell and with him all the other wicked spirits who wander the world for the ruin of Souls, Amen.* He felt the pressure ease in his chest, and he hurriedly recited the prayer again, then again and again. He focused on it so much that he felt less fear and more like himself. The Demon was gone from his chest, as was the pain; he quickly directed his eyes in a sweep, everyone else was back to wearing shirts or blouses, sweaters or hoodies and a single three-piece, somewhat rumpled suit. The Demon chorus was gone and Thomas knew he had almost been gone too, for good. He had never, not even in the worst drug horrors, felt like his mind was about to snap, but he knew that it had been. He knew what he had felt was real enough and that would have been all it took for a true descent into madness; faith in it being true. He was glad he had remembered faith of a different, more benevolent kind, at the last.

'So Thomas, would you like to share with us how you are feeling about being here?' asked Stan with a gentle voice. All eyes were suddenly focused on his chair and he straightened up a bit, hurriedly trying to remember if he had made an outburst or something similar to have drawn Stan's attention. 'No, just my turn' he said to himself, as he could tell by the expectant way most of the other addicts were looking at him, they had looked that way at every other person who spoken so far.

'Well I don't really know how to begin,' he said in quiet tone, 'except to say thank you to everyone who has told of their experiences so far.' This was met with varying nods of agreement and encouragement, so he forged ahead. 'I've been caught up in smoking crack for a while now, almost nine months and it's time to stop. Not that it was ever time to really begin, but it seemed like the thing to do at the time.' He got a few laughs out of that one, not that he was trying; he was still getting over the recent internal exorcism he had just performed on himself. He was reverting to type, the normal Thomas, the entertaining Thomas, the clown perhaps? 'Why have you decided to come here now Thomas?

Why is now the time to deal with your addiction and stop?' asked Stan with an intensity belied by his subtle lean forward in his chair. Thomas barely hesitated before replying, 'because it's going to kill me and I do not want to die like this.' This was greeted by silence, he knew he had struck a chord but he continued anyway.' I have lost my self-respect, the respect of the people I work with, the love of my life and my ability to say no to myself in many ways. I am not this person I have become, I was not raised to be the person I am right now and with the grace of God I may well be able to find my way back to who it is I am supposed to be.' He had used the expression 'with the grace of God' as a colloquial filler, quite common in the country and society he grew up in, but as he said it he knew it to be more than that. He had also noticed the atheists and agnostics in the room, subconsciously bridle at his saying it. 'Fuck 'em', he didn't care, he knew this was about him and what he needed to do to get better, to heal. 'There are no atheists in foxholes' he remembered the famous quote and nodded to himself as he visualized himself hunkered down at the bottom of a muddy hole as the Devil's own artillery pounded relentlessly down around him.

He said no more and after a few seconds Stan leaned further forward 'you are very precise in what your goals are Thomas, do you think they are realistic?' Thomas was considering the look in Stan's eyes as had delivered that question across the room to him. He saw no guile there, no judgment, just curiosity he replied 'At this point Stan, they have to be, my addiction has taken away most of my other choices so the only real choice left to me is to either live or die, and I choose to live.' The little surge of self-esteem he felt as the words came out of his mouth was indeed small, but it was there. For the first time in nine months, Thomas was actually just a little bit happy with himself. It was not much but it was a start. The Demon growled something internally, but Thomas ignored it, dismissed it, with a sharp slap of his minds rediscovered whip. He clung to the feeling; he had a beginning now he realized, something to act as a foundation for recovery. He would build on it. Stan studied him closely for a few seconds then said 'Very good Thomas, very good indeed, if you really believe that you will succeed.' Thomas met his gaze and simply said 'I know,' He was done with talking now and Stan sensed it. He moved on to the next target in the room and Thomas was aware that some in the room were still gazing at him intently as he tried to concentrate on the new speaker. He could see them out of the corner of his eye, considering both him and what he had said. He was still mulling it over in the vaults of his mind, when Stan pierced his reverie by saying 'Ok everyone, really good work tonight and I will see you all at the same time on Thursday, be safe and stay clean.' The addicts rose and some went to Stan to chat, others amongst themselves but the majority went out the door. Thomas decided to once again follow the herd while he processed his first session of rehab. In the lobby he went left to go out the front door as the herd went right. He walked out into the green garden space on the Eight Avenue side and sat on a bench to light a cigarette. The noise of the traffic was less now as rush hour was almost over, the bridge and tunnel crowd almost fully filtered across the Hudson by now.

He drew on the cigarette and inhaled, 'I liked what you said' said the ferret from right beside him on the bench. Thomas gave a start then looked at him 'Screw me you're a stealthy bastard aren't you.' This was more of a statement than a question. 'It's safer that way, for me, I've found. I'm Eric.' Thomas extended his hand

'Thomas' the ferret took it and shook it briefly 'I know" was all he said. Thomas continued to smoke, waiting for Eric to say more if he felt like it. He had after all approached him. When the cigarette was almost done the ferret said 'I liked what you said and I wanted to tell you, I'm going home now.' 'Which bit of what I said did you like Eric?' there was silence and the ferret looked intently at him. Thomas looked right back and said 'it's nice to meet you Eric, will you be here on Thursday?' the only reply he got was a faint 'Yes' over the noise of the traffic as the ferret turned and disappeared as quickly as he had arrived. Nothing was going to strike Thomas as strange after what had happened inside earlier. He refocused on his new little island of self-esteem and walked over to the pizza place on the corner for a slice and a coke. He ate it there at one of the stand- up tables, then walked the short distance to the subway to go back to Queens.

When he turned the key in the door he knew what he had to do. He filled the apartment with light and opened all the doors and windows and let the warm night air wash in and around everything. This was going to be difficult but he had to do it. Quickly, while his mind was still made up, he rushed around his stash spots and once he had all the material he had in his hands, he threw them in the toilet and flushed, he watched as close on five hundred dollars' worth of material swirled its way down to oblivion. There was a pang and a thought 'What have you done?' but that was ruthlessly suppressed and isolated from his consciousness. He would be clean of crack, he knew he could do it but it would be hard. He also knew it would be a long night, so he prepared himself for the onslaught to come. He took his phone out and deleted every number he had for a dealer or hooker who could get him crack. He had brief flashes of faces and places as he went through the list, the temptations were strong, but he remembered the female alcoholic who had blackouts and what his visions of her abuse had unlocked in him, he stuck to the task in hand. Thomas was a realist as well and while anyone else in the room earlier would have said he had to be clean of everything, he knew he was not an alcoholic and he would need to self-medicate in some way tonight to get through the coming storm. When all the crack was gone, he disposed of all the equipment in the appropriate way as well, the pipes were wrapped thickly in tissue paper and crushed beneath his foot, then wrapped in more tissue along with the little metal smoking screens, and flushed.

He satisfied himself that all of the hard stuff was gone. He rolled a joint and poured a glass of good whiskey adding a dram of water to it to *open it.* He turned on the news and settled in a very respectable manner in his brightly lit living room, evening air washing cleanly through the place taking away the stink of newly old habits that had seemed to always linger. He smoked some cigarettes and eventually the joint while arguing quietly to himself with *Amanpour* on CNN about something she had said about the War on Terror. He was feeling normal and he did not want anything else except what he had right now. His own war on terror was just beginning and he fervently hoped he made a better fist of it than George Bush Junior had. After all, Thomas couldn't call in the marines if he got it wrong. He was an army of one and he would fight the Demon, but not to the death, merely to a standstill, a point of peace where Thomas one day, would be invulnerable. This was the lullaby than ushered him to sleep, to dreams that led him back to happy joyful times in his youth with his family and friends, 'Blessed Michael the

Archangel indeed' was his last conscious thought. He was at peace.

Chapter 10

The Problem with Sex

Rain always made him pensive and this particular Thursday evening in Manhattan was no different. The slick sidewalk was beginning to gleam with the reflection of the streetlights and the neon that flashed on and off at every deli he walked past trying so hard to catch the attention of a potential customer. The wet hissing and splashing sound the innumerable car, truck and taxi tire's made as they pushed through the water to find tarmac all at the same time, was a swishing counterpoint to the honking horns and the clatter and tapping of thousands of pairs of shoes, hurrying home beneath a sea of tortoise shells, as their umbrellas bobbed and weaved.

Thomas was leaning against the corner of the pizza joint across the way from the hospital; he had a spot beneath the awning where he could smoke out of the rain and not get jostled by the crowd. The sea of cars and people never ceased to amaze and terrify him and he had never felt as lonely as he did right now, in the midst of eight million souls. He wondered if he would not have been better off back in Ireland standing in the middle of a green field with nothing but some livestock and perhaps a dog by his side and not a person in sight; he knew that he would be. The feeling of getting slowly lost in this mass of humanity was utterly terrifying to him. He visualized himself as a drop of colored liquid falling into this ocean from the end of God's pipette, watched as it was diluted, assimilated and was gone like it had never existed. He feared not having a voice, not meaning anything, not mattering. He knew deep inside that this was a big part of his addiction, it was his *escaping* of this ever more present reality, that he was becoming daily more aware of.

It was time. He shrugged himself from his reverie against the damp concrete pillar and stepped out into the crowd, not fighting its flow, just gently taking a polite diagonal across to the edge of the curb from where he could cross the street and enter the garden in front of the main entrance. He still had a wispy picture of the green Irish field in his mind, so the touch of a wet leaf with his right palm soothed him a bit as he passed through the garden to the front door, fully jammed with people coming and going.

The bustle inside was what he had come to expect. The first day it had been intimidating due to its strange newness reinforced by the reasons for being there. That was being replaced the more often he came, by the mind's knack of accepting the familiar and the known. People were similar but different in this regard, as they were living, breathing beings subject to all manner of urges, drives and demands. Places though, only seemed to change for Thomas if people actively modified or tampered with them.

All this reflection on seemingly everything had once puzzled and frightened Thomas more than a little bit. His first forays into drugs had only deepened the creeping sense of paranoia these same *ruminations,* as he called them now, caused him to feel as the tightness of panic in his chest. He stood with some others just slightly off the main thoroughfare of the lobby, patiently waiting for the elevator. He noticed a scent, female and alluring, that wafted across his awareness and caused a tiny stir of arousal. He looked discretely about and located the source, a fine, tall, slender brunette, wearing a pencil skirt and tight blouse, sensible heels and tan coloured pantyhose. As he took in the view and admired the slender strength of her legs he could feel the arousal growing to where his penis was giving all the signs it was about to stir. In his mind he could see himself pressing his face between her willing legs, her skirt discarded on some floor somewhere, her hands on the back of his head pulling his face in so he could nuzzle, smell, lick and experience her. Her imagined moans of delight had him almost fully erect now.

Ding! The chime that announced the arrival of the elevator shook him quickly out of his waking fantasy. He had not seen her face in his mind's eye, but then again he never did see any faces when he fantasized or masturbated. As everyone stepped into the car he allowed some others to enter first so he could regain his internal balance and also give his rapidly dying erection time to settle; a crowed elevator car was not for sharing one of those. The brunette caught his eye just before he did the pirouette to leave himself facing the doors as they shut. He blushed immediately, strongly, and kept turning to face the doors feeling his eyes dropping with embarrassment at what he had had going on in his head a few short seconds ago. She must have thought he was shy and cute because just as his eyes left hers he knew he saw a little twinkle of amusement and satisfaction there. 'How wrong she is' he thought knowing that if she knew what his life had been like over the last few months she would be screaming her way down the hallways at full tilt, flirting the furthest thing from her mind. He again felt shame for where his mind had wandered too, as he had admired the beauty of her shape, the symmetry of her proportions a subtle hint emerging through the woollen material of her skirt. Where did the normal admiration and hardwired desire a man should feel towards an attractive female begin to morph into the sicker realms of lust and power? He inwardly shuddered at the thought he might have been brushing that border with the feather of his thought.

The elevator seemed to stop everywhere on the way up, due to his *ruminations* time was stretched out to almost agonizing slowness. Thankfully the brunette exited on the fourth floor, another surreptitious glance in his direction but more questioning now, not hostile, just a curiosity as to why he had reacted to her the way he had. His eyes had remained strictly on the floor beneath his feet as she had brushed past him in a sea of femininity that again assailed his olfactory sense, he could tell enough from his peripheral vision to know that. The whole episode left him somehow saddened as he stepped out and followed the rhythm of his boot heels down the corridor of institutional pale greens to reception. No doubt she would have already forgotten him, as the next man she encountered with a pulse would admire her too. 'Must suck to be an attractive woman in a city, or anywhere for that matter, always objectified by evolution, before anything else about you is recognized or appreciated,' was the thought running through his head as he stood waiting at the midriff-height counter. The large African American nurse behind it was sternly dealing with the guy in front of him, her white nurse hat perched precariously on an impressive weave that would have been a costly undertaking, but it suited her features. Her uniform was at least two sizes too small for her and it seemed like it was straining to contain her. 'Objectification again my good man,' was his self-directed rebuke as finally her gaze settled on him. Her body language was not the friendliest but that was no surprise working where she did. No shortage of rudeness here one would imagine, or downright crazy either, came with the territory. 'Hello, I'm here for the six o'clock session with Stanley,' he said as he handed over the small green embossed card that marked him for what he was, an addict. She made no attempt to disguise her review of him, as she swept her eyes up and down and then back to his eyes again, with challenging intensity, judgment strongly emanating from her all the time. He had a sudden desire to yell at her ' who the hell are you to judge me woman, just do your fucking job!' but he did not, he stood calmly as she almost snatched the card from his fingers and ran it through the old fashioned counter foiling machine they used. 'Sixty-five dollars, insurance, cash or credit?' came at him from beneath that now leaning white hat. 'Cash,' he answered noncommittally, handing it over.

The manual machine rattled and thrummed with the force she applied to get it to produce his receipt, almost like she was taking out her desire to cause him pain upon it. 'Whatever her friggin' problem is, I want no part of it,' he thought while simultaneously taking the roughly proffered receipt and sweetly adding audibly to her 'Thank you Ma'am,' with his most unctuous *Go Screw Yourself Then* smile. Her look changed to a guarded surprise with a faint hint of shame in it but quickly returned to the fixed glare she had had for the other guy earlier. Maintaining his own rigid smile he turned away and crossed to the waiting room, he recognized no one so he sat in the first available seat to watch the rain on dirty windows, as the minutes ticked by to the start of the session.

Ferret arrived and after a quick scan of the people present he deposited himself soundlessly beside Thomas, 'Hello' he said quietly while briefly making eye contact. 'Hello' Thomas returned with a smile, his first of the day. 'How you getting on today?' he continued. Ferret looked back at him, seemingly satisfied that everything was in an order that was acceptable to him 'I'm ok, been busy being busy.' Smiling more now, Thomas said 'You do strike me as a man who is always on a mission of some sort!' Ferret let a smile of his own slightly out into sight, but said nothing more. They both sat there for a while saying nothing further, then just as suddenly as he had arrived Ferret jumped up and declaimed 'It's time' and was gone. Thomas couldn't help himself from feeling a bit better about the here and now, the little man just emanated this sense of no threat, no danger, an almost innocence that he had rarely ever come across before. Thomas got up and followed him the few short steps down the hallway past the now ludicrously-angled tiny white hat, glowering at her next victim. He ignored her totally and stepped into the room where the chairs were always arranged in a circle; that was how he thought of the space now, circles of chairs and thoughts, circles of addictions and excuses. Endless circles, round and round they went inside his head as he sat down. Ferret was elsewhere, not here, just elsewhere. No doubt he had entered and not liking the small amount of people already present, he'd exited by the second door at the far end of the room and was now no doubt doing another lap of the sixth floor corridors, killing a bit more time while feeling he was about something, 'Endlessly repeating circles,' he reminded himself.

He caught Stanley entering out of the corner of his eye, closely followed by a few of the regulars. Nods and polite greetings were exchanged, 'hello's' and 'good evenings' and smiles and nods, all the usual preliminaries that had to be performed and dispensed with before the dissection of their vicarious realities and addictions began in earnest. He danced the polite dance as he felt he was supposed to and just as the last bum was finding a seat, he saw the ferret glide in and alight on a chair as quietly as an owl would on a mouse. Again he couldn't help himself smiling.

'Well, now that we are all comfortable shall we begin?' announced Stan with a warm smile that took in everyone present. The usual roll of names being announced and the gathering repeating the name with welcome attached, passed round the room swiftly and comfortingly to Thomas's mind. He had indeed become used to being here now and he was in no doubt whatsoever that this was a good thing. Once the greetings were done, Stan invited Fart Boy, of all people, to speak. 'This will be good,' thought Thomas aloud to himself but at the same time resolving to pay attention, there was something indeed about this guy that bothered him greatly, not just his *obvious* dealings during the smoke break.

'My name is Jonathan and I use Crystal Meth, I've been clean now for six weeks almost and I feel I'm in a good place with all of that.' 'Bollix' thought Thomas angrily, he never could tolerate a liar, especially when he lied to himself, but he did not stir any more than that, this was not the forum and anyway if Jonathan wanted to lie about where he was at and what he was doing, that was up to him. His making a mockery of the circle did continue to bother Thomas though, so he simply sat, face impassive and nonjudgmental as any other in the room, while Jonathan droned on. 'So when I would be having sex the rush was always good and that was what kept me doing it, you know what I mean guys? It really just kept you wanting to push it and push it.' This hit a chord with the others and even though he loathed himself for admitting such, Thomas too. 'Every lie, has to have a grain of truth in it somewhere, well any good one that is,' he reminded himself as he contemplated the features on Fart Boy, shining now in the reflected glory he felt from everyone for agreeing with him. This thing about sex was exactly on par with what Thomas had been *ruminating* on earlier during and after his encounter with the stunning Brunette in the elevator. The thought that he and Fart Boy could share anything remotely like similar desires or whatever, repulsed him, but he had to allow that it might be so, in some ways. They were both addicts and that was as far as Thomas was willing to go on that one. Thankfully Jonathan was gay, otherwise if Thomas thought he might be doing something or living his dream anything like Fart Boy, he'd change his gender preference just to escape it. 'Nope, that's not true either,' he thought in parallel, the taste of one cock in his mouth had been enough for a lifetime, no matter how long ago.

Finally Jonathan's droning monologue of his exploits in bed while high ran out of steam, either that or he hadn't been expecting a positive response, so had only rehearsed that much. He totally struck Thomas as a mirror actor, standing in the bathroom rattling off lines and lies with equal abandon, totally and utterly impressed with his own eloquence and being stunned by how the world had not yet fully recognized his unique brilliance and rescued him from obscurity, to whisk him to the very tippy top of the ivory tower that was his, waiting on him, somewhere. He was forced to admit to himself that he did that, acted out scenarios to his own reflection all the time ignoring who he really might be, not seeing what was right in front of him. Was he truly, deep down where the real secrets were, any different? The truth made him shift a little in his chair, the only outward sign of the realizing pain within.

He was still well reeling just a little bit from that moment of self realization when the outside intruded, it was his turn to speak now, the eyes directed at him said so. The looks he could see in those eyes varied, questions, always questions, some happy, expectant, inquiring, weighing, attraction, repulsion. Everything you could really imagine, but to be fair, mostly friendly and expectant. He shifted again, more comfortably this time and began to speak.

'Hi everyone, my name is Thomas,' he paused as they all replied in their various ways, some nodding with a friendly 'I'm in rehab, I have to bloody smile...' kind of smile, that one always made him chuckle, so he did and his smile lit the room. 'I smoke crack cocaine, and that is the reason I'm here tonight, but not the why. I started to smoke crack about nine, more like ten months ago, I was with a woman and strangely enough she was not a hooker.' This last brought some chuckles from the expectant inquiring curious attracted folk in the room, and gained the rapt attention of everyone else. 'I was upstate on vacation with friends, and well, we partied hard at this ski lodge hotel place. I was stoned off my head on weed, had drank a ton of whiskey and managed to hook up with this woman, just kind of happened between the pool table and the bar, met her right out of the blue.' He paused for a second as he remembered that distinct moment, could picture it perfectly. 'She was pretty stunning and liked to party. Not long after bumping into each other, we were up in my room, smoking weed, dancing and drinking. I had a smoking room so once we kept the noise to acceptable *I'm-getting-laid-on-vacation-tonight* levels, we would be good to go. She produced a pipe from her purse, a stem. She said she was going to freebase, I thought 'sure I'd do a line or two' if she had coke. She did but she also had crack. After a few lines we started to screw, next thing you know I'm setting up for my first ever hit of crack and she's making me feel real good at the same time.' He paused again to let that one sink in; he was not trying at all to be a dick to the women in the room. He needed to reinforce that he was telling it just as it was, no bells no whistles. He resumed 'I took the hit and that was it, I wanted more and more and by the time the morning came I knew I'd go seek it out when I got home. But at that stage I thought it would be fun, it was for a while but as you all know eventually happens, I lost control of it and by the time I realized that I'd only ever had the illusion of control over it, it was too late to stop.'

Several people nodded their agreement and the attractive alcoholic asked 'Thomas, are you addicted to sex?' it was a frank and honest question, he could tell by the look in her eyes. 'No, I do not believe that I am.' Again the nods and knowing looks, did a turn about the faces present, more than ever paying attention, some still in spite of themselves but quickly getting caught up in the story and his telling of it. 'I said the *reason* earlier, but not the *why*; the why is *because of* sex. You see I have always been very sexually aware and that was mainly due to abuse I suffered at the hands of a man when I was very young.' Thomas did not say the man was a priest as that definition really made no difference to the facts, he felt also felt honour-bound in a way, to defend all the truly gifted and good men and women who had given their lives to a true vocation, to help others. 'I discovered early after I went through puberty that sexual activity felt good on a physical level, but I had no idea why I still felt dirty, I also had no idea that what had happened to me had really been about power first and sexual gratification second.'

Again he felt reassured by the level of absorption in his take he could see in his fellows in the room, he knew he had to be wholly truthful here and that that level of honesty was what he needed to get past all of this. Some of the women in the room had a look that Thomas could not explain, but he knew straight away what it meant, they too had been victims of sexual violence. Stan was regarding him intently and nodded encouragingly for him to continue.

'As I grew older I would masturbate a lot and the orgasms were sometimes the best feeling I had all day. I would constantly be looking at women through a kind of fantasy lens, the fantasy being great sex, love and safety all wrapped up in one, a completeness I was yearning for. Of course that sort of completeness does not happen easily or quickly and as a result a lot of my relationships could not bear the strain of my own expectations. I became increasingly more frustrated with my own sexuality and as I grew, to fully understand the nature of the abuse I had suffered, I needed to escape. My desire for answers happened to intersect with my discovery of weed and that satisfied my curiosity for a while and I would ask all the beautiful metaphysical questions, like some stoned pseudo-intellectual. I had developed to a place where I had kind of intellectualized sex as well, so on that night I first smoked crack while being stimulated, the combined physical rush of the drugs and orgasm, just felt extremely intense. I was transported, or felt I was, somewhere inside myself and for an instant thought I'd attained some higher level of consciousness. Of course I had not. When I smoked again I was alone and while I was thinking the big thoughts and trying to direct them towards the nature of existence and the universe, my place in it etc. my body just kept hitting me with wave upon wave of arousal. I was overwhelmed by it. It was a short step thereafter to buying crack and picking up a woman off the street or calling an escort to smoke it with, as the two seem to be inextricably linked. Soon nothing really mattered except sex on crack, the physical addiction of it had found a way to direct me to drive myself to use more. Eventually the road I was on led me here and I'm thankful for it too, the only other direction I could have taken – well I do not need to tell any of you where that would have led.' He had been leaning forward with his elbows on his knees so he leaned back now and took a deep breath.

Stan was again looking at him intently and said 'Thank you Thomas, you have a very good, and if you don't mind me saying so, Irish way with words.' Thomas didn't mind at all, used to all that. 'You explained very well the link between sex and drugs for you, do you think you can break or have broken that link?' Thomas chewed on that one for a moment, he had to continue to be honest, to be true. 'The last relationship I was part of, I found it very hard to have intercourse and not be thinking on a subconscious level of crack whilst doing it, have I broken the link? No. Will I ever break the link? I hope so, but in the meantime I have to try to manage it as best I can. I hope it fades with the passing of time.' Stan gave him another encouraging smile and said

'Thank you for your contribution to the group tonight Thomas. Any questions for Thomas?' Most of the people just imperceptibly shook their heads, the rest said or did nothing; it was obvious though that he had stuck more than a few different chords in the last few minutes. The eyes looking at him were all somehow softer of nature now, he felt acceptance from them he had not felt before, like he was a bone-fide broken person, just like everyone else.

The next speaker began and Thomas was split between listening and reflecting deeply on what he had just told the room. He had meant every word of it and it had been difficult to share, but he could already feel the change slowly growing within him. Perhaps someday he would indeed truly be free of his former nightmare. Six weeks was what he had now, six weeks of hard won, pillow-chewing-all-through-the-sweat-soaked-nights-of-withdrawal, cleanliness. He was proud of that and scared too. He was fragile but facing the realities of some huge things this evening had to help, 'hadn't it?' Thomas tuned back into the room and was disappointed by the current speaker, he was crying and sobbing as he described his crystal meth use in the bath houses of the village, the orgies and every now and then would reference some of the points Thomas had just made, while looking at him pleadingly to back him up, give a sign that Thomas was with him. Obviously his contribution had inspired this guy to a sudden epiphany. 'Seen this happen here before,' he reminded himself. Several times over the last weeks, newbies would come in and you could always tell after a session whether they were serious or not, whether they were there of their own accord or to placate families or loved ones at the end of their respective tethers. They would jump on the first bandwagon they came across in the room. 'Put the Devil on horseback and he will ride to Hell.' The old saying echoed through his mind as he regarded the spectacle unfolding before him, the false tears, the feigned regret, 'Blah blubbering blah!' Thomas reckoned this guys' type should be winnowed out, not allowed to make a mockery of the genuine work people were trying to do to get well. The crying methhead would last two sessions at the most, then disappear back to the bath houses of Greenwich Village Gaydom with a new patron to supply the ICE and bang him sore for a while, until they got bored with him, then he would be back again, to a place just like this. Straight, Gay or Bi, Thomas had seen this act from various addicts before and it pissed him off for its juvenility, its transparency. He pointedly ignored the guy's eyes when he glanced down the way at Thomas, by the looks of it others were cottoning on to him too. Stan was not happy but he hid it well, eventually as the blubbering fool began to repeat himself Stan interrupted, 'You are finding this very upsetting and that's ok, it's hard to share so much and especially with new and strange faces all around, thank you for sharing and take some time now. This is a place of discussion and peace, be at peace.' Thomas grinned a bit in spite of himself 'Oh very Buddhist of you Stan, well said and not a moment too soon.' He exulted to himself, and he could feel he was not the only one in the room feeling, thinking the same. Immediately he felt guilty though, he was in no position to judge, but he had just done so anyway. There was no doubt that he would be questioning everything for a while in life, most of his trust in anything, especially his ability to make correct discernments, had been burned out of him with the multitude of crack pipes he had used and the even larger multitudes of quills he had smoked. That was the real source of his annoyance, his reality, and gay-boy cry-boy had just happened to be convenient to hang it on. Now he felt worse. He had released torrents of primitive, chauvinist and homophobic bias, inside his head this evening so far, as he had tried to cope with the realities of what he needed to say here and actually saying it, normal understanding and tolerance of other ways, forgotten in a rush of base hypersensitivity. 'Regression instead of enlightenment, what gives?' he asked himself rhetorically.

The rest of the session went quickly and Thomas felt himself drifting his way to the end of it, lost in his own thoughts on what he had spoken about, the memories that went with them, the faces, the places and regrettably the situations of most of them. Finally it was time to leave and he stood and gave a nod to Stan, picked his chair up to place in the stack at the back of the room, did so and left the room. He was down the hallway and at the elevator even before the Ferret had made good his escape, which alone was impressive. The elevator arrived empty, so he stepped in and hit the button, the doors already closing while the rest of the herd were still milling around the reception area, struggling to organize themselves into some sort of unconsciously conscious entity with a common purpose. As the doors glided together he caught a glimpse of the white nurse's hat looking above the other heads, he could tell by how it moved that its owner was pissed. He was smiling again as the car descended to the ground level, uninterrupted on this journey. He was thankful, as the last person he wanted to see was the woman from earlier. He stepped out and was reaching for his cigarette packet before he even reached the front door of the place.

The rain had slackened off to a drizzle that would get you wet if you spent long enough out in it, but not so much if you just walked through it and ignored it. He wanted away for some reason tonight, just to get back home and be warm and safe, alone and happy for being so. He had some steaks to cook and there was a bottle of wine or two in the cupboard as well. The amount of groceries in the larder had greatly increased once he had stopped spending all his money on other things.

The traffic was quieter now as the main evening rush was over, so he stepped out onto the roadway as he lit his smoke and crossed over back to the real side of the city, as he thought of it. The four streets that formed the block the hospital complex stood on reminded him of a moat. The Marlboro filled his lungs and with that he remembered he'd need to get more when he got off the no.7 train in Woodside, he had enough for now. 'Yes, I'm going to enjoy cooking a steak and a good red to wash it down.' He thought as he dropped his butt in the gutter and hurried down the steps to the subway along with the other late travelling denizens of this increasingly, at least to him, anonymous city.

About a half hour later, he stepped off the old style Red Train Car on to the platform at Woodside and joined the crowd as they shuffled their way to the turnstile. He clacked through it and headed down the rain slickened, wide wooden planked steps with the yellow grip painted leading edges. The stairs ran down through a forest of drab, deep green, painted built-up beams and girders, trusses and columns, built up because that was how they made large scale structural steelwork back in the day, taking angles and flats and riveting them all together. It was lovely and archaic all at the same time, especially here as you could see the guts of the elevated railway. The community below had a feel to it that was much warmer than Manhattan; here people would have the time to know you, well, get to know you by sight at least. Thomas stopped under the awning at the Pakistani newsagents halfway up the block and bought two more packs of smokes. He liked the three brothers who ran the place, especially the oldest one who was in his late sixties and bedecked in gold rings that flashed as he passed out Thomas's change. He always greeted them with a 'Salaam' and they responded in kind then a jovial follow up of 'How are you today, Mr. Thomas?' delivered in the lilting singsong of their native land that they had not lost in twenty years in Queens. It was a small and positive interaction he enjoyed.

He bade them goodbye and hurried up 61st and then cut across to 58th and walked the two blocks to Queens Boulevard. It was ten lanes wide here. He waited on the corner outside the Rite Aid store for the lights to change and let him over safely to the other side where there sat a Staples Office Superstore. His apartment was just behind that. He made it safely across and then turned the corner onto 47th Avenue. He went through the front gate and opened the main door, turning to close it as he stepped inside. He shook off most of the rain and took off his overcoat. Turning again he started to walk towards the stairs, just as he put his foot on the bottom step, he was stopped dead in his tracks by a 'Hello Thomas.' He looked up and was totally surprised by what he saw. It was Joan and she was sitting on the top step at the first landing looking down at him with a smile. 'What the bloody hell do I say or do now?' he thought frantically as he took a very ginger second step. She stood up and he found himself saying 'Hello Joan, you look well.' And she did, God above how she did, with her eyes sparkling the way they did, her hair glistening with a combination of rain and conditioner, her perfume filled the stairwell, how had he not noticed that when he first opened the door? He didn't know, didn't care, she was here. Before he could say anything or even think anything else, she was down the steps and in his arms, hugging and kissing him passionately. 'Why are you here?' he thought as she continued kissing him but soon he didn't care, didn't want to know, she just was.

Chapter 11

The Problem with Love

Not long after falling in through the front door of the apartment in a tangle of each other, clothing rapidly discarded as they made their way across the polished wood floors to the first available piece of furniture, they lay spent in a tumble holding each other, heaving chests slowing down as their breathing came back to something normal. He was floating in a demi sleep, idly playing with strands of her hair as her head nestled on his chest. He was impossibly content in that moment. There was no light, except for the dim ambient streetlight spilling in through the insect screens of the open window. He would have to get up in a few minutes to turn on some light, but not right now; he had no idea how long she would be here for and he was not going to rush it, not a moment of it.

She stirred slightly with a soft moan of pleasure humming through his chest cavity from her cheek, it felt electric to him; he could feel the vibration tingle around his heart in an extraordinarily physical way. 'This is love,' he murmured to himself, but straight away a faint chuckle of the positive side of his conscience replied '

No, this is lust, excellent that it may be, but still lust, nothing more.'

He was saddened a little by the truth of that as he forced himself not to ignore it, he had fought long and hard within himself to gain some grasp, a handle if you will, on what their relationship really was and the feelings that had almost destroyed him, well added to the path he was already trotting down. He shifted slightly now that the magic of the moment had been dispersed a little by his thoughts. She was exhausted but murmured a soft 'hi,' nonetheless. 'Hi baby, how are you feeling?'

'Absolutely wonderful, thank you I needed that so badly,' she purred while shifting her arm to let her hand stroke the hair on his chest suggestively. 'Are you hungry? More importantly do you have the time to be hungry?' he asked somewhat tentatively. She turned her head so her chin was on his chest and was looking up into his eyes from under her perfectly plucked and ordered eyebrows through the edge of her falling fringe. 'I'm a fool!' he thought, accepted it and said nothing. 'She smiled as she replied ' Yes I have time, quite a bit actually, so,' as she said this she touched his penis and started to kiss his chest moving down slowly, until she had him in her mouth again, knowing how to arouse him to exactly where she needed him to be. Soon she was on top, reverse cowboy style, rocking with him on the way to the title.

After they had finished, he got up and went to the kitchen, leaving her dozing under a blanket he had pulled off the couch for them. She was happy, so was he for now. He showered and questioned, just a bit, the silly look of happiness in his eyes as he consulted his mirror briefly. Pulling on house pants and a cotton long sleeve he padded barefoot to the kitchen, turning on the down lights as he passed through the archway. He glanced over his shoulder again to look at her snuggled up, a foot protruding from beneath the blanket on top of the Persian floor rug, the fan of her hair and the curve of her hidden hip. The highlights of colours and textures of the tableau, struck him as the light from the kitchen spilled over her, the contours of her position casting shadows against the darker shadows of the room beyond her.

He fetched some new tea lights from the cabinet and started to light and position them around the place so it had a warmth and soft beauty that complemented the sound of the rain falling again outside. Earlier he had been sorting through some CD's before going to the city and he had found a compilation that he had made a long time ago so he put it on, not loud, just at the right level to accentuate the whole. He moved back to the kitchen and set about cooking. He always kept steak at room temperature in a sealed bowl, already seasoned with salt and pepper, lightly coated with oil. He made a salad and then a dressing of English mustard, balsamic and walnut oil. As he shook it to mix in a bottle the soft sounds of Dave Brubeck's *Take Five* washed through the air. He set the griddle to a high heat and released a pair of thick New York strip steaks from their confinement. While waiting on the griddle to heat he opened a bottle of red, a Zinfandel from Coppola Vineyards to breathe a bit, 'this is like a movie right now, life imitating art,' he thought to himself while reading *Francis Ford Coppola* off the wine label. That made an impression on him and he continued to mull it over as he crumbled feta and blue cheese into the salad and drizzled the dressing over it all.

The griddle had an almost indistinct wisp of smoke coming off it now, ready. He placed the pair of steaks at ninety degrees to the raised cast iron ribs in a rolling motion; they sizzled with a satisfactory intensity just like the aroma that exploded from them. The music was now moving into some *Morcheeba* as he poured two glasses of wine, taking a sip from one, enjoying it immensely. Joan stirred as he set some cutlery on the table along with the wines and some napkins. She slowly, beautifully, got up and walked naked through the candlelight towards him, her tousled hair over her face hiding everything except her smile. She put her arms round his neck and kissed him deeply. Pulling back she said 'Do I have time for a quick shower?' already stepping slightly away from him in the direction of the bathroom, a coquettish look sparkling in her eyes. 'Yes indeed you do, a few minutes' he replied as he smiled and turned to flip the steaks, they both liked medium tending towards medium rare. The sound of the shower hissed in the background as he took the meat off to rest and placed the salad on the table, serving spoons at odds to each other after he slid them into position.

'This is good isn't it?' he asked himself with an urgency that seemed to come from left field. He knew how he felt about her, this being in what he considered a normal set of events that any couple would experience, but they were not an ordinary couple. He was still trying to get a grasp on that like always, while he transferred the steaks to warmed plates and the sound of the shower died. She emerged wearing a shirt of his, the effect that had on him not lost on her. He held her chair and she sat after kissing him playfully once again. He placed her plate on the table in front of her with a theatrical flourish and was rewarded with a chuckle and a smile. After fetching his, he sat down. They both smiled and giggled as they raised their glasses to clinking height and said 'cheers baby!' both at the same time, making them laugh. The after-sex endorphins were in full flow all right, but that was just part of the deal. Happiness was what mattered and right now, they both were extremely happy.

A tune from the *Buena Vista Social Club* called *Chan Chan* came on as they were negotiating the passing of the salad bowl. 'Mm perfect music my dear, really perfect,' she said cutting hungrily into the steak. 'Not bad is it, I found the CD earlier today when I was trying to sort them all out,' he replied glancing across at the cardboard storage box in the corner of the living room with a few neat stacks of CD's beside it, a jumble of cases and discs still evident inside. 'I can see that, how'd you go then? Oh God, this steak is so good, you could always cook my love.' This sounding a bit muffled as she tried to speak around a mouthful, while smiling at him with pleasure in the food. 'Love on a plate, you know that.' She continued to chew then took a sip of wine as she swallowed contentedly. 'You always did say that, said it came from cooking for your family when you were younger,' he smiled sipping himself, the complex flavours of meat, cheese and wine entwining themselves beautifully on his palette. 'Yes that was how my Mother cooked and baked for all of us and that's how she taught me to cook, don't know any other way to do it, nor would I really want to.'

She had a look in her eye as she regarded him that was weighing and pensive 'you are the most completely complex, infuriating, intoxicating, dangerous and gentle man I have ever met Thomas, how do you do that?' He chuckled saying 'spoken with true female understatement that!' She laughed with him. They continued the meal and when they were finished he cleared the plates to some *Louis Armstrong* and popped the cork out of a second bottle of red. As he poured the ruby liquid in along the side of her glass he could see the candlelight dancing off it and in her eyes, as she sat more comfortably on the chair, one leg folded beneath her the other pulled up to rest her chin upon it.

'This had to be a dream really?' he thought to himself as he regarded her, she and everything about the evening from when she had kissed him in the hallway, to how she was sitting right now, had fitted the image he had always imagined that would be his life with a true love, his dream. 'Anyone's really' slipped out softly unconsciously from between his lips; she studied him over the rim of her glass kindly 'what was that you said babe?' He paused for a moment deciding what he should say now, as it could turn the whole evening on its axis because of saying what he had, more importantly the thoughts behind it. He was ok with how they ended before; he had made peace with all of that hadn't he? The old shrine to her had been discarded from his daily space; tonight was a gift, a totally wonderful gift. Everything that had needed saying had been said.

'I was just thinking how beautiful and stunning you look sitting there and that it was like a dream come true, then I realized it would be anybody's dream to share time and space with someone that beautiful, like we have and are tonight, that's all,' he continued to smile at her gently and with no hint of remorse or regret, only love for her in his eyes. He was letting her know he wasn't pushing any agenda, just reminiscing as friends. She shifted just a bit uncomfortably in the chair 'Oh Thomas, let's just be happy tonight ok?' she was still smiling but her eyes were slightly guarded now. 'How quickly the wind will shift in the sails of love?' He thought to himself. Her eyes were an azure, perfect summer sky that had just developed a very disappointing raincloud in the bottom left of his mind's eye. 'It's ok Joan, I'm not looking a gift horse in the mouth here,' he said laughing and she joined him, enjoying the old Irish saying he had taught her ages ago. 'Life is like a box of chocolates.' he continued in his best Forrest Gump and they laughed harder.

'So dare I ask if things are going well for you at St. Luke's, or would you rather not talk about it?' was delivered quietly across the table to him, softened by a smile. He considered his recent experiences there, how they had assisted in the ongoing shaping of a new him. 'It was difficult at first Joan, but as I got to feel more comfortable being there, it started to work for me on some level. Each time I go, I feel drained leaving but not from stressing anymore, from having done some hard confronting work within myself. Some things you face about your own reality or see reflected in the faces and stories of the others who are in the room, are difficult.' This last delivered with a frank look of truth. 'Go on,' she said softly a new look in her eyes now, calmer, satisfied somehow.

'I remember telling you once back when you were in the throes of divorce and all that went with it, that no matter how bad you were feeling at the time, someone, somewhere, would give anything to have your problems, do you remember that?' She nodded. ' Well bad and all as I had become, I realized pretty quickly that I had the strength and the grace of God, a whole wide experience to help me find a way out of the tangle inside my head and soul.' He grew silent for a moment, he reached for a cigarette offering the pack to Joan first and she took one. When they were both lit, he took a sip of wine and continued, 'Each time I arrived I was confronted by the fact I was there first, and the fact I was lucky to be there, thank you by the way for putting me in touch with St. Luke's, I will never forget that Joan,' she again nodded saying 'Welcome, go on.' He smiled back at her, loving the connection between them, the uniqueness of them and the complete incongruity of it all.

'First time I went I was terrified and I had the terrors, but then again it had only been twelve hours after a huge binge, so I was still well out of it really, even though functioning. I was seeing demons in people's chests, feeling my own wrapped tightly.' he trailed off to silence for a second taking a drag from the cigarette and exhaling long, remembering that night, still not exactly sure, in fact convinced that it not been all hallucination. ' Anyway, I made it through with frantic fervent prayers, there are no atheists in foxholes after all, and there was a little echo that kept telling me through the madness, *you have to stick it out, stick it out or die!* So I did and I was better the next time and the next, each time a little more sure, a little less fearful, a tiny bit more complete.' He paused again to refill their glasses before continuing 'I'm still very much working on it all and I expect I will be for the rest of my life. I don't talk in there for the others, just myself, I find myself tuning out when they share their stories, is that bad, wrong? I don't know. I feel like I'm overcoming the proverbial Irish and Catholic guilt by telling my dirty little secrets and in doing so expunging them one by one. I have caught myself about to lie a few times because I was always lying to myself about those things, and in those moments of catching myself I chose truth, I'm somehow proud of that.' She leaned forward intently and said 'you should be, don't ever forget that Thomas, you should be.' He took her hand and they both squeezed at the same time, 'Thank you Beautiful.'

They drained their glasses in a mutual toast and he rose once more to fill them. He chuckled as he realized the two bottles of the *Godfather's* best were done, so he fetched a good solid bottle of *Amarone* from his cupboard, setting it newly-opened upon the table between them. She smiled up at him and asked 'Any Scotch?' he laughed and said 'yes I do, want some?' she had mischief in her eyes as she replied 'not just yet, that *Amarone* looks amazing and let's save the scotch for these later' pulling out her leather cigar holder and separating it revealing four *Cohiba's*. 'You are without doubt an unconventional physician Milady, but I'm not complaining.' She giggled and took it upon herself to pour the wine this time round. 'I also thought we might watch a movie together?' He was surprised, very surprised and it showed. 'Why are you looking at me like that?' she laughed and he had no answer initially except to issue a rueful smile and a shake of his head. 'That is a surprise, I mean a welcome one but it's already late and I thought you would have to leave soon.' She was still smiling and gained this look of a mischievous teenager 'no, I was hoping to stay.' He smiled in spite of himself and their history 'you are always welcome.' Immediately he was cross with himself as he could already feel the consequences of this queuing up to assail him later, when she actually did eventually leave, could he put himself through all the emotions again, was he stronger now? He found himself hoping so.

They moved through to the kitchen, wines in hand and he became aware of the music again, *Lent* and it was sensual and healing, reflective. Without thinking he slipped an arm around her waist and soon they were lost in lovemaking again, totally lost in the drug that each of them had become for the other, it was a moment he knew would be forever with him and even though thankful beyond belief for it, the premonition was stronger by the moment, he would never share time and space with her, hold her, kiss her, make love with her again. These thoughts and feelings cascaded in a torrent through the very core of him and translated themselves into sheer raw intensity in their physical coupling. He knew from her responding in kind, that she was experiencing her own torrent of emotions and understandings. Tears were rolling down both their cheeks even as they smiled, even as they climaxed, together, for the last time.

They both needed showers again and she went first while he did the dishes and moved the wine, cigarettes, scotch and cigars over to the coffee table. He searched for a movie and elected to let her choose when she got out and he was showering. He took his glass out on to the balcony and looked up across the fence of the cemetary and picked out Jupiter in the heavily light-polluted New York sky. The clouds had resolved themselves into inky dark broken shadows, instead of a solid covering like earlier. He had been happy with his lot while walking home in the rain from the subway. He remembered the days and nights he had dreamed on this very balcony of all things Joan. He could still feel the memory of tears on his cheeks and all the other tears he had shed out here, quietly asking himself all the why's one could ever imagine having any reason to ask. Was he not over all of this? He knew that he was in the sense it would not, well he hoped and prayed, drive him to a low of self-esteem so as to start him giving permission to himself to go get some drugs and punish her unknowingly while destroying himself. He admitted to himself that he had been guilty of that, many times. He had spoken about it once in the room with Stanley, Ferret and Fart Boy. He had had to. All the times he would leave himself wide open, like a road upon which he invited her to find traction and purpose, but he was way too vulnerable then to do so, but he did leave himself open to her and in her search for her own direction and purpose, her tyres spinning madly to find that needed purchase, she had left acrid burning tyre tracks all over the road that was his heart, it left him impotent, lost and angry.

Several times she had arranged to come stay with him and at the last moment demurred, shortly after the text would have arrived, always a text never a call, he'd find himself calling his Cabbie or climbing into the truck if he had not been drinking too much and it was off to hell for a serving of 'Screw you Joan, look what I'm doing now BITCH, see what you made me resort to, BITCH!'

He shuddered at the memory of the pain that had manifested itself in that way; he never would have been able to say those things to her so he had acted it all out. That had been a huge lesson for him and one of the most important he had ever come to accept as true. In a way it had saved his life, his soul, yet here she was again. 'Was it all just about closure now?' he thought while lighting and beginning to smoke a new cigarette, 'it has to be I guess, it simply has to be.' He knew that no matter how much he or she would try they would never be fully able to build a life together. She had too much to lose and it would kill her to see the sneering, knowing glances of her peers if he ever screwed up again or merely at the fact of what he did for a living. Builders and doctors were not really socially compatible in society beyond what they already were to each other, and truthfully always had been, fuck buddies.

He drank a long swallow of the glorious wine and felt the past, all of it travel down with it, through the very core of himself. As he smoked, Jupiter disappeared and he searched the other cloud gaps to see if any other parts of the cosmos would reveal themselves - he was disappointed. 'I never could sort out the difference between sex and falling in love could I?' he mused to himself and he knew it was true. Sex already was a loaded deck for him and because of that he had tried very hard to be both good in bed and respectful, but he never did learn the knack of just screwing someone without developing a connection, nor had he wanted to, until he walked through the open door of crack cocaine that is. He remembered that Joan had promised to go on that trip and bailed at the last, 'well the rest is history,' and he shuddered again strongly at the memory; he could still taste it, right at the back of his throat, the crack, the seductive, wonderful, choking, puking, motherfucker that it was.

'Did someone just walk over your grave?' asked Joan as she joined him on the balcony placing a hand on his left shoulder with a smile, 'you shuddered just then like an army had done just that.' He turned and kissed her on the cheek 'Hi there, no was just thinking and well, that's all,' he smiled at her warmly dismissing her concern. 'Ok, I'm next for the tub so why don't you find a movie you're happy with and I'll be back to you in just a jiffy, deal?' She reached up and stroked his cheek and said 'I love you Thomas, I'm sorry about that.' He looked deeply into all that she was 'I love you too and I'm sorry enough for the both of us,' a shared nervous laugh followed making it all ok, they hugged briefly and he headed for the shower, wiping yet another tear from his eye. As he entered the bathroom he could hear the channels being changed as the search for a suitable movie progressed. He undressed and got into the shower, loving the warmth of it yet again trying to revive his spent and aching body. God, how he loved feeling like this after making love, properly making love, for hours. He luxuriated in the flow of hot water and over the sound of it splashing off his head he could hear the sound of the television and the beep of a car horn. He hoped it was good whatever she had picked.

As he lathered himself thoroughly all over, he began again to examine what it all had meant to both of them. He really could not get any answer to float to the top of his consciousness, except they shared an attraction and in another time and place, another life they would have met when they should have, married and had the 2.5 kids and the white picket fence. 'Maybe in the next life!' he smiled to himself as he turned off the taps and humming to himself, towelled dry. The movie sounded action themed with bangs and shots, shouts and screeching tires. 'She could be an awful redneck sometimes,' he chuckled to himself remembering some of the crap they had watched together at her urging. Stepping quickly across the hallway to the bedroom he fetched a fresh pair of house pants and his last clean cotton long sleeve, while doing that he gave the room and bed a once over to make sure he had done the job good enough earlier, he had, he was happy with his handiwork.

Happy with himself now, he headed back out looking forward to a cigar and a scotch. Reaching the living room he stopped suddenly, she was gone. 'Well fuck me dead!' he said to the now empty room 'she's bloody gone and done it, again!' and he started to laugh, and laugh. He ambled over to the coffee table and saw the half folded note sitting there, waiting on his hand to collect it. He ignored it and lit a smoke, took the last of his wine in hand and walked back out onto the balcony. He looked out to see if he could see a glimpse of her-; no sign. He remembered the beep of the car horn in the shower, no doubt she had called a car service and that had been its announcement of its arrival. The car service was based in Woodside so it would have only taken two or three minutes to get to her anyway. He still couldn't help feeling duped though. He briefly toyed with the idea of calling her cell phone but there was no point, he was not going to put himself there again, it was too dangerous for him, rejection of any kind. No, he would let it lie where it was. On the television someone was killing whole swathes of society by the sounds of all the gunfire so he stepped back inside to rectify that by turning it off. The silence was sudden and very looming, but he was already turning to put the music back on. He hit random and just decided to go with whatever the disc threw at him. He poured a really stiff scotch, opened it with a bit of water, took one of the cigars and lit it, then moved back out to the balcony and his observatory chair.

The pungent smoke was soft yet urgent on his palette and the whiskey soothed that away while lighting his innards. He pondered as he smoked what had just happened tonight, all of it. The music changed, it was *Lent* again, this time his impression of it was more in line with what the composer had no doubt intended, reflection, abstinence and a helping of penance, just what the religious period of Lent was about when he grew up. He snorted briefly to himself, almost laughing at himself; earlier he had found it sensual. But it still was seductive because it was telling him something, reminding him gently yet strongly as he sipped and smoked, there was a problem with love when it came to Thomas, and he almost had it, could almost grasp what it was. He decided to just float with the music and enjoy the afterglow of a most intriguing and enjoyable night, no matter how abrupt its end had been. He would figure this one out, eventually. He got up to get another glass of amber evocation and this time decided to take the note back outside with him to read, to see what she had to say for herself, this last time:

My Dearest Thomas,

I cannot tell you how very much you have meant to me and how much I love you.

It is hard to write this, do this, leave like this, but I feel I have to before I become trapped by you, yet again. I had to see you one last time, be with you and experience you. You see, I'm getting back together with my husband and I know that all I have done wrong these last few years, even before I met you, I have to leave behind. I go now to live the life of a dutiful wife, a professional and I will always cherish my love for you and how you loved me. I'm so sorry, really I am, please understand. I love you madly.

Xx

J.

'That is that then,' he said loudly but with no rancour, either in his voice or his heart, in spite of what he felt he should be feeling he smiled and was ok, perhaps it was best like this, he knew that it was. He glanced at the note again, *trapped by you again* jumped out at him far more than *I love you madly* or any other sentiment expressed or implied in it. He sipped pensively at the drink in his hand, lost in a moment of clarity as it unfolded in his mind. Love was indeed a trap, for the mind, the body and the soul in some cases. In his case being trapped or under the power of anyone was always a tricky one, ever since he had been overpowered and used, when just a boy. That was the crux of it really, that was the problem with love, he gave too much of himself in it, he had never learned how to put boundaries around or in his heart, he was either in or out, all or nothing, then when he was disappointed by the inability of the other person to reach his high standards of selflessness and devotion to it all, it crashed down about him like rubble from a bomb blast. In fact there really was no problem with Love itself; the problem was Thomas's understanding, experience and unconscious search for the acceptance and safety of it. He again was glad that he had purged himself, no longer willing to run out and rail against the universe when he was rejected. His days of rejecting himself were done.

He reached for his cell phone and pulling up Joan's number sent a simple text 'Thank You X'; he felt he could owe both of them that, he respected her choice and thankfully, finally her honesty. Now it was all about him having respect for himself. He lit the corner of the note and watched the bluish flame engulf it behind an advancing edge of black across the cream-colored paper. Dropping it in the ashtray to finish its own destruction, he decided against any further destructive actions of his own. He was glad the shrine was gone; he was glad that Joan had come and now was gone too. He was also glad that the echoes of her would remain with him forever. He had to navigate them correctly but they would always be there, indelibly burned into his memory by the times he was living in his life when they had known each other. Times of passion, fear, drugs, pain, hope and love. Someday he would be ok with it all; someday he hoped he would be able to love again. He laughed again as he realized she must have written the note before she arrived, when she planned the encounter, it had been too neat and well scripted to have been a rushed affair. He knew he should be annoyed at being used again, but instead he concentrated on hoping, that one day, in spite of her, he would in fact, love again.

Chapter 12

Decisions

The change in seasons resonated with Thomas in conjunction with the changes felt and directed within him. The last lingering spring evenings were lengthening into the early days and warm brighter evenings of summer in New York. Things were changing apace now, both around him in the external world and in his conversation with himself. He was musing, ruminating on all of this as he emerged from the Eighth Avenue subway stairs and felt a last, warm kiss of the slowly setting sun peeking through the skyscrapers, as it went to lay itself to slumber across the Jersey side of the Hudson. He very deliberately walked to the garden at the entrance, took a seat and sat down to smoke and think.

Several months now into his attendance at St. Luke's and the benefits of his time had become a cherished reality, a cornerstone of recovery and rebirth. There were no more illusions being cast across his vision and experience by the previous constant negative narrative he had been trapped inside. There was no other way to characterize all of the subtle complexities of his life up to that point that had combined, synergized if you will, to lead him to the very cusp of utter destruction, rock bottom. The real, stark truth revealed his former view and coloring of it, to have been skewed just enough to give unconscious permission to accept victim status for himself and through that to act out, tear and rend at himself, to expiate the shame he had always felt at who he was. Thankfully he was at an end to all of that and he prayed daily now that that was indeed so.

Over the months he had developed a system within rehab that had worked, for Thomas at least, by allowing him to express his inner fears, gauge reactions and accept criticism of how he had been thinking, pretty much about everything, from his addiction through to his perceived need for sexual contact, to his understanding of his own consciousness. That in truth was the big one, his consciousness. The raw, often misunderstood power, of the space he had been occupying for two hours at a time, twice a week was quite simple once he had distilled in down enough to be palatable. It was a place where people could come to confront their various addictions, mindsets and experiences, without having to be afraid or judged. It was a place where they could tell the truth of their experiences and share hope with others who had fallen or been pushed, into the same boat. He had recognized also, that for all of its having a feeling of understanding and collegiality about the place, it was an uncaring edifice, a necessary construct of a modern society, which had to be seen to at least be doing something about addiction. It was a place that offered no judgments, made no promises except that you would not be turned away, if you could pay or were being funded to participate in some way, shape or form. A place that in a dispassionately and clinically detached way told you, you could do it if you worked hard at it. However, if you did not, it would not be fighting for your survival on your behalf; you would not be sought out and recused. Thomas had seen plenty of new faces start, only to fall off the wagon and never be seen again, their name might be mentioned, once, at the session they did not show at, to see if they had sent word or reason for their not arriving and then they would never be mentioned again.

There was only so much room in the lifeboat and steering it no doubt required a Darwinian form of selection that focused on those who could cling on long enough, tough enough, to earn a seat by the oars that drove it forward. There was and never would be any apology for this. Thomas realized how truly blessed and lucky he was, to have managed just that, simultaneously accepting just how tenuous a lifeline it was and had remained, until now. He was done; ready to seek the rest of the answers elsewhere, strong enough he felt to leave this behind, this final lair of temptation that remained outside of him. He had changed his life radically from what it had become, gone were the phone numbers, the hookers, the people that he had associated with, all excised ruthlessly from his life out of an animal necessity for survival. The final lingering connection with that life was this place. In fact the sixth floor and its denizens were the only contact Thomas now had with the street world, the drug world, the only place he knew for sure he could source crack if he wanted it. A number could be found here that unlocked the combination required to relapse and disappear. Every time he had watched as that very scenario had unfolded covertly, had both angered and saddened him, but more importantly, it had terrified him. He had to be rid of the terror he now felt at the power of his former substance of choice. He had to be rid of all the fears he had once held on to so dearly as though within them, resided answers.

Glancing at his watch he saw it was time to enter this world for what he prayed to God would be the last time in this lifetime. People moved with a more elegant motion in the warmer evenings. They were unencumbered from the heavy clothing of bitter winter, so they flowed more easily through the doorways and spaces within. Gone was the oppressive blast of heat produced by the air curtain units ducted just over the entrance, which always struggled to keep the outside, outside, and inform your shivering body you were now inside. They were passive in this time between being needed to ward off winter and soon enough, to seal out the summer swelter. Men and women tripped lightly, happily along in shirt sleeves and blouses, unconscious smiles of momentary freedom betraying their skins' happiness to be neither sweating nor goose bumpy.

He glided with the stream heading for the elevators, and he was somehow detached as he was aware of his approaching them, walking on automatic feet that knew where they were. 'Will I miss this?' he thought as the doors slid effortlessly closed, only to open a brief while later at his destination floor. 'Will I prevail?' was crossing his conscious mind as those same automatic feet of his, guided him to reception and the precariously perched white nurse's hat that never sat above a smile. 'Will I keep this to remind me?' he asked himself seriously as his rectangular embossed green card was surrendered to the abuse of the counter foiling press, which had almost rendered it unreadable over its months of smoothening torment.

'What will I say tonight?' echoed like his heels on the hard, sterilized, floor as he found one of those heavy waiting room chairs for the last time. He had no real answers to any of the questions, he was not sure if they actually were questions. It was more of a recognition within his mind that it was a time of change, another beginning, 'I've had a few of those in my time,' he laughed uproariously, ironically, in his own head at that one, his mood betrayed to the outside world by a solid, happy smile, incorporating distant eyes.

'You look happy tonight,' said Ferret from the seat beside him. Thomas turned and regarded him with no alarm, somehow he knew the slight, anxious man, would intercept him here, therefore he was not at all startled by his pronouncement. 'Hello, I guess you're right,' Thomas replied while continuing to smile, this time at the ferret and the complete incongruity of the two of them sitting together, in this place. 'I guess I have made a decision Eric, this will be my last session,' he left that hanging as he wondered just how long Ferret *Eric, his name is Eric,* had actually been attending the sessions. 'Good luck Thomas, I will miss sitting with you,' he replied with a hint of regret in his already quiet voice. For a moment Thomas thought he would simply get up and leave, but he stayed put, contemplating the interior of the waiting room.

After a while Thomas asked 'How long have you been coming here Eric?' the reply was swift and quiet, 'Five years more or less, five Christmas-time's, yes five.' Thomas digested that answer for a brief moment and continued 'Have you been clean for all of that time?' Eric turned and looked at him with no emotion, no anything, really readable on his face 'Yes, yes I have.' Thomas had somehow known that would be the answer, 'Then why do you still come?' which seemed especially relevant to Thomas as he was leaving, after only a few months. 'You already know the answer to that Thomas, I am not strong like you are, I am strong in a different way, I have to come here, to be reminded of what I lost, so I will never lose anything ever again.' Ferret seemed almost surprised by what he had said and sat back just a little further, the opposite direction of movement Thomas expected.

'I'm leaving tonight because I feel my place is no longer here Eric, I need to leave it all behind myself, completely.' He paused for a moment before continuing 'I know people come and go here, give out phone numbers and the like, every time I see that happen I can taste it again, you know the crack, at the back of my throat in my nostrils, it scares me.' Ferret kept looking straight ahead 'I see that too, they are bad people taking advantage of wounded people.' The sheer childlike clarity of what he had said was striking to Thomas. It was so true; the wounded being picked off by the predators, the carelessly unconsciously evil ones. 'What did you lose Eric?' Eric turned towards Thomas at that one and replied 'My wife, my child, my life.' He had no more expression on his face than normal for him but Thomas could see the pain in his eyes; he said nothing, waiting for him to continue. "I got high after work once and drove to collect my wife and kids from the school, PS3 Lower East Side, you know it?' Thomas nodded that he did, he had built scaffolding all around it a few years before when he was still working in the field, back when he was clean and had a spark long extinguished.

'My wife and I were angry that month, we didn't talk much, just did the routine. She didn't notice I was high. I drove us north on the West Side Highway to get to the George Washington Bridge, she said I was driving too fast; her mother lived in Passaic County. I steered head on into a semi a half-mile from her mothers. They died. I lived.' Thomas was stunned but hid it well. All he could say was 'I'm so sorry Eric. That is a huge burden to carry.' Ferret went back to his study of the already memorized paint drip patterns where the wall met the ceiling in front of where they were sitting, he said nothing and just nodded in agreement. Thomas was reeling inside just a bit, he knew everyone here lost something, normally of themselves, dignity, self esteem, boundaries and morality, friendships and the like; but to be responsible for the death of a wife and child, that would have killed him with remorse, guilt and cowardice, he just knew it, he would have killed himself to expiate the self pitying shame at such a crime.

He cringed at the twisting sensation that coursed through him, almost making him want to puke his guts up right there and then. He remembered, he had come to almost crashing whilst driving under the influence; he had caught the slide of the car just in time by sheer instinctive chance, a fluke. He remembered the faces through the windshield, the man driving the minivan, the others were indistinct so he did not know whether they were men or women, children or adults, they had just been there and almost crushed out of existence by him, almost. He had shook then and he trembled inside at the memory. Even now, when he knew he was ready to move on, life reminded him that there would always be memories of all kinds and their arrival was neither going to be scheduled or in some cases, desired. They would just be. He faced back round to the Ferret again and asked 'So for five years since the accident you are coming here, always here?'. The reply was blunt 'I did eight years upstate for manslaughter first, then started here when I got out.' Thomas was not sure he wanted to pursue this line of conversation any further; it was proving difficult for them both. 'I am sorry you have to live with that Eric, really I am' he offered by way of concluding that particular train of thought. 'Thank you for talking to me, good luck Thomas.' And just like that the Ferret was up and gone, the circuit of the hallways before the session, that he obviously just had to do, his own OCD purgatory. Thomas understood more and knew less in that moment than ever before in his entire life.

He glanced down at his watch - it was time. He got up and again felt his feet become automatic as he made his way to the room for the last time. Stan was there, suit rumpled but clean nonetheless as he looked through some papers on his lap, glasses perched on the end of his nose. He looked up and nodded with his welcoming smile before returning his attention to the paperwork. Thomas took a chair in his usual arc - as he thought of it - it was always the same general area so that he could see most of the room in front of him and there was little space left behind him. He was unconsciously vigilant to things like that now, the space behind him he could not see, the sounds of both day and night distilled and searched constantly, for the sound that was out of place, the sound that might herald danger. His inner life had been forever changed by his recent past.

As he made comfortable in the chair Stan spoke to him,' Good evening Thomas, how are you?' 'I'm well thank you Stan, yourself?' Stan nodded that he was indeed well. 'Thomas, I'm going to ask you to lead off tonight, can you do that for me?' Thomas didn't even think as he said 'Sure, not a problem happy to do so.' He pondered again, like he had been for much of the previous two days, how exactly he was going to tell Stan this would be his last session. He had just been given the floor so to speak and that would be the best way, to tell his story one last time, say it loud and proud and wrap up with the news he was done. He still had no idea what he would actually say but was sure that it would come to him, as he needed it to. Ferret made his unique way in to join the circle and there were two others still down the back of the room at the water fountain, who would take a few more seconds to find a seat. Thomas found himself starting to pray for guidance and inspiration and he just went with it. It was the old prayer his Mother had taught him many years ago to recite before examinations in secondary school:

Come O Holy Spirit and fill the hearts of your faithful,

Kindle in them the fire of your love,

Send forth your spirit and they shall be recreated

And thou shalt renew the face of the Earth.

He felt better, as he had always done, after reciting it. He thought for a moment of all those innumerable exams he had sat in school; pen in hand and that prayer in his heart. He remembered that it had brought him grace then and hoped it would do so now. This was so much bigger a moment, now that he was almost at the edge of the jump-off point, than he had really thought it would be. The revelations of Ferret still echoed in his head too, adding to the growing din of change. He recited the prayer again, softly, in his heart and felt a calm descend. He was as ready as he ever would be.

'Well good evening everyone, I'm glad to see you all here safe and well and I hope you all have been enjoying the lovely change in the weather too' Stan said to the assembled with a warm smile. 'So if we are all ready to begin, Thomas will lead us off tonight. Thomas, if you please?'

170

The moment had arrived so he simply stepped off the edge and let go of everything. 'Hello everyone, my name is Thomas,' he paused for the expected chorus of replies to his greeting then continued leaning forward in his chair as he spoke. 'I have been coming here for some time now to deal with my addiction to crack cocaine and the consequences of that addiction. I have been clean of it thankfully, for all of that time. I still self medicate, if you want to allow me call it that, with weed and alcohol every now and then, but I never had a problem with those to begin with.' He could see there were two schools of thought on that one in the room and no middle ground whatsoever; it did not matter to him, not anymore. 'Every time I got high on crack I lost something of myself, felt it tear away from within me but it wasn't enough to make me stop. I acted out of what I thought was *my choice, my right* to go party, to call escorts and pick up hookers, and I loved it dearly – for a while. When I began it was all exciting and thrilling and I'd look forward to the weekend so I could go party again. I am a high functioning addict and managed to keep working at my job, hiding my addiction. Soon it crept into my working week and I gave permission to myself to use every second night, then it was every night, then it was too late to stop. This progression if you will, took all of three weeks, less than a month. By the end of the second month, my performance at work was being noticed, but I clung on. By the fourth month I had been warned and by the fifth I had to take a leave of absence to try to save both my job and myself. It was for three months and in those three months I lost any chance of regaining the woman I loved, most of my savings, my self-respect and grip on reality and almost my soul. I tried very hard to justify my drug use as an escape from the past but that didn't work; it didn't work because it wasn't true. I was an addict and there was nothing I could do, or think that would paint over the simple barefaced fact, I needed to get high. So I did. It kept going and going. If I had good stuff I would pick up a hooker I had come to know well and we would party; if it was shit material, I'd recook it and smoke on my own. I had all the excuses and I watched myself lie to myself more times than I care to remember. I ignored the disgust I felt at myself and just got high. I put myself in and sought out situations that became risker as my addiction deepened, I was now going to the crack dens and houses directly to buy myself; I knew the variations in price and quality to be found in the different areas controlled by different crews. I knew what times each spot would be open for business, which ones were to be avoided because they were too *hot* due to the cops watching them. I could walk down dangerous streets at night and be recognized by the dealers and welcomed by them because I always had cash. I felt a weird fucked up satisfaction at being able to do that, like some twisted movie plot line. I had a gun pulled on me one night but that didn't stop me. I almost got arrested another and if I had been I would have gone to jail I had that much crack in my pocket. I pushed and pushed the boundaries like I was unconsciously daring life to catch me out, thinking I was wining something.'

He paused for a brief moment to try and figure out where he was going with all of this; not exactly sure he plunged on anyway. 'Everyone I knew, knew there was something up. I didn't go out or return calls I was simply unavailable. If the lads came to the door at the weekends to see if I was going to go play some rugby in the park with them like I used to, I would be playing curtain cop until they gave up and went away, they stopped ringing my doorbell a long time ago. One day I went to the bodega to get cigarettes and beer and by the time I walked back, the power had been turned off by Con Ed, I hadn't been paying the bills. I sat in the dark all that weekend and got high. I paid the bill and when the lights came back on the following Tuesday I broke down and cried at the filth that was revealed in my home. It was trashed: shit everywhere, broken bottles in corners, crack bags everywhere and filth on the floors. I remember looking at my fingers through the tears and being appalled by the hardened and blackened skin at their tips, from cleaning screens from the crack pipes over the gas jet, then repacking them so I could keep getting high. I tried to call my parents in Ireland, to hear their voices, to remind myself I had come from a place far different than the one I found myself in. They answered but I couldn't speak, they knew it was me and I'll never forget my father saying *we love you son, come home* before the line clicked dead. Ten years in New York and I was throwing it all away. Eventually I screamed at myself and decided to be done, to give life one last effort and I found my way here.' Thomas stopped for a second and wished he had thought of getting a paper cup of water to keep in his hand as his mouth was dry. 'I cannot describe even to myself, let alone all of you here, what I felt like those first days of not using. The madness that gripped me to go out and just buy crack so I could get high again, the nights spent writhing in bed, being deafened by the pounding of my heartbeat behind my eardrums as I forced myself to stay there, inside, safe from my need to use, safe from myself. I told myself over and over that the longest hour of my life was still only sixty minutes long, but my God, those minutes felt like they were carved in my skin with a blunt knife held by the Devil, as I curled myself tighter and tighter into a ball of grief. After the first week or so, it got easier and being here in this place with people like you helped in that more than I can tell you. I had all the superior thoughts, the angers and all the other feelings that you have in a place like this. I soon learned to listen again, to understand that I was not special or unique, that others have addictions and reasons and stories too. I learned that each person who comes here is a valid human being in their own right and that I am so lucky to have regained my own validity in coming here.' It was time he felt, to say it, to give it reality through sound, to end it. 'That is my story, well the short version anyway, of how I came to be here, to be speaking to you all tonight. I am glad Stan asked me to start because I needed to tell you all that the work you can do in a place like this, if you let yourself, give permission to yourself to do, can let you see a way to save yourselves, because no one else is going to do it for you. It has to be you for you, and that being said it is also the last time I will be coming here.' There, it was out.

There were many more reactions than he had expected there to be to his pronouncement. Through the murmurs and comments Thomas noticed that Stan was looking at him very keenly. He returned his gaze intently, with neutrality that conveyed his mind was made up and he felt himself ready. He turned back to the room and said 'I have done what I came here to do and if I do not build on that by making the final changes in life I need to, then I will never be able to leave it all behind. I feel I am safe enough with myself now to let go of here and to make those changes. I have decided that I am leaving New York as well, because I know too many of her dark secrets, too many of her hidden places and as you all know from your own addictions, you cannot ever unlearn all that you know about the where's, the when's and the who's that you learned about to feed those same addictions. I know now that the price I have to pay for mine is to leave this city I have come to love dearly, because it will always hold too much temptation for me, if ever I was to find myself again weakened by time or circumstance. I am going home, back to Ireland to start again. I wish each and every one of you the strength and the grace of God to find your own ways to healing, to freedom from that which crosses you, to peace.' He stopped then and felt the tear run down his now smiling face. He felt so free it was indescribable.

The silence continued for a moment and Thomas could feel that he had made a very important connection with everyone there, even Fart Boy, who for once had a look of guilt on his face. Perhaps he would stop passing out phone numbers for the dammed now, but he doubted it. On impulse he stood up and approached Stan, holding out his hand to shake. Stan took it and Thomas said 'Thank you Stan,' as he shook his hand firmly. Stan just nodded and said nothing; he knew Thomas was done, but he did have a kind smile for him. Thomas said 'If you don't mind, I think I should leave now and I'd like to say goodbye to everyone on the way?' 'Not at all Thomas, thank you for your work and contributions here and good luck to you on your journey' was the warm and sincere reply.

Thomas nodded his thanks, feeling the emotions getting the better of him, but he was still happy, light even. He turned to Ferret and holding out his hand 'good luck Eric' the Ferret took his hand and nodded with a smile. He moved around the circle and as he did so they all stood up and clapped. He was stunned and just a little overcome by it all. His back was slapped, his hand shook and he even got a few hugs from some. Finally he made it to the doorway and looked back saying 'Goodbye, thank you and God bless you all' before he turned and walked out into the corridor and away.

He noticed a quizzical look in the eyes beneath the white nurse's hat as he passed and he nodded at them, he was rewarded with a sniff of disdain and a shrug. He allowed himself to laugh uproariously as he briskly followed the confident booming of his heels on the floor to the elevator. As he emerged into the warm air at the entrance, he headed straight through the garden, brushing his right palm against the leaves as he passed. At the curb he decided against a slice of pizza but wanted a coffee, so he got one for the subway ride, it was served in one of the ubiquitous blue cardboard cups every deli and bodega seemed to have in the city, emblazoned with stylized Greek writing proclaiming *we are happy to serve you* on the side. The white plastic top would no doubt leak as he drank, like they always did, but he didn't care.

All the way back to Queens he felt better with each passing second. He had had no idea within himself that he was going to say everything that he did, but he was glad. Most curious of all however, was his decision to leave New York, that was one he had not seen coming, one he had not even considered, but he knew it was what he had to do nonetheless, and he was ok with it, whether it was his conscience or his guardian angel or both, it didn't matter, it was good.

The views of the city from the number seven trains window after emerging from the blackness of the tunnel before Queens Plaza station, were very familiar to him. For years he had admired the colorful graffiti on the rooftops around the artists collective, a stunning counterpoint to the stygian darkness of the tunnel, the old *Swing line* sign on the redbrick of a former factory just after the *Silvercup Movie Studios* sign that had been destroyed in the first Highlander movie he'd watched as a teenager. So many times he had made this journey in all weathers and circumstances, happy and sad, on the way to or from work, in love or alone, but none of those journeys had the sharpness or clarity that this one seemed to have. He knew that in the instant he had acknowledged that inner decision to leave, it would be so.

The train trundled its way up the Boulevard and he watched some of the landmarks of his life in the city roll by, *Blooms Bar* at 42nd Street, the old dingy cinema across from the gas station at 43rd, *Sidetracks Restaurant* at 46th beside *Alpha Donuts*, the projects at 48th. He took it all in as the train changed from following the boulevard to chasing Roosevelt Avenue on its way to Woodside and the station at 61st Street. Just before he stood up to get off the train, he could see *Shane's Bakery* and the *Stop Inn* diner on the opposite corner from it, all the old air conditioners and chimney flues seemed to make up the entirety of the roof. Walking down the steps to the street he realized that one day if he were to take the same journey again, it would be as a tourist not a local.

He got his cigarettes as usual from his Pakistani mates and knew he would miss their smiling welcome of his business, their earnest happiness to serve the inhabitants of their community. He would miss it all, the faces the places and even, truth be told, all the races which made up the melting pot that was this city, which he had once called home. He knew he could no longer call it that. The sense that his mind was drinking in all the sights and sounds of the place, continued as he walked the short to the apartment. When he stepped in through his front door and switched on the lights and he realized that the clean and ordered apartment felt different too. It had been a canvas upon which he had painted many a painful scene but also ones of hope happiness and love. He could feel it saying to him *our time together is done*.

Thomas opened a bottle of wine, put his Massive Attack CD's in the changer, rolled a joint and retired to his observatory chair to reflect without thinking, to plan without planning. Tonight he felt free, safe from his former self, he was at the end of the something, of what he was not quite sure, but it was good enough.

Chapter 13

Taking Your Leave

The first thoughts Thomas had as he awakened were mainly centred around figuring out if he had loaded the coffee urn correctly the night before, without getting out of bed to do so. When he eventually did get out of bed, he found himself disappointed. 'No big deal' he stated with a stretch and a smile. He was content within as he remedied the coffee situation, setting off the chugging and puffing that filled the apartment with the aromas of monsoon greened hillside plantations, captured in the mystery of the ground beans. He puttered about the kitchen for a minute or two, and then went out onto the balcony where he stretched again and admired the early morning sunshine, warm and sweet on his recently less-lined face. Leaning on the perimeter railing, he looked casually around the visible slice of the neighbourhood he could see. Nothing was going on, out of the ordinary at least, there were a few souls about but he knew none of them, not even to see. The Asian trashcan Olympian was due in about thirty minutes, he realized as he checked his watch. He smiled at how for such a little old lady she could batter those trashcans into utter submission in less than thirty seconds, along with the auditory faculties of anyone close by.

The puffing and chugging subsided and he went back inside to fill his favourite mug, happy it was as good as ever, he grabbed his cigarettes and sunglasses and went back out to sit down. The hot smooth liquid caffeine lifted his head out of the last fogs of sleep and the nicotine from the cigarette finished the job. 'God the first cigarette with coffee is always the best, the best!' he declaimed lightly with satisfaction to no one except himself. He felt correct inside and out, the momentous decisions of yesterday had been made, the way in which they had resonated within him could not be ignored. They were correct; now he just had to implement them. He had tried to get a handle on how exactly he was supposed to actually do it: leave New York, last night but had decided eventually, like he had told himself when he had first sat in his chair then, to just let it evolve in his head today, so he had.

The first mug of inspiration never was a long drawn out affair for Thomas and he found himself back in the kitchen pouring another, while there, he threw on a few slices of toast and some eggs to boil. He loved the fresh cleanliness of the polished wood floors as the sunlight spilled in across them; he revelled in the scent of order that was now present dispelling the fractured memories of past mornings of pain and regret. He opened and chocked the bedroom door and pulled back the curtains to open the window fully, this would allow a slight but sensual breeze to pass through the space while he got both his head and his day fully up to speed. 'Mmm no rush,' he murmured contentedly as he shelled the eggs and buttered the toast, set his tray for breakfast on the balcony and switched on NPR to catch the news as he moved back outside. He settled back and listened to the voices of New York discussing an aspect of the world as it was today, while eating happily.

Soon he was back to a cigarette again as he enjoyed his second big mug of coffee - lo and behold there she was, struggling out between the front door and the fly screen attached to it, trash bags tied up in advance and three to a hand. Down the steps she came as the slight chorus of Korean floated up to him, he recognized none of it but by the tone of it she was swearing, profoundly. He smiled in appreciation of the drama she made of this simplest of chores. Approaching the bins she unceremoniously dropped her six tied bags and proceeded to kick the cans one after the other, knocking off the lids. 'No way,' Thomas laughed as he said it, all the time he had lived here he had only ever seen the operation from halfway through, what he was seeing now was priceless and explained the racket he'd always heard.

She must have heard his chuckle and fixed him with a glare that could have stripped paint off steel. He waved and offered a cheery 'Good morning' in return. More expletive Korean was released and she went back to her, now understood, purposely-noisy task. 'Maybe she's taking revenge on the neighbours?' Thomas thought as he watched grinning and fascinated. After a rearranging of the trash cans, which turned them every which way that was noisy to get to, they were set back in their original positions, then the six bags were picked up one at a time and flung with an overhand type motion to clatter into the depths, each twirling throw was accompanied by a grunt a female tennis player serving an ace on centre court in Flushing Meadows, would have been rightly proud of. This thought made Thomas laugh a bit again, but quieter this time for fear of more paint-stripping looks. Once the bags were all in she bent as only an octogenarian Asian could, knees and elbows akimbo, to pick up the lids. They were banged down like cymbals into an acceptable position and he wondered at the strength of the wee woman.

She straightened up as best she could, glared and no doubt swore at him once more, turned and disappeared back inside with more alacrity than when she had emerged. Thomas would not be able to explain why, but he was completely delighted by the whole show. It reminded him of the old farmers, well set in their ways, who would come into his father's business and harrumph and give out about everything and anything, leaving themselves wide open for a good slagging in return, but remaining always confident in their belief that they had worked hard all their lives and they owed nothing to anyone. He smiled again as he remembered that those same big, tough, gruff sons of the land were normally capable of being taken down a peg or two by their equally tough wives. Thomas wondered if the old lady across the road still had a husband or had she battered him into submission decades ago. 'Not a problem I'm set to have in life by the looks.' He said knowing that the chances of him ever being actually married were at this stage of his life at least, extremely remote indeed.

Going back inside he decided that after a shower he would take a walk into Woodside and buy the newspaper. He was sure that as he walked in the sunshine, he could begin to get a handle on how exactly he was going to go about uncoupling himself from this city he had called home for so long. After he lathered his short hair into luxurious foam, he then spread the suds over the rest of his body, realizing as he did so he was gaining back his definition, which had been lost as he lost weight to his addiction. He resolved that he would use his ability to take the sun well, to tan up his front and back so he didn't have the look of a cadaver with lower arms looking like they had been dipped in a bucket of creosote. There was no doubt in his mind that when he did set foot inside the door in Ireland, he had better be looking his best. He knew his folks would have been sick with worry for him and he needed to look healthy for them, to give them even the smallest bit of peace regarding his recent past. A drop in the ocean he knew, but an important one nonetheless. Towelling off, he checked his watch again and it told him it was eight thirty, he liked that he would get the full day and that he was starting it well. He had so much to be thankful for now and that filled him in a way that felt right, but not overly out of control as though he was bipolar, just right.

He dressed well as he always did, and as he splashed on some cologne he saw the wooden rosary beads his mother had given him, draped on the corner of the mirror he had once feared to consult. On impulse he put them in the pocket of his cargo shorts along with his phone and keys. The pocket on the right got his cigarettes and wallet. He looked in the mirror once again and welcomed the small moment of narcissism as he regarded himself. Unchecked it would be a negative, but in his case it was a reaffirmation of his position now relative to where he had been, he shook it off and with purpose, was out the door and down the stairs to the outside. The apartment seemed to be already just suffering him until he was gone, no longer welcoming him to lounge and waste time, tolerating him. He did not let that thought dampen his enthusiasm for what he was about. He was doing the right thing and would be leaving the space better than he had found it when he moved in.

As he walked briskly down to the corner of the Boulevard, he watched the traffic swish by until the lights halted the flow, a few leakers who ran the red light illuminated in spite of the sunshine, by the strobe lights of the traffic cameras taking snapshots of their plates. 'Yummy yummy $300 dollar fine each time' he thought as he stepped into the now stalled river of cars to cross over to the older, more settled heart of Woodside. The crosswalk was one of the longest in the city and he was mindful of the cars now twitching against their brakes, as their owners tickled their automatic transmissions with the throttle, impatient to be where ever it was they had to be. He wouldn't miss driving in New York, it was frustrating in its gridlock on the surface streets and as thrilling as NASCAR when barrelling along at eighty miles an hour on the Brooklyn Queens Expressway or going door-to-door with a semi trailer around the curve approaching the Triborough Bridge, the braking ripples and corrugations in the road surface just waiting to catapult you to an instant demise beneath its wheels. No, he would not miss it and put those thoughts out of his mind as he enjoyed the walk down past the laundry and the bodega beside it.

The patron of the family store waved from his chair beneath the corrugated steel awning that all bodegas seemed to have in New York. Thomas grinned happily; he often spoke the rapid-fire immigrant Spanish with the old man and his family in the shop. He would miss that too, banging on in a variant of a language he had learned in his time here. A brief cloud passed over his thoughts as he remembered speaking fluently with Mama G, Dena, Lowell and all of that crew. Knowing the lingo had been both a blessing and a curse in that time, got him in places, got him out of trouble a regular gringo would not have survived speaking Anglo. He shook that off, understanding it was in the past. He smiled knowing that his Spanish would never be accepted in Spain, it had too much Ecuadorian, Peruvian, Porto Rican and Dominican laced into it for the inhabitants of the centre of a former empire, to accept. 'Kind of like the weird relationship the French had with the Quebecers when it came to language' he mused as he continued his journey. The Spanish would always be with him though, a legacy of his time here. Just down the street he passed the old radio station on his left *WABC*, recessed back in slightly from the street, its attendant AM broadcast aerial now only telling of its life as a roost for pigeons. Down further, the noise of the subway as it clattered back and forth, to and from the city, started to have a larger presence the closer he got to it. The dark green paint of its structure shined a bit in the sunlight telling lies about how dirty it really was.

Directly at the corner of 58th and Roosevelt stood the Catholic Church and as always at this time of day, the doors were open. It was a reassuring link with times past, to see the old ladies with their hair covered with lace, going in to pray and recite the rosary. Irish, Greek, Italian, Latin's of all nations, Asians; Woodside was indeed a stew of the history of this city. He blessed himself as he walked past and took note of the sign which detailed the times Mass was celebrated, he decided to make either one or the other, one PM or five PM. He turned right at the church and walked past the *Starting Gate* pub and the Chase Manhattan bank, which no longer had anything worth talking about belonging to him in its accounts. He kept walking past and bore slightly to the right passing *Sean Og's* pub on the next corner. He remembered when he first came to New York it was called *The Horse & Jockey*. 'Call it what they may' he thought to himself, 'it was still only a business out to separate as much hard-earned cash from the inebriated as possible, nothing more nothing less.'

He knew that cynicism of any kind was counterproductive to his current joviality and purpose, but some realities of the Irish diaspora were not as fairytale as one might hope; fights and ugliness with lots of drink and sometimes drugs involved, were part of the story too, so was he. In another minute he was swinging left down towards the newsagents and he went inside to get the paper, instead of going to the window. The greeting was warm as usual and he was glad to have gone in as he left. He would miss all of it he knew. On impulse he decided to have a pot of tea in Shane's Bakery and ducked inside the doorway, which had been richly decorated in a Celtic fashion by the owner's cousin, a tragic, gifted artist who had committed suicide. On the walls inside were more of his works, landscapes and still lives, portraits and studies. They were beautiful and haunting, made more so by the knowledge they were from a soul now departed, who had left ripples of beauty behind. Thomas loved that Shane kept them on the walls, a memorial to a happy childhood in county Cavan together.

He exchanged pleasantries with Sinead the young Irish girl behind the counter as she made his pot of tea; the array of custard slices kept tugging his attention, so he ordered one of them too. As he sat on a high stool up the back at the long shelf affixed to the wall, he was perfectly positioned to both read his paper while watching the comings and goings of the young and old, the short time students here for a summer on a J1 visa and the long termers like him, who came and lost track of the years as they flew by, which they did here, like no place else on earth. He read The Times avidly, loving the overseas coverage that only a big paper like it could carry these days. The quality of the writing had always enthralled him and it read in his mind with the perfect clear diction, that only an American news anchor had. The paper was a weekend institution and in fairness, a whole day could be invested in getting the best out of the Sunday edition.

The tea was beautiful and rich with all the crispness of its origins and the unique flavour of Lyons, which was the taste of home for him. In Ireland you either drank *Lyons* or *Barry's* tea and if ever there was a place on earth more addicted to its tea and more likely to force its consumption upon you than his native land, he had no idea where that might be. Memories of having innumerable cups of tea in houses of friends and neighbour's flooded his mind as he bit quite deliberately into his custard slice, its creamy filling squeezing out satisfactorily as he did so. He enjoyed this little indulgence and washed it down with the taste of home. In the background the rising and falling of those myriad voices from every county of Ireland, seemed to be melding into a melody that softly repeated to him *Time to come home*. He felt ok with that minor fantasy of the mind, while relaxing in a place that was familiar. He glanced again at the paintings hanging above and around him, all that beauty of talent and perception had not led the artist home, rather the opposite, Thomas was once again thankful to God above, for he at least would make it home. With that thought echoing he drained the last of his tea from the mug before him and stood to leave, sliding the high stool back beneath the shelf on the way. He threw a happy wave and smile at Sinead on the way out and she beamed back at him the way only a young, untrammelled soul could.

Taking a quick left he walked the half-mile or so up to Grand Avenue to go see the travel agent nearly all the Irish used. It was an old school New York family business, more than one trade was plied beneath the same roof and the place even had an office for the local congressman who was a scion of the family. Thoughts of the Irish connection to the city's political history made Thomas smile as he walked in the door, Boss Tweed and Tammany Hall, the five points and directions to vote early and often. 'Hi Thomas,' shook him back to reality as the feminine voice called his name, he smiled in spite of himself it was Carol and they had shared a moment many years ago when he had first arrived in the city. They had always remained friendly though and now that she was married with a few chickens in the coop, she always did have a glint in her eye for a harmless flirt with Thomas. 'Hi Carol, looking beautiful as always' he stated with a wink, she blushed pleasurably and leaned in closer than she would for anyone else across the counter, her cleavage not exactly being disguised by the motion; he couldn't resist, 'the twins are keeping well I see' he delivered while maintaining eye contact. She blushed even deeper and laughed as she said 'You're a brat Thomas, talking to a married woman like that' that didn't stop him grinning back at her, both knowing full well it was just a bit of harmless fun.

'My Dear Carol, much and all as I would love to spend the afternoon exchanging pleasantries with your wonderful bosom and yourself, I have things to be about!' he delivered with aplomb. She gave him an arch look and said sweetly 'well you missed that particular boat didn't you young man' it definitely wasn't a

188

question but he answered anyway enjoying the banter 'if memory serves correctly I didn't miss the boat entirely, just the last sailing, and I have a memory like an elephant'. She couldn't help herself laughing, no doubt remembering a few of their steamier moments herself. 'What can I do for you, you bloody chancer?' she asked lightly, happily. 'I need you to get me a ticket to Dublin from JFK next week please, if you can, one way and with your usual attention to detail when it comes to price.' There he had said it. Someone else now knew or was about to that he was leaving. 'One way?' was the curious reply 'Are you leaving us Thomas?' He looked at her seriously and replied 'Yes Carol, I am. I'm going home for good and leaving all of this behind' signalling the city with an unconscious wave over his shoulder. She looked at him intently with genuine concern in her eyes, the concern of a true friend. 'That doesn't really surprise me you know.' He regarded her in turn 'how so amigo?' 'Well the last few times I seen you driving in that electric blue truck of yours Thomas, I could tell you were not happy, you were just floating along not seeing anything or anyone around you. People do notice you Thomas, you are hard to miss after all and you just fell off the edge of the earth it seemed about a year ago, one weekend you were out and about in the pubs and restaurants in Woodside and Astoria like the rest of us, the next, no sign of you and here you are walking in to buy a one way ticket home, what happened?' she said the last with genuine concern in both her eyes and her voice. He regarded her with warmth and thought for a second or two before answering, 'A lot has happened Carol, a lot that wasn't good, but I'm over it and its just time to move on. It can't ever be the same for me here again, I had my shot at the title and I blew it. To be honest, when I think about it, I'm not really sure if I ever really felt like this was home or just tried really hard to convince myself it was.' He smiled to soften the hardness of what he was telling her. She smiled at him 'You were always a good man Thomas, you remember that whenever you go, now get out of my office and come see me Tuesday to collect your ticket.' He could see she was just a little upset but he had no idea if it was for him or because of him, probably a bit of both.

He chuckled at her friendly dismissal saying 'Thank you gorgeous, I'll see you then. Say hello to the congressman for me' this last punctuated with a wink. 'Out Rogue!' was the mock scandalous reply that ushered him out the doorway back to the sunlight. He liked Carol, and would miss the little friendships like hers he had forged in his time here, but all things end or at least change. If there was no change there was stagnation and Thomas had had enough of that to do him a lifetime.

He lit a cigarette and decided that he would continue up Grand Avenue and loop his way back to Woodside on his side of the boulevard as he thought of it. He crossed the road and approached the barbers - he could see the big, gruff and friendly Uzbek, which owned and operated the place waving out at him. He had to stop. For years, every Saturday he had not been working had been a day for a hot towel shave and an hour or two of smoking cigarettes, reading the paper while waiting with the odd shot of vodka supplied by the owner surreptitiously, to favored patrons like himself. It was a place that only New York could have in all its perfect incongruity. The big mullet wearing Uzbek had moustaches that could only be described as spectacular, as they drooped in luxurious waves at each side of his face almost as long as the mullet went down his back.

His riotous red silk shirts were always open far enough to show off the hairy chest bedecked with gold. Thomas was always amazed at how many gold rings he could wear and keep his fingers clipping scissors all day. There was no doubt in Thomas's mind that his barber had a healthy dose of Gypsy in him, which only made him all the more fun in his eyes.

'Ah my friend, come in, come in' this delivered in his heavily accented English around a bear hug that revealed at least three different brands of cologne Thomas could recognize and quite a few more he couldn't. 'Hello Staz, good to see you' replied Thomas equally heartily while returning the back slapping hug. 'You here for shave? You need shave, come sit, wait, talk, smoke, we not long before you get shaved, I get you tea.' Thomas let himself be ushered to the ample black leather couch that filled one side of the shop; one end of it piled high with magazines. Staz had a samovar constantly in a state of brew in the corner of the shop, right beside the rarely used disinfecting tub filled with combs and old discarded scissors. He poured a Russian style glass of what he called tea, it was coal tar black and a similar taste was only alleviated by the natural sugar lump on a stick he dropped into it before handing it over. Thomas accepted it graciously and settled back to take in the place. Staz returned to the old man he had in the chair, apron tightly clinched around his scrawny neck, and adroitly picked up the conversation they were having about yet another dismal baseball season for the Mets. Thomas liked everything about the place and the man who ran it, it was an upturned finger at those who said the local and old school barbershop was dead. Anachronistic would barely describe it. He lit a cigarette and noticed the shadows outside from the parking meters, lengthening as the afternoon started to wane. The walls were stained yellow with decades of nicotine and scattered haphazardly on that background was a collection of headshots, mostly in black and white, showing hairstyles that only a Gypsy could love, sculpted breaking waves of hair rising inches above foreheads and long flowing tresses that would have suited a Jacobean Cavalier. Thomas doubted anyone ever sat in one of Staz's chairs, pointed up and said 'I want it to look like that!' Thomas also doubted that Staz would have given a shit for what they would have wanted anyway, he liked that about him too. He either liked you or he didn't, if he didn't, you would be foolish to let him near your head with a tool of his trade in hand.

Thomas sipped the liquid masquerading as tea, politeness was important and even though he had come here for years, he wouldn't want to offend Staz. That brought him onto many thoughts about how he had conducted himself, even during the bad times and manners had indeed saved him many a time. He crushed out the cigarette butt in the ashtray and leafed through an old National Geographic. There was an article on Ireland in it that extoled the virtues of the Emerald Isle. Thomas was struck again by what he saw as these subtle little messages that seemed to be popping up at him all over the place now, little nudges that he was indeed supposed to go home. 'Am I deluding myself or is it just a weird sort of prescience?' was the question he posed, which he just couldn't answer. 'Perhaps there simply is no answer,' he thought as Staz was wrapping up the chat on baseball, while brushing off skinny slumped shoulders with a big horsehair brush. The old man left a wafting stream of scented oils and pomades in his wake, along with whatever else Staz had slathered into his thinning hair during their conversation. 'Come Thomas, come, I ready now you shave!' was the expansive invitation accompanied by a sweeping gesture complete with a slight bow, in the direction of the chair. Thomas smiled in spite of himself, again the image of a Gypsy filling his mind's eye. He sat in the chair and relaxed back into it, letting his head be adjusted on the backrest, before he and the chair were tilted back to a working position with a solid stamp on the peddle by Staz. 'So how you my friend, you not come see me for long while now?' this delivered with a look that said this state of affairs had caused great and lasting pain 'I'm good Staz, I've just been very busy is all, you're right though it's been too long.' He got a snort from the Uzbek that told him this was an acceptable answer albeit not a fully satisfactory one, but it was the only one he would get. He busied himself with fetching hot towels and then wrapping and pressing them around Thomas's head and face, the heat almost burning, but not quite.

He drifted a bit as Staz gave him the run down on what had been happening in his extended families' lively lives. He got the details of the latest wedding, a huge deal in Uzbek life and photos were fetched and admired in turn. Between the lathering and the shaving a pair of shot glasses were produced, shots of pepper vodka had to be consumed for the good health of the newlyweds, 'well six months ago they were newlyweds'. Thomas chuckled to himself knowing full well, Staz needed a slightly plausible excuse to produce the vodka. He closed his eyes and bantered with Staz happily, as he felt the strong fingers pull and arrange the skin on his face, their passage closely followed by the keen, almost exciting feel of the razor. As he drifted in his thoughts while chatting, he realized he just couldn't tell Staz he was leaving. It would lead to an immediate closing of the shop and a session of tearful vodka that would last all night, but apart from that, he much preferred the thought of Staz grumbling to other regular customers about Thomas's' betrayal of his art with the razor and his shop. After all, it far better suited how he truly was, it was better to give him that than to give him reason to mourn.

When the last towel had been pulled tight then flapped like a courtesans' fan in front of his face, Thomas allowed himself to be plied with all kinds of scents and oils that were in bottles along the shelf, they looked as though they had been transported through time from an apothecary. No doubt after being blessed with their contents, he would smell like a whore's handbag. But that was all part of the unique experience that was Staz. He would never be able to tell this big, friendly, out of place character; just how many important points of Thomas's life in this city had been accessorized by a shave in this very chair. His first interview for a job in the office instead of humping steel beams and planks by hand in the field. The following week, another shave the night before he had to make that transition from hammer holder to draughtsman, with a pencil instead of a double headed nail between his fingers. The evening he had taken a taxi out to La Guardia to meet Alia off her flight from San Francisco had started with a shave in this chair. The first official date he had secured with Joan, the new clothes he had bought, gleaming he felt, as he had settled in to be groomed by Staz. Each time he knew Joan would be about he had sat in this chair. He smiled at the memory of the few dates that had actually ended well, conscious that the last unplanned one had ended the best of all; he had not been left broken hearted. The time his younger brother had come out to visit he had brought him here. The young lad had both been fascinated and appalled at the shop and its flamboyant owner. Many years and many memories were tied to his visits to this chair and he felt a twinge of real regret, as he was tilted back upright by a final depression of the pedal, by the solid right foot of Staz.

'Now my friend, you look like prince ready for the princess, yes, yes, you do,' he said as he fussed Thomas out of the chair in a courtly way while simultaneously directing him towards the cash register. Business was business after all and Thomas knew how to tip. After he paid he said 'Staz, let's have one more toast, to your health this time my friend.' Staz did not really need to be asked twice and he grinned like a bold schoolboy as the tall shot glasses were produced and filled with effortless aplomb. They were raised and clinked and Thomas said 'your health Staz, you are a good man.' Staz raised his glass to his lips and just before quaffing it said 'To Me, my friend!' with a hearty booming laugh. Thomas put down his glass, the peppery aftertaste changing to a slight but pleasant burn down his oesophagus. He turned for the door and was engulfed in a back slapping perfumed hug once more, this time not sure where the scents from Staz ended and the ones from him began. 'Take care my friend, goodbye' he said as he walked out the door. 'Never goodbye Thomas, only next time' was the reply from the moustache beneath the glittering brown, intense eyes. 'Next time then it is Staz. Next time.'

He walked away up the road and felt the twinge of sorrow again only just a little stronger than before. He thought about it as he turned the corner and decided to grab the train for one stop back to Woodside instead of walking, he had lost the appetite for it really and it was getting late. He jumped on the F train and a few minutes later found him heading down the heavy planked steps again, to the street outside the bakery once more. He was still happy but the more he was aware of the repetition of his coming and goings here, the more he wanted it over with. There were just too many ghosts imprinted in everything he knew about the place. The earlier review of the art left behind by a suicide echoed still. He needed to go. He just knew deep inside, that if he stayed, death would find him here, somehow. Walking the reverse course he had earlier travelled, he looked at his watch seeing it was almost five pm. He looked up and saw he was just approaching the church, so he went in blessing himself with holy water from the font as he did so. He knelt first in the pew he selected, then sat back and waited the few remaining minutes for evening Mass to start. He was content. He produced the rosary beads from his pocket and unconsciously ran them slowly through his fingers as the bell intoned the imminent arrival of the celebrant. He stood with the rest of the congregation and felt himself lose his uniqueness and blend, slowly, evenly in with all the other faces present hoping for the kiss of the grace of God. He knew he already was in receipt of that, the mere fact he was alive and miraculously intact was testament to it. The beads had a texture of peace as they moved through his fingertips and that same peace spread through the rest of him. The constant denial in earlier years of this seemed so pointless to him now as he remembered the Sundays he had come here, somewhat reluctantly, to join his older brother and his wife when they had lived in New York. At the time he could not get far enough beyond his present to appreciate the true permanence of his faith from the past. He prayed for them now as he did all his family, he prayed for every soul he had met in his decade and more, of life in New York. He included everyone, hookers, dealers, pimps, therapists, employers, and happy Pakistani newsagents, Staz got a mention too.

His thoughts drifted into the peace and the familiarity of the liturgy as the readings gave way to the gospel, then on through the Eucharist and finally as he followed the rest to communion. He could not deny the power of faith or the guilt of having denied it for so long, disguising his need for it in anger, retribution, love that was not true, power that was corrupted by the nature of its source and most importantly of all the loneliness of ignoring himself. That one pained most of all and he acknowledged it for what it was and felt it pass as the wafer melted on his tongue. He asked for forgiveness and safe passage home. One he would recognize when the wheels of the jet bumped down on Dublin's runway, the other he would have to accept as having been granted by his still being alive. After Mass was over, he waited respectfully for the Priest to leave the altar before genuflecting at the end of the pew and turning to walk out of the Church. The Priest was there, shaking hands and exchanging pleasantries with the congregation as they left. Thomas took his hand as it was offered and said 'Good evening Father, thank you,' the reply was gentle 'Good evening and God bless you.' He smiled at the man of the cloth 'Thank you Father' and walked past him, giving the next congregant the chance to say the same. As he walked home he felt that his whole day had been about one thing and one thing only, in his own unique way Thomas had been saying goodbye. 'Taking your leave is what you're about' came the confirmation inside his own head 'just taking your leave.' He blessed himself one last time, he was thankful he could do so after all.

Chapter 14

The Reality of Arrangements

Mondays were never a big part of Thomas's list of enjoyable things. There was no doubt that he had had many enjoyable Mondays during the course of his life, but as he had gotten older he found those to be few and far between. This particular Monday was no different and for good reason, he had lots to do and he had only allowed himself a day to do it. First on his agenda was to drive to the Bronx so he could tell his recently long-suffering employer, that he was done. He liked the people he had worked the last two years for greatly and had completed some spectacular projects for them, but he had also fallen by the wayside and his output along with it. They had been tolerant and fair and he had still been paid his commissions for the scaffolds he had secured and designed for them. His salary had always been paid too and he was thankful for that, it was effectively all that had kept him. His electric blue Dodge V8, which he loved so much was theirs too and he hoped they would let him have it a few more days, until he got everything he needed to, done.

As he drove down to the lights he decided to take the FDR drive on the east side of Manhattan, instead of the BQE to the Triborough Bridge, so he indicated and turned left accelerating along the boulevard towards Sunnyside then down the slight hill to Queens Plaza in Long Island City, where he would be joining the rest of the morning rush over the 59th Street Queensboro Bridge. He made his lane choice early, so he could get onto the single metal decked lane on the north side of the bridges lower level. This was for two reasons really. The first reason was for the view it would afford him of Roosevelt Island and its attendant cable car and of the Upper East Side of Manhattan itself; beyond the sluggish brown waters of the river. The second reason was that most commuters avoided it as too narrow and the noise of the metal rungs through which you could see the water far below, was off-putting for most. It was the province of taxis and guys like him, who knew all the fast ways, because they spent so much of their working lives driving from site to site in the city. It was also perilously narrow, with a crash barrier only a few feet high. To Thomas it just added to the thrill, just like the sudden choke points at the bridge towers where the crash barrier stepped in an extra two feet or so. He loved it, smashing the throttle with the window open and the quick, sure flick of the wrists on the steering wheel, which both negotiated the choke points and corrected any slide from the vehicle, all in one instinctive motion. It was quite the thrill at seventy plus miles an hour, as his brother had found out when he had come to visit all those years ago. Thomas smiled at the memory, he would be seeing him again soon now, along with his other brothers and sisters, the smile widened. After the crossing, he swung down north then east across to York Avenue where he could slide onto the northbound FDR.

It was perfect as most of the traffic was heading the opposite way. Soon the engine note was roaring with the confident rumble of a V8 as it echoed back in through the window, rising even further as he flashed under the extension of New York-Presbyterian Hospital, supported by its massive concrete pillars, and then the note dropped again as he re-emerged on the other side. He noted the brief glimpses of envy at his rapid progress that he caught from the sullen faces as they flashed by on the far side of the median, where the traffic was crawling.

It had not taken him long to figure out the subtleties of getting into the city from Queens when he had first started driving here. If he left Sunnyside at 7:00 am he could be over the bridge and heading down onto Second Avenue by 7:15 am, however if he left Sunnyside at 7:10 am, no later, it would take over an hour to get over the bridge and nearly the same to get to his first stop of the day. That had always struck him as so random at first but he had learned why with time. The morning rush hour commuters, from as far out Long Island as exit 55 on the Long Island Expressway, some even further. The herd would arrive on Queens Boulevard like the breaking leading edge of a Tsunami at 7:05 am, regular as clockwork. Soon he was past the smart part of the Upper East Side and passing the exit for 125th Street, which transected Harlem neatly from east to west. He continued until he got to the small bridge across the Harlem River at Willis Avenue, which got him back over the river to head east onto the Bruckner Expressway. He was almost there. Within a minute or two he was pulling up at the rear of the office just a block south of the surface street part of Bruckner Boulevard. He was a little nervous, but it had to be done, he had called ahead to announce his arrival. He walked around the corner and hit the buzzer for the office door which was steel reinforced. He smiled up at the security camera whirring round on its axis to peer at him. The buzzer clicked and he stepped inside. There was a second door that had to be opened in the same way too, but it was mostly glass. This was a part of the Bronx close to Hunts Point, surrounded by projects and desolation and let's just say, not a family friendly place. But it was perfect, just like the old factory yards in Queens where he used to work, for industrial space hungry operations like scaffold or lumber companies. The area was full of multi-million dollar service companies perched on the outskirts of their biggest market, Manhattan construction. The locals who lived nearby were so far removed from all of that it was nearly unbelievable. Some of them would never have been further south in Manhattan than 96th Street, if even that far. Beyond there was a world that belonged in movies, it was not for them.

Upon passing the final barricade, Thomas waved and said hello to the few juniors who were already at their desks, doing phone sales for rentals and the like. He said hello to the girls at reception and accounts and headed straight for the general manager desk in the corner. He liked Tony; they had always gotten on. They shook hands and Thomas sat easily in the chair by his desk, waiting for Tony to wrap up what was no doubt not the first phone call of the day for him. Construction was an occupation for early risers and self-starters. Thomas thought about that, he often received thirty to forty, or more, calls a day while driving from site-to-site, meeting-to-meeting and had to make many more. The two-way Nextel radio system that was part of his phone, would be going full on as well, with its chirping sound announcing questions from the yard on load lists for trucks to be dispatched the following day, foremen on his crews asking questions he had already explained while laying out the job for them, the girls in accounts asking about billing cycles and for him to make time to call or visit a slow paying account.

It had always been an exciting sort of life as he had risen to Project Manager, he had no doubt that the fast pace of it all had contributed to his shattering and falling apart once the pebble had hit his metaphorical windshield, that defined the boundary of his bubble within life. He knew that was why he liked driving in the city so much, he was in the bubble of his truck, the work and the day flew by with intensity and yet the city and its numerous lives and stories, slid effortlessly by the outside of the windshield, across the surface like a sitcom, his lonely, noisy, crazy bubble. Tony coughed to clear his throat as he put the phone down. 'Morning Thomas, how you doing?' was his opening sally. 'Good morning Tony, good to see you. How's all going with you then?' Tony considered him for a moment 'It would be going a whole hell of a lot better if I had you out and about doing the magic.' That was what Tony had called his skill set, the ability he had to price, draft up plans, load list, direct construction and collect the money at the end of it all. He had been good, very good, but no more. 'Well that's what I'm here to talk to you about Tony, I'm afraid I'm done, finished. I got to leave New York man.' Thomas had decided there was no other way to say it, except straight, the man deserved that, as did the company. They had been more than good to him, more than understanding, compassionate even. Tony studied him again with eyes that had no judgment but they were definitely weighing him up, looking for the chink in the decision Thomas had just announced, which would allow him to convince Thomas otherwise. Tony had once been a master of the magic too; hence he was where he was. Thomas could tell he was disappointed and unable to find that chink, as he slumped his shoulders in resignation just a fraction, almost imperceptibly. 'Come on, let's go in the back and have a coffee' he said getting up and moving round to the Seventies style laminate door the led into the conference room and from there out to the workshop. On the way through, Thomas was proud to see the series of framed photographs of some of the more intricate scaffold installations he had designed. The interior of St Thomas' Episcopalian Cathedral on Fifth Avenue stood out. He had been so proud of that project and the company had too. There were others but that was his favorite. He followed Tony out to pour two mugs of *Chock-full o' Nuts* which was the coffee of choice for this percolator. It was good, a real NYC-style brew. They sat on one of the old benches and they both lit up smokes, taking a second or two to gather their thoughts. 'So,' Tony said after a bit 'What gives?' Thomas regarded him warmly 'Tony, you know what I've been going through for the last while,' at which Tony just nodded for him to continue. 'Well that's all come to an end now and I cannot stay here in New York, too many memories, too many opportunities to screw up again. I don't think I will screw up, but I can't take that chance either, you know what I mean?' Tony kept looking at him for a moment and sighed as he said 'I was afraid this was what you were going to tell me when you called earlier. Are you sure about all this? I mean you've been here for years, know the city and the business inside and out, why not give it a chance, yourself, another chance?' Thomas shook his head gently but emphatically 'I am giving myself a chance Tony, a chance to not fall again, taking the chance God gave me to escape the nightmare once and for all. Anyway since 9/11, I've never felt the same and you know that, lost too many good friends, can't get them back. I have decided to take my chances and just go home to Ireland, see the family, make a life for myself if I can, before it's too late to start anything new.' Tony looked away and sipped his coffee, he remembered that day too they all did, but Thomas had been down there. Thomas in turn, could see it, smell it, like it was yesterday and realization washed over him like a wave. It was not long after that he had gone skiing, taking a needed break to escape working at Ground Zero and the city rank with fear at the time, and subsequently had smoked crack for the first time, felt abandoned by Joan. He had fought not to recall those weeks and months of funerals with empty coffins, the city as tense as a bowstring, his friends dead and lost forever. He had never mentioned that in rehab, or therapy. There had been no point, talking about it could not bring back the dead.

'Thomas, you ok?' said Tony, he looked worried as Thomas tuned back in to the conversation. 'Yeah I'm good, just got a little sidetracked there is all.' There was no more he could say, or Tony could say for that matter, it was what it was. 'I was hoping to keep the truck for another day or so, move some stuff, give away furniture and the like, will that be ok with you?' Tony nodded saying 'when are you flying?' Thomas chuckled 'I don't actually know yet, would you believe. I'm collecting the ticket tomorrow. I'd say it will be a day or two after that.' Tony laughed 'Fast, yeah kid you never did hang round much once you made up your mind, here's what I can do, call me tomorrow and let me know when the truck's coming back, leave the phones and laptop in it of course and when you come up I'll have a check with your last salary, commissions and holiday pay etc. I'll get Segundo to drop you back to Queens then, best I can do.' Thomas smiled genuinely as he said 'That's more than I would have asked for Tony, you are a good man and I'll always appreciate that.' Tony waved him off and said 'Look Thomas, I have always liked you, but you seriously pissed down my neck while telling me it was raining for a while there, I respect the way you came clean about things and got sorted. Also the work you have done here lately has regained a lot of good will for you. The family acknowledges that and wishes you well for the future.' The family being the owners, first generation Irish success stories and good people who worked hard and honest, unlike some of his countrymen he had come across in his time in New York. 'Please give them my respect and my thanks Tony. You know you have that too don't you?' Tony smiled at him 'You're damn right I do or else I never would have put up with you this long,' he paused and looked at his watch 'Right I gotta go back out there and keep this mad house running, so with all due respect Thomas, fuck off and don't waste anymore of my time today please!' Thomas laughed and shook his hand as they both got up. He would miss this man he was a good soul. He drained his coffee; he would miss that taste of *Chock-full o' nuts* too. He followed Tony back into the main office and as they entered, one of the girls was already paging him on the intercom to take a call, so he picked up the phone to answer it as he swung round his desk to his chair. He held his hand to the side of his head mimicking 'Call me' as he spoke into the phone. Thomas threw his best GI Joe salute and smiled as he turned and left, Tony's voice booming instructions down the phone as he made his way out through the security doors to the street outside.

'Well that went well, better than expected' he said to himself as he lit another smoke and ambled his way back to where the truck was parked. Sun was getting bright as it rose above the high rise projects on the far side of the street from where he was, so he slid on his sunglasses as he hopped into the truck, key sliding into the ignition and turning the engine over almost before the door had fully closed behind him. 'Muscle memory is a beautiful thing' he complimented himself, as he pulled away from the curb and executed the U-Turn he needed to, so he could get back on the expressway and head for the Triborough Bridge, and Queens. As he drove towards the bridge he could see down below, from his elevated position, some of Hunters Point or *Hunts Point* as the locals called it. It was a produce and wholesale market for the city by day and a famous hooker and drug hangout by night. He had had his moments there too, the memories made him glad of the path he was now taking. He could also see the top of the expansive and vividly colored tent, expertly pitched on Governors Island where the *Cirque du Soleil* were undertaking their now customary New York run of shows. He had gone once and been impressed, but in truth actually spent more time admiring the cleverly designed rigging that held up the structure, than the acrobats themselves. He approached the toll barriers at a reasonable speed, for him, trusting in the *EZ Pass* stuck to the inside of the windshield to do its magic before the barrier smacked him in the face, it popped up just at the last moment, perfectly judged as always, his own contribution to keeping the traffic flowing smoothly.

Right after the booths and barriers, the road narrowed back to a few lanes each way and he let the truck take its set through the long curve that led onto the Brooklyn Queens Expressway and Queens. Pretty soon he was sliding across to the right hand lane to take the almost hidden exit for 58th Street and Queens Boulevard, and just like that he was back where he had started only an hour or so beforehand. "Pays to know your way round' he laughed to himself as he parked and shut off the engine, almost regretting the silencing of its confident rumbling vibration. He would miss driving the truck, for sure he would, but even that was not a reason to stay here any longer than he had too. When he got inside the apartment he offered it a greeting 'Hello House' which was a superstition he had picked up as a young teenager, who was terribly impressed at the time with all things legendary, mystical and magical, which was easy to understand based on the culture from which he came. Ireland was awash with fairies and tales of the supernatural, some of it had to have rubbed off on him. He realized as he said it this time though, that he was hedging his bets just a bit. The apartment felt defiant in its needing of him gone now, he was happy to oblige. There existed an uneasy truce between them, now that he had already started to pack things up in the boxes scattered about the floor. It felt to him that the walls and floors would hold their memories of what had taken place here, from him, for a short time at least, until he was gone and some other souls resided here. He knew that within a week of his leaving, it would be rented out again and it would be like he had never darkened its doorway. He busied himself with the last of the packing. The clothing he was keeping was stacked for a later run to the laundry, the rest of it stacked and bagged for donation; the same went for the boxes and boxes of books he had accumulated in his years here. The CD's had been winnowed out to those he wished to keep, the essential range of music he truly loved and felt his soul was richer for having discovered, the rest were going the way of the books and unwanted clothing. Soon he had that task well in hand so he made a pot of coffee, realizing he would miss that puffing chugging monster of a percolator also. Aer Lingus was not going to take pity on his desire to maintain a relationship with a coffee pot by letting him have it as a carry on, so it was going too.

He sat and flicked through the news channels for a while until he settled on NY1, the local cable news outlet that focused on New York. The anchor was introducing some goings on at City Hall with the mayor's staff. He watched only as a way of soaking more of the place up he reckoned, not out of any desire to update his political awareness. He tired of it pretty soon and realizing he was procrastinating just a bit, forced himself to jump up with some vigor and let out a medium level 'Arrghhh Thomas boy, get on with it!' as he quickly stretched and got back about the task at hand. He saw that he was almost done. Once he had all the keeper clothes bagged, he started to move all the things that were going, down the stairs and out into the bed of the pickup. He was neat and ordered about how he did this, mostly because it would be more efficient and mean less trips, but also it was more him to be ordered than disordered, a recent rediscovery. He was surprised that he managed to get everything in tightly, in a double depth stack. The clothes bag he had for the laundry went in the cab, on the back seat. As he secured a cargo net over it all, he could not help noticing it represented a life, ten years' worth, with all of what went with that, and now it would soon no longer even be his. Shaking that one off, he went back inside and grabbed his smokes and keys, wallet and phone, off the counter top along with the flyer he had found for the furniture reseller who was not far away.

He drove across the boulevard to the laundry and dropped off the bag, taking out the shirts and telling the little Asian lady he needed them folded after pressing instead of on hangers, otherwise he'd ruin them when they were packed in his travel duffel bag. It took a while to get the idea fully across. He then drove the few short miles to the Salvation Army in Long Island City and he had no shortage of assistance in unloading the truck. Some of the residents had to be told not to climb into the bed of the pickup. He managed to keep some semblance of order to the proceedings but still could not ignore the slight pain he felt in his chest as he watched his former possessions being pulled and rifled through by grubby, uncaring, greedy hands. One of the staff, a long suffering volunteer, took charge of the boxes of books and CD's, they were salable items if only for a dollar or two a piece, but the residents could get high on a nickel bag for five, Thomas knew this all too well. The confluence of more of his unwanted knowledge and the sight of things from his life being pawed through and argued over like spoils, was almost too much. He accepted the volunteer's thanks, declined the tax receipt offered and was back in the truck and driving away almost quicker than his muscle memory allowed. He felt tears running down his face as he drove back up to Woodside, shame, regret, whatever it didn't really matter anymore, he was just simply upset and he took deep breaths to help it pass. Those were the feelings that were dangerous, those were the feelings that reaffirmed he needed out of New York ASAP. As he rolled with the traffic to the hub of Woodside, he called the furniture place, getting the number off the back of the flyer. The Spanish speaker with bad English was delighted to deal with an Anglo who could speak his lingo. By the end of the call it was agreed he would be up at Thomas's apartment at nine the following morning, to check over the furniture and give him a price for it. He would move it out and resell it at a good profit Thomas knew, but he didn't have time to advertise and go through all the usual bullshit, it had to go and the money, whatever it was, would be handy. In New York, when you rented an apartment you got clean bare floors and bare eggshell white walls and that was how you were supposed to hand it back. You also never got your security deposit back, so as it was worth a months' rent, you just didn't announce your leaving until that had been almost used up. Thomas had learned that one the hard way and he was not giving any headspace to needless stress, ever again.

He looked about the place and considered how empty it already felt. The furniture was all that remained and soon even that would be gone. He leafed through the assorted bills and made a list of all the numbers he had to call to end services, cable, power and phone. He made the calls and gritted his teeth a bit while navigating the phone trees of each organization, yelling into the handset at one point 'Give me a fucking human being not a FUCKING choice of numbers!' He was actually not really mad, just hopeful that indeed his call was *being recorded for training and quality purposes.* He smiled at the thought of some call center trainees getting an earful of that, at an orientation somewhere.

Soon even all of that was done. Now he had to go, no choice except to leave. By Friday night the apartment would be dead in the water, no lights, no power in its outlets, no hot water in its taps, no life in its connections to the crooked wooden pole outside, that had always leaned somewhat drunkenly into the edge of his view across the green of the cemetery while it had connected his voice, to the rest of the world. It was all over now bar the shouting and tomorrow, after the furniture was gone, all he had to do was go to Carol's office and collect his passage home. Then it would be really and truly final. It all had taken a few hours to do and now he needed to get out of the place again. With that decision he also plumbed for a shower, then dressed well and walked to Woodside. He went into one of the many Irish Pub / Restaurants and took a stool at the counter; it was not too busy being a Monday night, most of the regulars having blown their drinking money from the previous Thursday though to Sunday. He decided on Guinness and had two pints while waiting on the steak he had ordered to arrive for consumption. He pondered what had happened while talking with Tony earlier. He realized that after his only really good, true friend had died in the tragedy, as he called it, *That Day in September,* he had in fact being truly lonely. Yes sure he had his family to talk to on the phone and his brother and sister-in-law living in the city for a while, Joan when she decided to grace him with her presence and of course all the hundreds of people he interacted with on many levels each week in his work, but he was alone and had always felt so. The Guinness was cool and crisp, familiar as it slid down just like the thoughts slipping across his consciousness were. Thomas had been alone for a long time now and the power of that understanding made him get up to go out and have a cigarette.

The smoke tasted good over the stout on his tongue, he felt like an observer as he watched the streetlights overcome the last of the daylight beneath the carcass of the subway above. The rhythm of Woodside pulsed around him in waves that washed up against him repeatedly but could not, had not, wet him in a long time. A part of him still longed to be drenched and soaked with the vibrancy and life of the place, but he could never shake off the stink of the more shadowed pools he had recently almost drowned in. Back inside the warmth and sameness of the bar was good, reliable and safe. The food arrived and he ate it while letting his mind wander, as his eyes followed the Rangers skating after a puck he couldn't see against the ice. It was one of the innumerable re-runs that ESPN had to fill gaps in the busy schedule of live sports that abounded in America. He would miss them all in a way and remembered fondly his trips to World Series games to watch the Yankees at their eponymous stadium in the Bronx and once up at Fenway in Boston, that had indeed been special, the atmosphere like All Ireland final day in Croke Park in Dublin, jam packed and sizzling with the electricity of anticipation. A few souls came and went in the easy quiet of a Monday night and he made polite, if brief, conversation with the bar man as plates came and went, empty pints were cleared away and fresh ones delivered. After he had a small but content buzz he paid, tipped and left stopping at the off license to get a bottle of Lagavulin 16 year old, a final luxury. He had bought Joan a bottle once to bring to her parents as a gift when she was visiting them, back when he thought they were a real couple, only to find out later she had delivered it to them with no mention of him. That one had hurt, more than a bit. He walked home happy enough, decided past slights would not affect his enjoyment of one of her left over cigars, he still had two from the last visit, and a few snifters of peaty heaven.

He re-entered the now uncaring apartment and realized he cared less himself, went to the toilet, washed his hands and kicked off his boots. He consulted the mirror and was content enough in what it had to tell him tonight. After pouring and watering a generous measure he sat down in his observatory chair to contemplate his lonely night sky one last time. The chair leaving tomorrow would be the hardest thing to have to let go of he decided, but he had also decided there would be other chairs and other views of the cosmos to be contemplated in what was left of his life. The cigar puffed to life with an ease born of practice and it tasted that perfect counterpart he knew it would, to the fiery dark amber of the scotch. As his eyes adjusted he could make out Cassiopeia and Orion and he raised his glass to them both. He looked forward to sitting on the top of Loughcrew, near the town of Oldcastle, when he got home to watch the stars with the Megalithic passage tomb behind him and a clear, dark sky above him. He willed his mind to take him there now, the highest point for five counties and home to over three thousand years of magical, mystical history. God how he wanted to be there right at that moment, instead he soothed himself with the knowledge it would be soon.

'One more drink' he said to himself as he shifted and discarded the now spent cigar, he would keep the other for tomorrow and the majority of the whiskey too. He refreshed his glass and fetched his cigarettes, turning on some classical music as he did so, the stereo would be gone tomorrow too. That reminded him of the stark reality of his arrangements that he had been about all day. He reckoned that he had made a pretty good fist of them after all. 'Arrangements' he muttered, feeling just a little sleepy now, as the whiskey added to the stout and the food to make his eyes heavy, 'arrangements for my New York funeral, that's what I've done today.' So he had, and as he fell asleep for the last time in his beloved observatory chair, he knew he was alone, perhaps he always had been, perhaps he always would be? He wasn't sure and Mr. Sandman didn't really give him enough time to think on it before he was snoring.

Chapter 15

Emigrating Home

Waking up somewhat stiff and just a touch worse for wear was counterbalanced by the scent of fresh cut grass and the sound of excited finches, as they busied themselves eating the newly revealed menu left behind by the passage of the tractor and its gang mower. Thomas stirred in his chair and stretched, with a satisfying clicking and popping running down his back. The grounds men in the cemetery liked to get the grass cut early and as he glanced at his watch he saw it was so, just after six. The sun was again dawning brightly into a cloudless sky and he admired the peace and quiet before the rush of the day's commuters began in earnest. It could be surprisingly peaceful once you learned how to filter out the low-level traffic noise at this time of day, along with the various window-mounted air conditioners some people had on this time of year, others hadn't bothered yet. The finches were a flurry of joy as they hopped and flapped, bustled and jostled each other for the tastiest morsels that early summer had to offer. He had always liked birds, but right now they reminded him that he too had to be busy today for it could be his last, he wouldn't know for sure until he saw Carol.

He could have called of course, but that would no doubt have spoiled his own surprise, he felt just a hint of excitement begin to build. He had four hours yet to kill before he would know as they only opened at ten, then it would all be happening. He would have to call Tony and instigate the agreed handover of equipment and then hand back the keys of this place which, as he woke up more, told him he was already forgotten by it. He made his way to the coffee machine and as he prepped it, stopped for a second, this would be the last first pot of the day he ever made with it. 'When did I buy the damn thing?' he asked himself and then he remembered, it was the big snowstorm of '96, back when he had been living with Alia in the one bedroom on 42nd Street in Sunnyside. He smiled at the memory, trudging home with it under one arm, her under the other, as he barged a path through the drifts for the both of them. He was glad he could smile at it, the memory, because it had been a lifetime lived long ago. He resumed the loading and charging of his most valued weapon against the fog of sleep, and simply watched it in all of its simplistic majesty, as it spoke to him in gurgles and chugs, puffs and trickles, one last time. He stood there, determined not to feel time lengthening as though he was watching a kettle that wouldn't boil as a kid. He smiled again, that had annoyed his father no end when he would do it, especially if the man was busy and had only ten minutes for his morning tea break, which was normally the case. The fact that, by his watching it and feeling it could elongate the perceived time involved, could in turn be transferred like some contagion to his father had only made him do it more. He was a junior scientist at that stage after all, searching for empirical evidence of the

215

truth. Thomas frowned though at that thought, his search for truth back then had been to hide from the real truth, the Smyth truth. 'Enough, enough of that now' he softly reminded himself as the level of the coffee reached a point he knew well. It was at the stage where it still had a long way to go in filling the jug, but if he tapped off a mug now it wouldn't be as strong as all damnation which would affect his coffee consumption for the rest of the day. He remembered a line for the *Bull McCabe* in *The Field* by John B. Keane 'We can't have that, and we won't have that!' Thomas smiled again displacing the previous frown; he had a very loving, yet dependent relationship with his coffee, and the shakes were to be avoided at all costs, especially today.

Back out on the balcony he thoroughly enjoyed the first cigarette of the day, when it was right; the combination of first caffeine and nicotine simply had no peer. The neighbourhood was waking up a bit more and the finches had moved their squabbling circus over the green horizon and out of both sight and earshot. It was truly a lovely day and the hum of the traffic was starting to grow perceptibly louder. He looked down at his beloved electric metallic blue pickup truck. It was squat and muscular and looked fast even sitting still. The paint was starting to gleam in the sunlight that was not yet directly falling upon it; the windshield still had a slight fog of dew upon it as a result, adding to its mystery, its power, at least to Thomas. Across the street the twitching of a curtain caught the corner of his eye, he did not see which window exactly but knew the general area, it had to be the bin lady. He smiled again; no doubt she was disgusted with his recent and obvious residency on the balcony, which just had to be messing with her routine, and her noodle, just a bit. He felt guilty about smiling at her discomfort, but not for long, eccentricity like that simply had to be enjoyed, applauded even, at least to his mind. The more he thought of her the more he thought he should say thank you, in some way for the guilty pleasure her eccentricity had provided. How exactly to do that though? Without being flayed alive in a sweltering barrage of Korean obscenities that would no doubt be covering her fear of being approached by him if he did so, in the first place. He would not like to do that, frighten her in any way, this was after all, more her place than his now, in fact for far longer than he had lived here he expected. He went and filled another mug of coffee and as he sat down in his chair to ponder this, then it came to him, the chair. He would leave his beloved, comfortable observatory chair, on the steps by her equally beloved, battered long suffering trashcans. He was very happy with that particular epiphany.

He checked his watch and saw that he had time yet before the percussion section of 'trashcan symphony orchestra' made its entrance onto the stage that was his former street. Fetching his good diary pen and some equally cherished writing paper from the bureau inside, he wrote a quick note that simply said *Enjoy* in large fluid writing. He folded the note and put it in his back pocket. Reaching for his mug he drained his coffee with a quick toss of his head and turned to implement his impromptu plan. 'No time like the present' he said to the uncaring space that was the apartment. He pulled back on his boots and heaved the chair up and close to him in a fluid motion. Sometimes he was surprised at his own strength but then he realized he shouldn't be, he was a big man who had worked hard all his life after all. With a mental tilt of his cap towards heaven for his regained vitality, he manoeuvred the chair in through the sliding door and across the floor to the main door, where he placed it carefully on the floor. He regarded its slightly faded and creased leather upholstery one last time against the backdrop of this place, he now considered *formerly* his. He had oiled it against the weather regularly and bombed it against bugs taking up residence in its interior. In winter it came inside so as not to rot and overall it was actually quite the piece, for something purchased for fifty dollars at a garage sale a lifetime ago. He had no doubt that the little old lady would be able to get someone to lift it inside and that she would be able to almost curl up in its embrace. He hoped she would think good thoughts as she did, just like he had mostly done, escaping to the stars. He opened the door and blocked it so, then went downstairs to do the same at the main door. Quickly he bounded back up the steps and lifted his chair easily again and carried it downwards and outside. He moved with the rapid short steps of one carrying a load and careful of not tripping on the opposite curb, reached the point he had in mind. He set down the chair and placed the handwritten note carefully on the cushion, angled just so. As he regarded his handiwork, he again caught the twitch of the same curtain out of the corner of his eye, but he was careful not to look up. Smiling like a naughty schoolboy, he walked back across the street and inside to await developments.

He poured the last cup of coffee he would ever make in his beloved jug, from it. He checked his watch again as he stepped out on the balcony and there she was, coming out the door but with no bags in hand. She approached the chair cautiously, peering at the note, which she grabbed while looking up at him. Thomas made what he thought was a universal open handed giving gesture towards her, with a slight bow for good measure. She studied him and then disappeared quickly back inside, note in hand. Thomas was a bit flummoxed and just on the point of being pleasantly offended, when the door across the street opened again to the staccato of harsh commanding Korean. 'No way' he said incredulously, as for the first time ever, he saw who had to be her husband and she was directing him to hold open the door. Next thing he knew she was down the steps, gave him a curt shallow bow and placing her aged hands on the arms of the chair, hefted it up the step and inside, quick as a flash. Thomas was absolutely stunned 'No Friggin way!' he said again in complete disbelief at the feat of strength he had just witnessed from the old lady, then he just laughed, thinking as he did so, that he wouldn't want to be the fella who tried to pinch her purse on the subway. He was completely tickled pink by the whole thing and was still laughing as he decided to take a shower and did so. He was just out and dressed again, when the doorbell rang and he knew it would be the furniture guys, so he opened up for them. He had been expecting just the man himself, but he had the whole shooting match with him, rigid body truck and four strong lads of short stature, from somewhere in the Peruvian Andes by their accents. 'No messing around' thought Thomas, 'he's here to do business for sure' Greetings were exchanged and the assessment began. Everything was going: beds, TV, couches, stereo, rugs, tables, pots and pans, coffee maker, the lot. It only took ten minutes of discussion and haggling to seal the deal, Thomas knew the guy would make back the two thousand three hundred dollars in cash he paid, twice over. It had all been good stuff, some of it very good. Thomas had a twinge of regret as the last piece descended the stairs and entered the rear of the waiting truck. He shook hands with the men and watched pensively as the truck pulled away and disappeared around the corner, gone. He had no time now to be sentimental; he couldn't allow himself to be. He went back inside and the starkness of the space struck him, so big when empty, all the life that had been lived there both in good times and bad, seemed to be leeching out of the very walls and drifting past him and out the open door like invisible smoke. It was as if the place was exhaling at last, ready to inhale in hope again when the next inhabitants arrived. He stepped inside almost tentatively and noticed that the only thing remaining in the kitchen was one regular glass and one snifter beside the still three quarters full bottle of scotch, the last cigar resting at the edge of the big clean ashtray his cigarettes, lighter and keys beside it. He felt the wad of cash in his palm that he had counted and counted again, to be sure of its value and shuddered. Six months ago that would have driven him straight over to Bushwick and Mama G's to smoke crack, lots of crack while Dena sucked and licked his cock and he watched Tray lick Mama G's pussy like a dog licked water out of a bowl, or whatever messed up combination thereof. The disgrace he felt at having involved himself in such a way with women was very real, the shame he felt at having being a part of bringing them down, using them as much as they were using him in return. Those memories would forever be a reminder of just how far he had travelled from the center of who he had always believed he was. 'No More!' he shouted into the empty space before him, hands tightly clenched by his side, knuckles white with the effort. This was exactly why he had to go. He knew it would take only one brief second, to decide wrong, one step left instead of right and he would be obliterated by the minefield that was his recent past. He went in through to the bedroom and pulled the bags that were travelling with him, out into the safety of the open plan living and kitchen area. He could feel it, an oppressive tightening of the walls as those memories, those desires; the very lustful compulsion that had once ruled him, taunted him now, with the chuckle of his old demon, the sensation of taste returning to the back of his throat. He bowed his head and prayed as he cried, he didn't fight it this time though, he just let it flow, releasing it finally. He continued to cry silently for a few minutes, then sated, shook it off.

Thomas stepped into the bathroom and washed his teeth to banish the phantom flavour and his face to do the same to the tracks left by his very real tears. There was no sense of pain anymore, nor even of regret, it just was as he was. He consulted the mirror, gazing intently, closely at his pupil to see the tiny image of himself floating there. A friend once at a time of need had shown him how to do it, to remind himself that he was real not just some fragmentary construct of his mind, he had reality and with it came renewed purpose, safety in the tangible, the seen, the now understood. He splashed water on his face once more, towelled it dry. He felt better, still shaky but better, the bulge of cash in his pocket, no longer invoking spectre's to be fearful of. He stepped quickly out and across to the kitchen grabbing keys, lighter and smokes. He felt good to have a purpose for the next little while at least.

Once downstairs and behind the wheel again, he drove the looping back way past the police repair shop, to get to Grand Avenue. Parking was easy right outside where he needed to go. It was just a few minutes after ten and he was the first customer of the day. Carol looked well as she smiled. 'Good morning Carol' he said brightly trying to disguise the slight uncertainty he was sure would be in his voice from the recent tears. Her reply gave no hint of that being so. 'Good morning

Thomas, here for your ticket?' he approached the counter 'yes indeed I am, what have you got for me beautiful?' she blushed just a bit at the compliment. 'Well you did say this week Thomas, ASAP. And one way correct?' he nodded in the affirmative 'so best I could do was Delta leaving JFK at 3:00 am tomorrow, landing Shannon about six local time then on to Dublin landing about nine or so' she looked almost apologetic as she said it from the other side of the counter, he breathed a sigh of relief from the breath that he had not realized he had been holding. It was good that it was this fast, he wouldn't have to stay in the apartment tonight, he was not sure it would have him, or he it anymore, in fact he knew it was so, after earlier. 'You my dear lady, are a legend. What's the damage?' she made a small wincing smile 'Thomas you know Delta are more expensive than Aer Lingus right?' he nodded again 'I know Carol lay it on me babe' this last delivered with aplomb. 'Eight fifty six' in spite of herself she couldn't help wincing again, that was the return price for Aer Lingus booked a few weeks in advance. Thomas didn't bat an eye and pulled out the wad from his jeans, quickly counting out nine, crispy, hundred dollar bills, one after the other. Carol seemed relieved that he wasn't upset and handed him the envelope with his ticket. 'Thomas, remember to be out there at check in at least three hours before ok? Delta suck when it comes to security you know.' He knew, 9/11 had changed many things and those ripples went worldwide. He was an experienced traveller though and it was not going to bother him one bit. He looked her square in the eye and said 'Carol, thank you and take care of yourself, you are one of the people I have been very happy to have met in life, truly you are.' She looked at him with a tear glistening and came round the counter to give him a strong, holding

222

hug that was over almost too quickly. 'Take good care of yourself Thomas boy, you hear me?' He did and kissing her quickly and respectfully on the cheek, turned and left saying 'God bless you Carol, always' over his shoulder as he did so.

He shrugged himself together and got into the truck, starting it up and moving off to join the city bound flow on the Boulevard, so he could get to the laundry. It was happening fast now and it was already ten thirty. He had to call Tony, hoped he would be able to do what he said he would, with short notice like this. He parked outside the bodega and quickly went into collect his bag of laundry and he was happy the shirts were folded as requested. The bill was twenty-two and by way of thanks he gave her a fifty, no doubt making her day. He dropped off the laundry in the middle of the floor of the living room when he got there and picked up the phone to call Tony. The conversation was short and to the point, basically come right now. He locked the place up and for the last time slid behind the wheel and gunned his blue lady of many an adventure in life. He was on the BQE fairly quickly and he felt good. The truck did not disappoint as he pushed the throttle to the floor and blew the speed limit away, loving it, knowing somehow that a traffic citation right now would be the least of his worries, he wouldn't be back and they were not going to seek extradition for a speeding fine but he did keep it within reason and well short of a ton. After parking and getting buzzed in, he was met by Tony at the inner door, 'Hi kiddo, you all set to go?' he shook his hand replying 'Hi Tony, all packed and ready. The phones and the laptop are in the back of the truck and the company fuel card is in the lap top bag as well.' Tony handed him an envelope 'It's all there kiddo, a nice egg to leave with, you'll be ok. Make sure you get on that plane though, I don't want you being tempted with a fat check in your ass pocket.' He was only being half serious Thomas could tell, 'Have no fear Tony, I'm hitting the airport as planned,' he paused for a moment then simply said 'thank you for everything Tony.' Tony stepped in and gave him a hug saying 'Thank you Thomas, we learned a lot together and made some good money too. Keep in touch and let us know how you go ok? I expect Christmas cards, and whiskey.' Thomas just nodded and slapped him on the shoulder 'You got it, can Segundo take me back or do I need to get a cab?' Tony was all business again 'Naw, he's good to go, but you better drive back to Queens if you wanna get there today, you know how he is.' Indeed Thomas did, many a day a crew started late because Segundo was so terrified of the flatbed trucks with a full load on board, he wouldn't cross twenty mph. Tony turned to leave and stopped saying 'That doesn't mean you get to scare the living shit outta him on the way either Thomas.' He smiled at Tony's knowing wink, 'Ten Four Tony.' Was the two-way radio, old school reply. 'Take care Thomas, be seeing ya kid' was all he got return.

Thomas threw a general wave at the rest of the office and buzzed himself out. Any of the items he had here were best left here, for the next *kid* who came along. Once Thomas was out back on the street and trying to find Segundo, inside it was like he had never been, except for the photographs on the wall, life would go on, it always did. He found the man in question and ushered him into the passenger seat over the excited tumble of Spanish he had for him. All the field guys really loved Thomas, as he looked after them. He answered as politely as he could and drove at the same time, but there was no stopping the jovial stream of chatter out of the little man, until they got past the barriers on the

Triborough that is. The last Thomas heard from the seat next to him after the barrier swung up, just in time as usual, was *Madre con Dios* and then nothing. By the time he parked at the old apartment about fifteen minutes later, poor old Segundo was traumatized. Thomas gave him a hundred dollar bill, to ease the pain and by way of thanks. It had an amazing restorative power on the man and soon he was trundling off happily in the electric blue truck, Thomas watching wistfully as it disappeared. 'What now,' he said to himself, checking his mental list of things to do. 'Food' yes, he was hungry but that could wait a bit then he remembered 'Bank,' so he turned and walked quickly down to Woodside opening Tony's envelope as he did so. 'Yes' he exulted to himself as he read the amount, he would indeed be ok and there was enough to keep him going for a good while if he was smart. 'Imagine what you have wasted, and could have brought home if you hadn't messed up?' echoed across his mind, 'It is what it bloody is, and how much is my soul worth after all?' he asked himself rhetorically, dismissing his self-recrimination ruthlessly. When he walked in the door of the bank, the queue was short, so he filled out the deposit slip and got in line. Soon he was handing over the check and that was that. His working life in New York was done. He had plenty now to get the hell out, start again, how lucky was he for that? He knew exactly how blessed he was.

He went outside, taking a long last look at Woodside in the daytime before he walked to the *Stop Inn* where he had one last encounter with their famous Full Irish Breakfast. Their coffee wasn't bad either. After he finished the heart attack on a plate, he left and walked home the long way, careful to not pass the old haunts as he had already said goodbye. He went into the church and blessed himself and knelt. He took out his rosary beads and he said the rosary in thanks, prayed for a safe journey and a happy ending to it all. Perhaps he had no right to ask those things? But he had too; it was what he truly felt. After one last look at the interior and the altar he would most likely never see again in this lifetime, like everything else he would rest his eyes upon for the rest of today, he left as quietly and as quickly as he had come. He made good time getting back to the apartment and that was that really, everything that he had to do was done, now it was only a matter of time. He had several hours to kill and with no phone now of any sort, no transport and a bare apartment, he decided to sit and have a whiskey and the cigar. He sat with his back to the wall, knees half drawn up comfortably and the bottle resting on the floor beside the glass between them. He puffed the cigar to life and poured a generous measure, opening it with some water splashed in from the other, far less glamorous glass he had filled for that very purpose. He chuckled as he took the first sip, there were the only two pieces of anything left in the place, and even all the plates, cups, knives and forks were gone. He twirled the drinking glass between his fingers as he smoked, looking out past it with his head sometimes back against the wall, sometimes not, as the slight breeze ruffled his hair and kissed his cheek. He remembered Dena walking barefoot through candlelight here, then Joan doing the same. He could see his old friend from upstairs whom had once worked for Cantor Fitzgerald, sitting and laughing on the balcony in the late afternoon sunlight. He looked out across the green to where the tops of the Twin Towers had once been visible, past the cemetery. He raised his glass in that direction in a silent salute. All the ghosts, good and bad, were acknowledged and laid to rest, he hoped. He sat like that for a bit taking in the fact that everything was changing, this time by his choice, albeit a somewhat forced choice. After a while he got up and busied himself and did the final check of the bags and polished his black leather boots to a lustrous shine his grandfather would have approved of. He missed him more than anyone he had lost in life and that would always be so he felt, until time called all those closer to him, but up to now he was the one that had mattered more than any other. Thomas hoped he was not too mad at him for what he had done and that he was happy he had turned it around and survived his own stupidity. He hoped so, but guessed he would only be sure once he died himself and met him again; he had to believe that he would.

He undressed for the last time in this now Spartan place bereft of anything except memories and showered. His shave from Staz was still good to go, as he felt his chin smooth beneath his fingers. He dressed very well and pulled on his gleaming boots and donned his black leather jacket. The towel was discarded on the rack. He packed the final things, his toiletries and the clothes he had just taken off, and he was pretty much done. Checking his watch, he saw that he still had almost forty minutes before the town car from Caprice would arrive to take him to JFK. He poured the last of the whiskey into his glass and watered it well; there were at least three of his big fingers in there before he did so. He lit a cigarette and whiled the time by leaning on the balcony rail. Finally it was time and the car arrived turning around just past his door to come back and park in front of it. The horn sounded once, the usual announcement. He drained the glass and stubbed the smoke out in the ashtray. He brought his bags downstairs and once they were in the trunk of the big Lincoln, he went back upstairs one final time;, he walked from room to room saying nothing inside or out, but saying goodbye nonetheless. On the way back out he brought the two glasses, the empty bottle and the ashtray and put them in the bin by the curb. He locked the door and hefted the keys up onto the balcony from the street below, he had had no intention of dealing with a landlord today and he owed him nothing anyway, so he had omitted him from his earlier plan of action. It was finally done, as he heard them jingle on the concrete above him.

As he got into the car and closed the door, he saw the little old lady hold back her curtain and wave at him, he waved back, it was almost too much but in the time he thought that, the car was already moving, taking him home. The driver took the Grand Central Parkway to the Van Wyck Expressway and had him at the Delta terminal in pretty good order. He got out and paid while one of the ever-present *Red Caps* took charge of his bags. He followed him inside and as he was earlier than most, got checked in pretty quick, no doubt the ten-dollar note he slipped him, helped with that. Once the bags disappeared on the conveyer belt checked all the way through to Dublin, he had a choice, have a smoke or go through security. He decided to smoke and then he had a second one. The sounds of engines coming and going as they powered their aircraft raised and fell in an unending crescendo of noise. He liked it though, for him it had always been the sound of hope, of new beginnings. Eventually he went inside to face the disrobing and probing, with all of the other shoeless people who were travelling. The experienced ones like him were ready by the time they got to the final stage of the x-ray machine and metal detector, footwear in hand, keys, coins and wallets in jacket pockets, jackets folded over one arm ready for the tray. Then there were the idiots who pretended they didn't know the shoes had to come off, or the watch, or the belt and they had to go through three or four times before they got it right, pissing everyone else in line off as they did so, getting shamefaced and catty themselves with everyone else in return. Thomas ignored it all; it was merely to be endured.

He passed through eventually and the Transportation Security Administration employee had a few straightforward questions about where he was going and why, that he had asked a thousand people in the same voice, the same way, all day long. Thomas answered, not bothering to point out he had no business asking the why after the where, reminding himself the poor guy could make more in McDonalds. 'Security in the wake of 9/11, smoke and god dammed mirrors' he reminded himself as he answered in monotones, glad he had had a few whiskeys to take the edge off the tedium of it all. Once he was through, he allowed himself to feel just a little excited. The terminal was both new and old and finding anything was a bit of a chore, he normally flew Aer Lingus or British Airways and they were located in a different terminal, equipped with signage that directed you somewhere you might actually need to go. He had no carry-on luggage, so he was unencumbered as he walked past and through the various duty free outlets, pausing in one to buy Marlboro reds and a piece of jewelry for his mother in another, but that was all. He had two hours to kill before boarding so he found the bar and restaurant combination that still had smoking area attached. He ate a good steak and fries with creamed spinach washed down with a couple of pints of Sam Adams Boston Lager, probably his favourite American beer. He soaked up the accents and the voices of America as he did so, from those around him and the numerous television screens all vying for everyone's attention. He heard his flight called for boarding, paid his check and had one more cigarette before heading to the boarding gate. He lined up and smiled that polite but meaningless smile everyone used in places like this, as the steward checked his boarding card. Walking down the ramp he saw it was an old 747 they were operating on the route, that suited him fine, plenty of room and from what he could tell, the flight was nowhere near full. He was directed down one aisle and took his allocated seat by the window. He watched the other passengers fuddle and fumble their bags in and out and back in again of the overhead lockers. The headphones fit pretty well and he put them on while he waited to be off. Soon the music was interrupted by the safety demonstration he pointedly ignored, he always felt bad looking at a pretty young stewardess, who had to mime blowing into the manual inflation device on the life jackets and always looked either pissed off or mortified at having to do so in the first place. He realized he was in luck, no one else had alighted in the two seats next to him 'Score' he thought happily as the aircraft lurched slightly as it was finally pushed back from the gate, its Auxiliary Power Unit noticeable by its labouring wail, as it helped the main engines to spool up into effective life, 'Number one, two, three and four, the journey has begun' he said to himself quietly as he watched the marker lights slowly slip by at the edge of the concrete apron below him. He was forward of the starboard wing and could see both nacelles, if he craned his neck just a bit.

After a few minutes they were the next to take off and Thomas blessed himself as he always did for take offs and landings 'The only two times in a flight you had to be really concerned' he reminded himself, but that thought quickly disappeared as the engine note rose quickly and the big bird started its rumbling acceleration down the runway. Faster and faster and Thomas correctly guessed V1, then the moment the pilot would pull back on the yoke to rotate the aircraft nose up, while no doubt hoping the ground speed and the wings would finish the job, with a bump they did. Thomas closed his eyes for a second as the reality of his having just left America hit him. He took a breath and held it for a moment; he prayed that he was truly free. He looked out the window again at the lights of Far Rockaways, the area where the airport was located. He hoped for one last view of Manhattan and the rest of the five boroughs as the plane banked into its turn that would take it to Newfoundland and then out over the Atlantic proper, he was not disappointed. He picked out the skyline and had a second or two to imprint it in his memory, before the low clouds swallowed the Boeing in their embrace. He checked his watch and knew that in about seven hours, jet stream permitting, they would touch down in Shannon on the west coast of Ireland. He laid his head back with a small prayer of thanks on his lips to wait for the service cart to arrive, it did in due course but he was already fast asleep, instead of a beverage, he got a blanket placed over him and beneath it he found the true peace of sleep that had eluded him for over a year. It was over.

Chapter 16

The Prodigal Returns

The aircraft bumped and dropped, alarmingly so for someone who was asleep and woken by the sensation. Thomas flicked his eyes open and took in what he was feeling was happening, the other passengers were calm, but mostly all awake and alert as far as he could tell, they exhibited no signs of panic, so he was immediately off guard again. He slipped up the window blind and was rewarded with the beauty of the blazing dawn across a sparkling ocean far below. He could tell by the slowing engine noise that they were descending now. The captain's voice came over the intercom to confirm what he had just thought. It would not be long now before they would be on final approach. He got up and stretched to loosen himself up, before heading to the toilet, as he came back to his seat he stopped at the galley to ask for a bottle of water, which he received with a smile. He stood there in the extra space the area afforded for a few minutes while he drank the water, doing some low key side to side movements to gently stretch his calves and hamstrings, it was good to help the circulation after being asleep. The fact that he had the three seats to himself for all of the flight made a difference too. Quite a few of his trips home had been spent wedged between people with screaming babies and they were long missions indeed. He sat back down and dutifully buckled the lap belt again, but not too tight. Out below, he thought he could see land on the horizon, but he had to really strain his neck to try and see it properly; the pilot would be adjusting course again soon and he hoped that that would reveal what he was hoping to see. The engine note changed again and he felt the big aircraft bank, slowly and gracefully to starboard, his side, and as the wing tip rose again to steady them on their new heading he could see it: land, Ireland, home.

He smiled inside at the sight. The Atlantic was not very rough but he could see the waves breaking into whitecaps as they approached the edge of land, the black line of rock face like a ribbon along the top of those same waves, separating the sea from the land. There it was sitting on top of the rock, stretching away inland as far as he could see, the brilliant emerald summer green of his homeland. The plane swept in over the boundary and as it lost ever more altitude, he could see the patchwork quilt of fields that made up the farms that were the beating heart of rural life. The small cottages and bigger houses spaced haphazardly along the winding country roads, which followed the contours of the land itself. He could see the sheds of the bigger farms and even some tractors moving amongst the green, working hard this time of year, making the most of the long summer days and longer evenings. He smiled to himself again, it would be silage season and that was full on for farmers and contractors alike. He could almost smell the cut silage as it was transported, to be ramped up into silos, the molasses placed on it and then covered with plastic to basically ferment. In the coming winter, the dairy and beef cattle his land was famous for, would munch their way through tons of it, while they were kept off the fields, so their hooves would not turn the wet soil into a moonscape the summer grasses could not grow on. They were much lower now and he could see villages and small towns flash past as the wings flicked up and down gently, making minor corrections to the glide slope they were following. The captain came on again, 'cabin crew, prepare for landing.' The excitement grew in him even more now, and in a few short seconds they were over the end of the runway and there it was, the gentle bump, which said he was home. He blessed himself as he always did on a safe landing and looked back at the two engine nacelles he could see; they were oscillating up and down a bit, as the reverse thrust was applied and the big Pratt & Whitney's blew clouds of condensation out and around for a few seconds, as the remains of last night's rain was dispelled from the runway beneath, then the engines softly dropped back to an idling note, as the aircraft began to turn left onto the apron to reach the terminal. The local time was announced with all the usual stuff like, 'Welcome to Shannon, if this is your final destination may we recommend our worldwide hire car or hotel partner?' and so on. The head steward also said there would be a forty-minute layover before the short hop to Dublin that would be for him.

He could see a host of aircraft parked at various angles to the terminal proper. Some were smaller Boeing and Airbus types, belonging to Aer Lingus and various other European airlines. There were also several other large jumbo jets and other wide body types, they were painted white and had tail numbers, but that was it. Thomas knew what they were and what their presence meant would be inside the terminal. He didn't care, he was back in the land of his fathers and that had to be the best thing right now. He was not worried at having been away for so long, except for a week or two here and there at Christmas and the like. He knew this place, 'It would be ok wouldn't it?' he had left for economic reasons like most of his generation, but also to see the world, have new experiences. He smiled wryly to himself 'Well I've certainly had a few of those haven't I' as the plane finally came to a complete stop and the engines spooled down to zero. The *Bing Bong* of the seatbelt light going off was like a starter's gun, everyone up and rooting in the overhead lockers like someone just yelled 'FIRE' but he stayed seated, no one was going anywhere until the door was open and then only at the pace the width of the aisles would allow people to flow at. As soon as the expanding in the forward direction concertina effect had almost reached him, he finally stood up and out into the aisle, grabbing his leather jacket as he did so from the overhead and joining the flow outward. Soon as he was out of the fuselage, the air smelt and tasted different, richer somehow, not just because he was out of the recycled air of the interior, but because it connected with him deeply, as it always did when he landed in Ireland. 'The air I grew up in.' was the happy thought as he emerged from the tunnel onto the orangey red coloured carpet inside the building. He followed the lane that said EU Passports and was amused no end by the nonchalant series of 'Howya, welcome home, yeah good, howya,' emanating in a thick melodious accent from the Garda who was manning passport control, barely glancing at the passports presented, 'only in Ireland after all,' he smiled to himself truly delighted. 'The difference seven hours and three thousand miles make' he noted to himself as he continued past and out into the big arrivals hall proper.

It was crowded and as he had suspected when he had seen all the unmarked aircraft, it was crowded with hundreds of fit young men and women, in desert camouflage fatigues. He sighed as he skirted past the mass of soldiers, all sitting or standing quietly and respectfully in one huge group between the bar and the famous duty free shop, first in the world if his memory served correctly. He was genuinely saddened to see them all there. It didn't take a rocket scientist to figure out where they were going to or coming from, it would be Iraq or Afghanistan. How many of them would make it back? Or how many would be maimed for life, by a war that was proving to be unwinnable in reality, but then again he reminded himself that his grasp on reality back at the height of his problems was probably better than George W. Bush's and Dick Cheney's combined. He remembered the face of Gen. Colin Powell, then Secretary of State, as he had to stand at a press conference and agree that some aluminium tubes in a photograph were indeed evidence of weapons of mass destruction in Saddam Hussein's arsenal, even though Hans Blix, the UN weapons inspector, said there were none. He recalled the mad rush to war in the wake of 9/11 in Afghanistan and while he could agree with that due to the Taliban sheltering Bin Laden, the face of Colin Powell said it all when it came to Iraq; it was bullshit, it was an empty justification to topple Saddam and they had made a complete mess of it, disbanding the Iraqi national army and filling the ranks of the insurgents as they did so. 'How many of these brave, loyal, unique and special young lives would be forever lost or changed by those decisions of greed, power and stupidity?' he thought to himself as he passed the last of them by on the way to the main entrance.

He was still mulling that one over, when he stopped to get a black coffee from the small outlet barista cart, set up by the doorway. He smiled as he paid in dollars, he would get euros in Dublin. He stepped outside and was delighted by the full fresh air of his homeland as it filled him. The rich tangible density of it, laced with the faint aroma of cattle dung and cut silage, was so good. 'The aroma of Country Life', as his mother used to call it on days it would frustratingly imbed itself in the freshly laundered clothing on her clothesline. The coffee was perfect, black and not too hot and he found a chair not far to his left, where he could take a seat and light up a smoke. It would be one after the other, for at least three he reckoned, to get his nicotine back up to effective levels after the flight, but he enjoyed the second one the most. As he was mulling things over, he heard a chanting coming from a good bit away, faint but noticeable nonetheless. Standing up, he walked round the corner and there it was, the source of the noise. Across the far side of the airport was a tight group of maybe a hundred protesters, hemmed in by ranks of Garda in their bright yellow jackets. They had signs and banners; he could read one *End Extraordinary Rendition NOW*! Thomas had read a good bit about so called *rendition flights,* landing for refuelling on the way to or from *somewhere,* operated by the CIA and the other shadowy intelligence arms of the US Government. Ireland was neutral, but for as much as the UK might have a special relationship with the US, Ireland had a very unique one. Ireland had twenty million plus voters on her side when it came to having the ear of Congress or the government at large; being Irish or having a connection to those roots was an edge for any American Politian. Ireland on the other hand, would never, could never, turn its back on America and the business they did together, let alone the tourism. Ireland would never openly agree or disagree, due to its neutrality, but in reality a blind eye would be turned if the call were made from Washington, in this case it obviously had been.

Thomas was ambivalent on this issue, torture, in all its forms, was neither permissible nor required in a structured, ordered, civil society, governed by the rule of law as far as he was concerned. But then again, neither was the choking dust and stink of burned flesh and despair, the all pervasive fear after the Twin Towers had crashed down heralding a new world order of aggression and suspicion. He was doubly glad now as he walked back inside, for the 'Howya, welcome home etc.' cursory approach to fear and security here. He walked past the soldiers again and wondered how they felt about the choices their leaders had made. One of them made eye contact as he passed and he nodded and smiled, trying to be welcoming and encouraging all at once. He was passed before he found out in return, if he had achieved either. His flight number was called and he made the gate in plenty of time, no pulling off boots and belts required. Thomas resumed his seat and buckled up, in short order the now even emptier plane, was pushed back, turned and was roaring down the runway for the short hop to the east coast and Dublin. He took a coffee from the stewardess when she came by offering just that and he watched the land unfold below him as he sipped it. There was a deep abiding correctness about how he felt, as the patchwork of fields grew smaller and the old midland mountain ranges, worn down by eons of Irish weather, rolled by. It seemed they had no sooner stopped climbing, than they were descending again and the same call for the cabin crew to prepare for landing was issued.

The jumbo approached Dublin from the western inland side but obviously due to the wind conditions on the ground, it had to swing out in a wide arc over Dublin bay and the Island called Ireland Eye. Thomas was delighted, as he got a wonderful view of the city and bay, from Howth all the way down the coast to Bray and the Wicklow Mountains beyond. He knew every place he saw now and that resonated with him deeply. His family home was only an hour's drive from the city, in the middle of County Meath, beautiful rolling countryside famed for its history, farming and horses. Grand old country houses, both occupied and abandoned, were everywhere in his home county, echoes of the colonial landlords and the Anglo-Irish ascendency of over a century, and more ago. The Hill of Tara, the ancient seat of the long disappeared High Kings of Ireland, Newgrange the magical, mystical, Megalithic tomb, also a world heritage site and his beloved Loughcrew, 'A smaller Newgrange, on a much higher hill,' he smiled to himself as he said that. He was lucky, very much so. All those wonderful things and places were with a fifteen-mile radius of where he grew up. He would be on top of Loughcrew to watch the sunrise tomorrow, as he always was the day after he came back to Ireland. The plane landed and taxied to the gate, it took a while longer this time, as this was a major international airport and much busier as a result. Tail fins from all over the world glittered like the flags once had to him, outside the UN building in New York. People from all over the world were coming here to share in the richness of the Celtic Tiger boom. He had missed all of that, of course and reading about it, or seeing reports of it, on the news was no doubt very different, to the experience of living it. He hoped the core of whom his people really were, had not changed.

He would find out soon enough. Once the aircraft was docked at its skyway, it was a much quicker disembarking this time round; he counted less than sixty people on board. He walked up the tunnel and then down the steps and around to the passport lanes and smiled again as he was just waved through, no hassles, no bother. 'George W and some of his cohorts should come through here and see this' he thought but then corrected himself, George would be on a private jet and his world would never reach this low a level, or that of the footsloggers recently encountered in Shannon, he so easily dispatched to wreck and ruin.

He entered the baggage hall and waited at the carousel for his pair of big olive green duffel bags to arrive. He did not have long to wait and he walked out through the blue customs lane and through the one-way doors that opened to the arrivals hall. There was a rectangular barrier spaced back about ten meters from the door and people were packed five deep against it. He smiled; there were so many Irish working and living overseas, that there was always someone coming home or leaving, and they were normally family events entailing an escort to the airport and long sad goodbyes and hug filled hellos. He had never been one for that really, but he was just a bit wistful as he watched tears of happiness roll down parental cheeks and hugs and kisses of genuine love and affection were exchanged. It was a lovely, if just a little overwhelming, atmosphere, but he managed to be happy about being on his own, as he rolled his cart through the gap in the barrier and out past the press of well-wishers. He had decided somewhere along the way that he would not be announcing his arrival, it was his decision and nothing could be allowed to sway him from it, so he told no one. Still he had to admit to being just a little jealous of all the filial love on display around him as he walked through. He headed straight out the door to have a cigarette and take in the pulse of Irish capital city life. He had never seen the airport so busy. People were going everywhere and a look at the departure boards was quite telling, several flights to Dubai, and tons to London, Greece, Spain and Turkey, on and on, the list of destinations almost boggled the mind. All the places Celtic Tiger Ireland went to play or buy property. He observed the men and women; the expensive nature of the clothing, jewelry, and handbags was just as high end as you'd see on the Upper East Side. Thomas observed the cars that drove past the drop off zone he was smoking beside, BMWs, Mercedes and Audis were ten a penny and their number plates proclaimed them to be all no more than two or three years old. He heard it before he saw it, the rumble unmistakable and there it was, a brand spanking new Maserati. Then he saw a Bentley. In fact the closer he looked, he could see the trappings of a wealth that only a very few had had here, when he had left over a decade ago, this reinforced by the stately progress of several Porsches intermingled with the rest of the German automotive contingent, all passing in the length of time it took to smoke a second cigarette. He had to admit to being just a little wide eyed by it all. 'American soldiers in Shannon and Saville Row suits and Bentleys in Dublin, what gives?' he mused as he moved back inside. The initial crowd of welcoming well-wishers was dispersing now to be replaced with others, for the next series of arrivals and departures. He was quite taken aback really, at the sheer volume of movement he was seeing, but he filed it away to process later. The rental car desks were busy and as he had nothing booked, it was a simple matter of choosing the desk that had the smallest queue, which happened to be Avis. He was served pretty quickly and was taken aback again, at the price of a mid-size car that he could actually sit in without bending his legs like a pretzel and rubbing his head on the roof cloth. The matter of fact way the price was presented told him it would be the same across all of the desks, so he agreed and paid without further question.

The directions he had gotten along with the keys brought him out through the multi-storey car park in front of the terminal, to the far side of it, which faced the old maintenance hangers. His old friend Alan still worked in there and Thomas looked forward to calling him tomorrow to let him know he was home. The man was a truly gifted artisan, when it came to working on aircraft and had more *type* licenses than any other engineer in the place. They had known each other for over fifteen years at this point and that was something special, but he would see him tomorrow, he had to get home today. He fished out the rental agreement and checked the bay number he was looking for again, he was in the right spot and he couldn't help feeling just a little forlorn for his blue Dodge V8, as he looked at the Toyota that would have fit in its cargo bed. 'Ah well' he sighed not totally unhappy, as he filled the boot of the 'thing' as he thought of it, with both his bags. 'At least it has a two liter engine,' that engine capacity was quite respectable for Europe really. 'Gas,' no, he should say 'Petrol,' was dearer here by a long shot compared to the good ole US of A. He had the 'thing' for a few days anyway and fully intended to flog the shite out of it, to find out what kind of guts it really had. It was a rental after all. It was also a putrid mustard yellow, green colour. 'Jesus, the fucking colour of it, it's a vomit comet,' he said loud enough to make the guy fetching his own disappointing, tiny European rental in the next bay laugh out loud, 'Ain't that the truth buddy, at least you'll fit in yours' Thomas gave the expected polite smile and nod in his direction thinking 'Remember which side of the road you're supposed to drive on BUDDY!' at the same time, not knowing really why the poor sod had annoyed him. He got behind the wheel and it was strange, he was on the wrong side of the car, he'd have to remember which side he was driving on himself 'Karma' he said, quickly followed by ' Ah Here!' irritated as he tried to figure out just how to start the 'rice burner.' He thought about that for a second, 'why in God's name am I getting emotional and racist over a friggin' rental car?' That hung for another second or two, 'No bloody idea, don't care either' was the abrupt and decisive reply to the interior, which thankfully, did not reflect the exterior coloration. He got it going, eventually, after he figured out which slot to slide the key card into and which button to push, even though it was clearly marked *start* now that he knew where it was. He gunned the engine, just a bit, by way of chastisement, then felt bad and let off the throttle, it was a cold engine after all and his father's long years of nurturing his mechanical sympathy couldn't be ignored, especially now he was home.

He pulled out of the parking spot and went through the barriers that led onto the airport's main thoroughfare and soon he was at the big roundabout by the main entrance - exit with the sculpture, if you could call it that, which looked like a cubist interpretation of a shard, pointing at the sky. He had two choices here, first go towards Dublin and the M50 ring road, then on to the M3 which was the direct route, but at this time a nightmare with traffic; or secondly, left up the M1 Belfast road to Swords and cross country to the N2 which would bring him to the outskirts of Navan, a bit more cross country, then join the M3 and hit Kells about ten minutes later. He grinned, the second option was the way to go; he had missed the backcountry roads he had learned to drive on many years ago. They were challenging and fun, the thrill of chucking a car quickly and smoothly around the curves and through the narrow bridges was one of life's great pleasures as far as he was concerned. Thomas made good progress, but was really surprised at the sheer volume of traffic he encountered. Trucks and cars, lorries and tractors, there was a feeling that everyone was in a huge pressured rush to get somewhere, or their world would fall apart. He could only describe it to himself as akin to what it felt like to drive in New York, only with different scenery and on the opposite side of the road. There was an impatience bleeding out of all the other road users and so he just went with it, observing and deciding that he would have to curb his desire to explore the limit of the rental cars guts after all. As he drove the smaller road from Ashbourne across to Navan, he was overtaken in crazy places at crazy speeds by several idiots, who could have had no idea just how blind some of the corners and dips ahead really were, one or two were even on their phones as they whizzed past. 'The place has gone friggin' mad!' he said to the uncaring interior of the car. He switched on the radio and flicked through the old familiar stations, via the buttons on the steering wheel. The talk shows were full of people complaining of being 'well off but time poor' he could see the truth of that in how they were all driving, property and the pursuit of property, stories of people being gazzumped when buying property off plans before places were even built. 'Gazzumped? Have to look that one up,' he reminded himself. The whole lexicon of modern Irish society was alien to him based on what he was hearing. He may as well have been a tourist for all he knew of what was really going on. The government was spending money, apparently like it was going out of fashion and during the ad breaks the big banks were advertising financial products as though they were vital to your survival, almost a sense of 'everyone else is doing it and you'll look a dumbass if you don't as well!' Open houses for new developments were big advertisers too and overseas property expos for the coming weekend at one Dublin hotel or another. 'The old sod's gone stark raving mad!' he said once again to the equally uncaring interior. He couldn't take anymore really and was just about to turn off the radio when he heard 'And now the Angelus,' from the RTE Radio one announcer, quickly followed by *Bong, bong, bong*, the sounds of the Angelus bells that always rang out at twelve noon and six in the evening from the national station, and every Catholic church bell, in the country at those same times. He was greatly relieved, it was the first thing apart from the landscape itself and the happy passport control Garda that had the sense of the Ireland he came from, the place he loved and remembered. Everything else could not have been more different, alien almost. The bell continued to ring and he recited the Angelus prayers as he drove, it was automatic, like blessing himself every time he passed a church or a graveyard, even the small crosses erected in the verge by the road, that marked a place where an accident had stolen a life. It was a part of being Irish; being who all his generation and the many before had been simply brought up to be.

The bells subsided after sounding the traditional three sets of three, followed by the uninterrupted nine. He remembered pulling the chain on the bell at the church in Carnaross as a young boy during summer holidays, having rode his bicycle the mile and a half to do so, laughing as he and his friend would get lifted off their feet by the reciprocating motion of the chain as they pulled it as hard as they could, the laughing terror one day, for having being too enthusiastic in their efforts and the bell toning a few extra times before gravity slowed it down enough to stop the hammer striking. No doubt the good Father was not impressed but he and his friend were already peddling home like mad as soon as the first extra *Bong* resounded out across the village. Thomas smiled at the simple, safe memory then realized he would not be cycling a bicycle as a kid on these roads, no way.

His drive around the ring road in Navan and then onto the road to Kells, was more of the same, he found himself doing the best he could to notice and appreciate the sights and places he recognized over the constant frenetic rush and push of the relentlessly 'going somewhere, need to get there' mentality all around him; it was palpable, intruding and pervasive. Still he made a concerted effort to just enjoy the newness of being home and at the same time, ignore the newness of the place which was at total variance to his memory of it. Soon he was approaching Kells and the first sign of it was the Round Tower standing sentinel at the highest point of the town, a relic of the monastic golden age and its battle to survive the ravages of the Viking raiders of the 8th, 9th and 10th centuries. The sight had always evoked a strong sense of homecoming in him, even as a child sitting in the back seat talking incessantly with his father or mother, whoever was driving, sometimes both at the same time. Next he was passing the golf club and he could see the old courthouse and the hotel beyond it, the traffic was not as bad as he feared it would be and soon he was driving up the steepness of Carrick Street to head out the far side of town to home. He was only minutes away and he was truly excited now. He had been surprised to note there was a traffic light outside the bank now, big changes indeed. The last three miles were a truly revealing few minutes for Thomas. The joy he felt, the relief that it was all finally over, that he had survived, recovered and made it back. The hope he had, for seeing his parents and his brothers and sisters, bursting within him and he tried so hard to rein it in, to keep it under a modicum of control. The waves of memory were almost overpowering as he made the turn that would reveal his family home, take him across the metal cattle gridded boundary, that was the edge leading to everyone he truly loved without question in his life, that truly loved and accepted him for who he was no matter what. There it was, its white walls a very testament to the purity of all its memories, all the souls nurtured within. He was home.

As the front wheels clattered slowly over the bars of the grid, he could hear a deep *Woof Woof* of both inquiry and warning, that heralded the approach of Ben the Great Dane, as he was revealed in all his huge blackness trotting around the corner by the kitchen window, having been disturbed by Thomas's arrival from either his perch on the step of the back door or his lounging on the grass close to his mother, as she worked in her beloved and beautifully tended garden. Thomas parked beside the gable of the house behind a couple of cars that could belong to his family, or anyone for that matter due to the nature of country living. He decided to let Ben take his time to check out the wheels with his nose and make his way round to the driver's window, it was as much fun to surprise the mutt as it was the human members of the family. He wasn't disappointed as the raised hackles and slightly arched back behind upturned floppy ears, gave way to a puppy like bounding on the spot and a high pitched half-bark, half-whine of delighted greeting for a returned pack member. Thomas got out of the car and was instantly reminded of just how big Ben was, by him stepping on the toe of his boot and leaning into him to be rubbed and scratched, while his tail battered both him and the side of the rental car with a whip like intensity. It was so good to see him but he quickly gave up on trying to save his jeans from the ribbons of drool the dog seemed able to fling at people with unerring accuracy. As Thomas moved away from the car to walk around the back of the house, Ben took it upon himself to take the vanguard, escorting him the last few steps to reunion. He popped his head up to the kitchen window and was rewarded by the surprised and stunned faces of his Mother, Father and one brother as they sat at the octagonal table having lunch. He could see the sheer joy on his Mother's face as she mouthed the words 'Thomas' from a smiling face that was rapidly changing from pale surprise to red-faced tears of joy. He waved happily in at them and could feel the grin stretching almost to his ears as he turned and walked to the back door and inside. His mother was in his arms before he knew it and all she could say was 'Son, it's so good to see you' before her emotions overcame her ability to speak. His Father stood up and had that smile which crinkled the laughter lines at his eyes that Thomas loved and his brother also got up and had a big grin of welcome for him too. His mother released him, a tissue already damping at her eyes and nose, he knew she would be unable to speak for a few minutes until the shock had passed and she settled again. He shook his father's hand and they exchanged the awkward hug of fathers and sons that all men of his generation did in Ireland. It did not reflect the deep and strong bond of love and respect between them though and he was happy to see Thomas too. His brother was engulfed in a bear hug and Thomas was struck by just how big and strong a man he had grown to be, in his twenties now and Thomas was proud of him in that moment as he was of all his siblings. The emotions were high for a moment then normality began to make its comeback as he was directed to a chair at *his* old side of the octagonal table, a mug for tea and a plate to make a sandwich on appeared in front of him too and his brother poured the tea. He loved this table, a side for each of them, the six children and both parents, all facing each other equally, all part of the one family and he couldn't wait to meet the rest of them.

The conversation was happy, rapid fire and excited and in that excitement the back door had been left open and Ben had entered the kitchen unnoticed, which of course was off limits, his father stood and shooed him out, the dog looking disgusted at this indignity and his Dad equally so. His mother was placing ham on his plate and passing the bowl of fresh salad leaves, making sure the plate of bread was near him too, all the while touching his arm as though to confirm he was there and she was not dreaming, his brother was talking animatedly getting him back up to speed, as his father sat down again from his banishing of the dog, joining in with his brothers voice as they all talked together, over each other, laughed together and it was like he had never left. His father laughed the loudest as he said to his brother in a brief lull 'Get the phone out Michael, tell the rest of them that the Prodigal Son has returned.' Thomas laughed the loudest of all, his father God bless him, had never spoken a truer word; Ben could be heard barking his agreement with that outside.

Chapter 17

Exile

The predawn chorus of birdsong, which pervaded the twilight outside the window of Thomas's old room, was both incredibly loud to his urban attuned ears and delightful for what it represented. He sat up and pulled the curtain slightly aside to take in the slowly brightening sky. At the height of summer in Ireland, it really only got dark for a few hours and he had about an hour or so before the sun rose proper. He realized he still had time, if he left now, to keep that most important of appointments, sunrise on the summit of Loughcrew. He rose swiftly and dressed quietly, in shorts and one of his favourite woven long sleeved tops. The day already promised to be warm, he could tell by the clear sky outside. He pulled on his socks and took his comfortable sneakers out of one of his still not fully unpacked duffel bags, holding them in one hand as he opened the bedroom door quietly and tip toed down the long corridor. As he passed one of the doors he could hear his father's buzz saw snore, which made him smile, his father swore he didn't but everyone knew it was not so. He was careful to step over the creak, which had always been in the floor by the base of one of the radiators, so as not to disturb anyone. He touched the picture of the Sacred Heart high up on the wall with his fingertips as he passed it, entering the kitchen, equally careful as he turned the doorknob not to make noise. Once inside, he closed the door and allowed himself to breathe again. He put the kettle on to boil, while he pulled on his sneakers and made a mug of instant coffee when it did so. 'Have to sort out the coffee situation shortly,' he mused as he sipped and did up the last of his laces. Coffee was nowhere near as important as tea in his family; he chuckled to himself at that.

He made sure he had everything he needed as he slipped out the back door, locking it quietly as he went. He didn't want to wake Ben up in his house either, as he'd bark the birds to silence and everything else to wide-awake. He loved the fey greyness of the twilight and the monochrome richness of the leaves weighing heavily on the grand old ash and beech trees around the house. He glanced down over the immaculately trimmed lawn and over the wall that led to the fields where his imagination had offered escape and the fields had provided it, decades ago. He could see the first rabbits of the day, newly emerged from their burrows to steal a march on their fellows and get the freshest grass shoots. Thomas decided to gently push the car in neutral, out over the cattle grid and a few yards down the road from the house so not to disturb anyone when he started it up. Once he had done so, he drove down the road towards the village. When he was far enough away from home, he changed down a gear and accelerated happily, he had the road to himself as it was only just after four in the morning, but based on what he had seen the day before and what the extended discussions with all of his family last night about how Ireland was now, told him that that would not be the case for long. A few miles down the road he made the left turn that would bring him towards Oldcastle, crossing the River Blackwater as he did so. He loved the sights and sounds of the countryside vigorously waking to a new day, as he drove down the well-polished tarmac alleyways walled and roofed with hedgerows full of flowers and scents and life. The large trees cast their boughs across the road like oaken beams and rafters supporting a roof of luscious greenery and the creatures that called it home, happy to sing about it. All of this flooded in through the open windows and he was happy as he raced the arrival of the sun to reach his destination.

As he made the next few turns he could see his destination as he drew closer to it, its looming silhouette a black mystery against the ever-lightening sky. Thousands of years of history were hidden in those shadows the sun would soon banish, he could never tire of the magical pull the place had had on his soul, from the very first time it he had climbed it with his family as a young child. The last mile or so of road went quickly, as it was mostly straight, except for a real bastard of a humpbacked bridge that would catch you out if you let it, and you could find yourself a part of the scenery very quickly. Thomas was ready for it though and he grinned as he felt the car grow momentarily light beneath him crossing the crest of the bridge, as the roadway fell rapidly away from the wheels for thirty yards or so. He was hoping to keep that feeling of lightness within his chest for the rest of the day, perhaps even the rest of his life if he could.

Finally, he came to the junction which allowed him to make the left and the subsequent right, which led him onto the weaving narrow road, more of a *boreen* than anything else, that was not much wider that the car. It was tarmacked, but little tufts of resilient grasses grew up out of the centre of it, where tires never laid a thread. This led to a parking area about halfway up the body of the hill itself, which was deserted as he got out and locked the car. There was a covered sign that was there for the benefit of tourists and it gave a good plan of the hills, there was more than one but he had only ever bothered to climb the main one really. The sign also gave an overview of the known history of the burial mounds and the peoples who had built them, eons ago. He took off up the stepped pathway that led over the first little ridgeline to be negotiated; at the end of it was a turnstile arrangement which let humans into the field where the steepest part of the climb began and kept the sheep in where they were supposed to be. He delighted in the almost silent scattering of a flock of them as he started up the final portion, the soles of his sneakers slipping just a bit on the dew-damped grass. The view was already impressive and beautiful; it would be to a stranger coming here for the first time but for Thomas it connected like a plug in a wall socket, he felt ageless here and more so the closer he got to the summit. He looked eastward and he realized he would have to push the pace a bit to be sure of getting there before the sun. He half-walked, half-jogged and loved the feeling of strain in his legs as he did so; he was earning it, which was important too. He made it to the top and negotiated the small fence that formed a perimeter about the very top of the hill and the monuments there. It was to keep the livestock out and prevent tourists from having to negotiate piles of cow dung or sheep's marbles, to find a suitable spot for their picnic blanket. He was excited now; his head full yet empty as his thoughts dispersed to nothingness and his soul seemed to hum with the energy of the place.

Against the backdrop of the now rapidly brightening sky, the main *Tomb Cairn T* as the archaeologists referred to it, reared up with the serrated edges of its outline announcing the stones used to construct it and at the same time, seeming to meld its presence into the sky beyond. He continued straight ahead, up the flank of the tomb passing the massive Mass Stone on the way and ignoring the iron barred entrance to the Tomb further round to the side, until later. He reached the top, which put him probably an additional five to eight meters above the summit grasses of the hill, and he breathed out a long sigh of happy achievement, he had made it, just, with a few minutes to spare. The land of his native county spread out below and all around him, it night-time blanket starting to recede, but still studded here and there with little jewels of light that showed homes and farms, islands of human security in the midst of the magic of the night of this ancient land, the land of fairies and heroes, giants and the demons they had vanquished. He turned and looked down across the saddle of the hill where the sun would finally appear, the standing stones there still indistinct and mysterious, maintaining the life granted them by the imagination of the viewer and the ancient power of this place. There it was, rising fire that suddenly splashed out and framed those same giants, giving them shape, movement and form and in that instant the legends came to life, they lived in the land that had spawned them once again. The moment seemed to last far longer than it did, a trick of the mind, as one became aware of that trick, it robbed the moment of its true magic and the stones were simply stones again, framed by the rapidly rising sun, reminders now, no longer the shades of moving giants. *Slieve na Calliagh* in the Anglesied Gaelic, the Hags or Witches hill, named so for a reason he remembered, but he knew he had nothing to fear here, except himself. Thomas inhaled deeply on the summit, his arms outstretched and his eyes closed for a moment as the new warmth of the sun breached the final barriers and the hidden places of history become awash with its revealing light. He felt its vibration through his feet, his skin, as he surrendered the last of the hidden places within himself to the cleansing power of its light, the healing power of this place, the magic of feeling as though his genes had been doing this very thing on this very spot, for a very long time, a feeling of belonging, connectedness that he felt nowhere else he had ever been, or would ever travel too. 'Thank you' he said to God, the universe, the hill itself and his ancestors. It was a statement that had no single direction but encompassed everything he felt was right, had learned and forgotten and relearned once again, to believe in. He opened his eyes and lowered his arms again and felt himself diminish just slightly as he did so, the moment passing its initial intensity but its magic would remain with him. He let his eyes adjust to the glaring brilliance of the only star he would ever feel the influence of in this life and as they did so, he looked down at the view revealing more detail every second around him. Slightly to his northwest the spire of the church in Oldcastle was piercing the newly revealed quicksilver shape beyond that was Virginia Lake, nestled between the ancient glacial carved hills that held it. The shadows were rapidly receding from all the smaller hills and dales revealing more and more detail as they did so. The day racing to banish the night, the endless cycle revealing its true majesty that could only ever be fully appreciated from a place like this.

Between his vantage and the town beyond, one swale held a Bronze Age hill fort, guarding still the land it had once been built to defend, its circle almost perfect and untouched by hand or plough, 'Bad luck that,' Thomas reminded himself, 'to disturb the ancient ones.' He reflected on that, on whether a lot of his life was bad luck or simply just was. He also knew that he had just been incredibly lucky to escape the recent trap of addiction that had snared him for a while. As he looked around and took in the majestic vista of this most beautiful place he gave thanks to God for having had the strength to endure, to overcome, to begin to heal. He started to step slowly back down the flank of the tomb and paused at the big block of the Mass Stone, almost up to chest height and a few meters in width. The crudely carved Christian Cross with the Celtic adaptation of a circle centered upon it, well weathered into the rock now, part of it. He traced its outline with his fingertip trying to feel the devotion that had once placed it there, believed so strongly in it that it had risked all in those penal times, so people could commune with what they believed in. Thomas knew he believed again, had felt that grace returning, being remembered, in his hour of greatest need, and he believed in the power of this place too. He walked from the Mass Stone around the base of the mound towards the entrance and its attendant curbstones framing the mystery within. He placed his hands on the old iron barred gate and rested his forehead against them as he peered inside. The passage was narrow and he could see the swirls, large and small, singular or in groups of three, carved by a human hand millennia ago, that had neither beginning nor end, infinity as expressed and captured by that same hand, in a time when bears and wolves still roamed this land. Others were cryptic, unknowable, in their representation of ideas and spirituality. He thought about that, as he always did when he came here, what it would have been like to live when Oak forests covered vast swathes and those same bears and wolves roamed and owned both day and night. Men would have lived short, sometimes violent lives, curtailed by sickness and war. Living in defensive redoubts like the one he had admired earlier in the dawn, yet they made time for what they believed in, found majesty and beauty in the world they knew and expressed and preserved their understanding of it in the monuments they left behind. 'What is to be my legacy?' he thought as he reached in with his right hand, straining to reach the carvings and as always, they were just out of reach, perhaps like all things divine, meant to be just so. He smiled; he was content to be that close to understanding, to enlightenment, it encouraged its further pursuit.

Thomas turned and continued his circumnavigation of the Megalithic understanding of the divine, as he thought of it, all the while letting his gaze admire the place itself and the view it afforded him. The sun was well up now, its diameter having shrunk back to its normal size after its earlier supernatural entrance and equally supernatural size. Those same short life spans that had built the place, had also had the time to figure out how to orient the entrance and the tomb itself, so that sunrise on the March and September equinoxes washed in to transport the spirits within, just like the more famous and massive Newgrange did, at Midwinter's dawn as the sun broke over the valley of the River Boyne. He had been there, in 1989, inside the tomb, with his father and the twenty or so others who could fit within its confines, an extremely rare privilege that very few would share. The weather had been cold with a heavy frost but a clear sky and Thomas still was awed, as he had been then by the shaft of sunlight entering through the massive stone box above the doorway and advancing like the finger of the Gods themselves up the passageway, its very walls and their planned positions focusing that light, shaping it, to a powerful mysticism that could not be explained, could only be experienced, like the bond of father and son.

He thought of how good it was to have seen and shared time and space with his father again yesterday, indeed all his family, who had descended upon the house not long after his initial arrival, to join in the welcoming of him home. He had been happy, so very happy as they had. They were surprised when he announced he was home for good, that raised a few eyebrows and understandably so. The elephant in the room as to why and the bigger one of why he had been in such sporadic contact over the last year was ignored for another time. Thomas had not elaborated either, as those truths would be easier to digest if revealed slowly and gently to minds unprepared for the reality of what he had experienced, the reality of what he had done. He stepped softly away from the tomb and walked the short distance to one of the smaller satellite tombs that were positioned at cardinal points it seemed, about the top of the hill. Their corbelled stone roofs long ago collapsed and removed, revealing the floors of the passages themselves and how they were planned and constructed 'Hence the term Passage Graves' he reminded himself as he sat on top of one of the stones lining that same passage, his legs dangling over the graveled floor. He traced his fingers around the swirls and curves of the carvings still visible on these stones, but every year diminishing just a bit more, in the face of the dual ravages of time and weather. He pondered again what his legacy would ultimately be and he realized he truly had no clue, no plan. As he had driven from Dublin home, the changes to what he had remembered, had been almost overwhelming to him, not because he could not understand them or see the need for society to progress, but because he had been robbed somehow of his idyllic vision and memory of home. He in effect, had built up what he had expected to encounter, until it was a fantasy that would never, could never be real. This saddened him greatly, both for the way in which he had allowed that to happen and the reality of things it represented. 'I had needed that though, hadn't I, to believe?' The carvings he was unconsciously tracing with his finger seemed to convey eternity to him through their texture as he did so. He realized then that his unfocused search for a purpose, his still childish understanding of his past for all of his pain and suffering while trying to do just that, echoed back against the eternity and folded it all together into one understanding, he would never actually know. Thomas sat a while not thinking now, as that sunk in. He stirred after a bit and got up to walk the perimeter fence that defined a boundary between the spirit world and the real for him. The sheep were ambling across and clipping grass as they went and the chattering of swallows as they swooped and dived was all around him. He watched them for a few minutes and decided that no other creature displayed, what was to him at least, such sheer joy at their own existence. 'Could I ever achieve that?' he was not sure, in fact he knew that he would not. Perhaps that joy was a gift to the smaller creatures who lived short bright lives, while for humans it was a path to be discovered, a series of lessons to be learned on the journey.

Thomas entered the swinging turnstile in the fence and started his way down the hill again, leaving the glory of the dawn in that place there and carrying the feeling of it within himself. He stopped at the small single bench that looked in the direction of Oldcastle and lit a smoke, his first of the day. He smiled at the position of the bench, located just short of the summit, a last place to catch your breath before a push to the top. He chuckled at the memory of some of the larger tourists he had seen struggling up the hill over the years, reaching this bench and clinging to its solidity like a drowning man to a rope. He sat there now and knew that he too had clung to his memories of this place when he had been drowning in his past and his present, as he confronted it. There was no denying it for him, he was lucky to be alive and lucky that he had this place to cling to. But that was what it truly was, a signpost along the road to recovery and escape, not the destination itself. That made him sad, more than just a bit. He was over not feeling like he belonged. All the time he had been overseas he had busied himself with what he had thought he was supposed to do, not actually knowing what it was he had to do. This place had been his once, but now he understood it was no longer that, just like he had realized when he went to sleep in his old bed last night, that it would always be a part of his story but was no longer his or in his future. He was home as he once knew it but it was not *his* home any longer. He had never truly belonged in New York because he allowed himself to be an emigrant as it was convenient to do so, helped him fit the bill. Now he had effectively emigrated home, only to discover it was no longer the home he once knew and apart from the history of the place, like here on the hill of Loughcrew, was no longer truly for him. He had once termed his time in New York and other places as his self-imposed exile from the horrors of a past he was not yet strong enough to confront and therefore understand. He realized as he sat there that he was in fact the exile that had yet to find a place he could call home, a place and a purpose that would be safe, for him.

Thomas stood up and stubbed out the cigarette, putting the butt in his pocket. He turned and looked back up to the top of the hill, once again he stretched his arms out wide as he called out for the ancients to bear witness 'I may be The Exile, but I am alive!' he dropped his arms and started back down the hill, knowing where the faint grassy path was leading him now, but after that he had no idea where his path would lead, he was determined to follow it though and to keep himself as he did so, no matter where his exile took him.

The End